Bella Andre has always been a writer. Songs came first, and then non-fiction books, but as soon as she started her first romance novel, she knew she'd found her perfect career. Since selling her first book in 2003, she's written sixteen "sensual, empowered stories enveloped in heady romance" (*Publisher's Weekly*) about sizzling alpha heroes and the strong women they'll love forever.

She is the author of: *Wild Heat, Hot as Sin* and *Never Too Hot*, all available from *Rouge*.

www.bellaandre.com

BELLA ANDRE

WILD HEAT

1 3 5 7 9 10 8 6 4 2

This edition published 2012
First published by *Rouge* in 2011, an imprint of Ebury Publishing
A Random House Group company
Originally published in the US by Bantam Dell in 2009,
a Division of Random House, Inc. New York

Copyright © Bella Andre 2009

The Random House Group Limited Reg. No. 954009

Addresses for companies within the Random House Group can be
found at www.randomhouse.co.uk

A CIP catalogue record for this book is available from the British Library

The Random House Group Limited supports The Forest Stewardship
Council (FSC®), the leading international forest certification organisation.
Our books carrying the FSC label are printed on FSC® certified paper.
FSC is the only forest certification scheme endorsed by the
leading environmental organisations, including Greenpeace.
Our paper procurement policy can be found at:
www.randomhouse.co.uk/environment

Printed and bound in Great Britain by Clays Ltd, St Ives PLC

ISBN 9780091948795

To buy books by your favourite authors and register for offers visit:
www.randomhouse.co.uk

For Paul

ACKNOWLEDGMENTS

FOR THE past year, I've had the time of my life writing about wildland firefighters, who are some of the bravest men on the planet. And I'm very lucky to have so many wonderful people in my life who've helped get this series off the ground.

Huge thanks to Joe Edwards for telling me all about his exciting summers as a Hotshot, and his wife, Elizabeth Edwards, for giving me so much insight into what it's like to love a firefighter.

Again, I couldn't have done it without my lovely, fabulous, and brilliantly talented friends: Monica McCarty, Jami Alden, Barbara Freethy, Anne Mallory, Carol Grace Culver, Candice Hern, Tracy Grant, Penny Williamson, Veronica Wolff (who went way above and beyond the call of duty with a very careful eleventh-hour read that made such a difference!), and Christie Ridgway.

Big thanks to Catherine Coulter, Brenda Novak, and Allison Brennan for reading an advance copy of *Wild Heat* and saying such lovely things about the book!

Thanks go again to my fantastic agent, Jessica Faust, who started it all off with her (not so) innocent comments about "hot" firefighters! And, of course, much thanks to Shauna Summers, Jessica Sebor, and everyone at Bantam Dell for being so excited about my Men of Fire series.

Thanks to my parents, Louisa and Alvin, and my mother-in-law, Elaine, for offering to watch my kids so that I can write. And thanks to my sister-in-law, Linda, for helping me time and time again. You're the best.

And I want to say thank you to everyone who has picked up one of my books and enjoyed it! Your letters and e-mails always make my day. I can't wait to hear what you think about these very sexy firefighters and the women they'll do anything to protect ... and love forever.

Enjoy!
Bella Andre

CHAPTER ONE

MAYA JACKSON was going to find the bastard who'd killed her little brother and she was going to make him pay.

But first she had to take care of the details. The stupid, goddamned details.

She turned the key in the lock of Tony's cottage on the edge of the Tahoe National Forest and her throat grew tight. How could he be dead?

Gone.

As of Tuesday, November 15, 2:09 A.M., Tony was nothing but ashes, the remains of his bones and skin and spirit lost in the rubble of an apartment building on Lake Tahoe Boulevard. Three days ago he'd walked through flames to save a couple of stoned ski bums. And he'd died a hero.

At twenty-three.

Tony's landlord needed the place cleared out to show to potential tenants. He'd been nice about it; if she couldn't come for a week or two he'd be happy to stash everything of value in a storage shed behind the building. Maya had wanted to throw the telephone through a window.

Everything of value was already gone.

Standing on the top slate step, Maya forced herself to open the cottage door. All she needed to do was pack up Tony's T-shirts and jeans and books and shaving cream and she could get the hell out of there. But it wasn't that simple. Because the last time she'd been in Tahoe it had been her brother's birthday. Two months ago he'd been having the time of his life up in the Sierras, fighting fires, bagging babes, hitting the slopes when the powder was fresh.

Images of her brother and father tangled up inside her head as she held on to the doorknob like it was a lifeline. Judd Jackson had also been a firefighter. A hotshot, one of the elite who put out the fires everyone else ran from.

As a kid she'd marked time by her father's presence. For six months he'd be there every day. Making her breakfast. Taking her to school. Kicking a soccer ball with her and Tony in the backyard until they were called in to dinner. She'd loved falling asleep to the rough sound of his voice as he read from storybooks, then closed them to make up stories that were even better. For the other six months of the year he was gone. Fighting the worst fires that had ever been. The Wheeler Fire in Ojai, California. The Siege of 1987 in Oregon. Judd Jackson was a national hero, time and time again.

Maya knew kids with hotshot fathers who left one day with a smile and chainsaw and never came back. She learned to dread every late night phone call and unexpected visitors at the front door. Her dad always came back, thank God. But he couldn't shake a brutal cough. And then, a year ago he'd been diagnosed with aggressive lung cancer. All those years of sucking in ash and black smoke had taken their toll.

She was still recovering from her father's death when Tony's fire chief had called. One less Jackson in the world.

Maybe, she thought, if she and Tony had an antagonistic brother-sister relationship like so many of her friends it wouldn't have hurt so much. But he'd never been the kind of little brother who pulled her pigtails and messed up her things, and even though she was four years older she didn't treat him like a baby. They'd been friends as well as siblings.

Their mother, Martha, had lived on pins and needles whenever their father was away fighting fires. And since organization and details weren't her mother's strong suit in the best of circumstances, Maya had been in charge of making sure Tony signed up for teams and had his school projects done on time. It was nice to be needed, so she hadn't really minded taking care of her brother.

And then, when their father had died, everything had flipped around, and Tony had taken care of her.

Now he was gone too. She hadn't cried yet. How could she when her chest felt like a block of ice?

Her girlfriends were trying to say all the right things, but none of them really understood. Her boyfriend, Dick, a San Francisco firefighter, was completely out of his depth. He'd practically seemed relieved when she'd said they should take a break. And Martha was a complete wreck, alternating between crying and sleeping.

There was no one else to take care of Tony's things. Only Maya.

She'd made a list, knew she needed to pack up Tony's clothes to give away, gather important letters and pictures, close his bank accounts, collect his mail, and tell everyone Tony had loved—and everyone who had loved him—that he was gone. But she couldn't move. Couldn't force herself to take one single step into Tony's house.

Desperation tore at her. All she wanted was to close her eyes and forget for one second. Somehow, some way, she needed to get away from the pain ripping her in two, needed to forget everything. Not just that she and her mother were the only ones left. Maya needed to forget her name, who she was.

She didn't drink much, never had, and she'd never before turned to alcohol for deliverance. But now that Tony was dead everything had changed.

She'd changed.

She shut the door without having yet set foot inside

the cottage and walked past her car in the driveway, heading down the pine tree-lined street at a steady pace toward town. Tony's house was at the top of a steep hill and Maya's walk soon turned into a sprint. She gasped the clear mountain air into her lungs, running long past the limits of her endurance, every step an effort to get farther away from her pain. Her jeans and white tank top clung to her body as she tried to run away from her grief.

The casino towers on the Nevada state border rose high in the sky off to her right—with enough booze to drown in—but they were miles away and Maya didn't have much more distance in her. Still, she ran. Praying.

She knew she should be praying for a church so that she could fall down on her knees and find some solace. But she didn't want to believe in a God who could take away a barely grown boy just trying to do some good.

Please, God, you took Tony away. You took Daddy. You owe me this one small thing. It's all I'm asking.

A fresh wave of anger jolted her. *Actually, I'm asking for a hell of a lot more than that. I need to find Tony's killer. And I need you to lead me to him.*

The soles of her feet burned in her sandals as she took a sharp curve. And then she saw it: the Tahoe Pines Bar & Grill.

Thank you, God, she thought. And then, as another flood of bitterness descended, *But I'm still not even close to forgiving you. You still owe me.*

She sprinted toward the restaurant, running to purge

her demons, even though she already knew sweating and panting wasn't making anything better, that it wasn't going to bring Tony back to life.

After a cursory glance at traffic, she crossed the two-lane road, coming to a dead stop in front of the restaurant. Sharp pains knifed into her stomach as she bent over her knees, sweat dripping from her forehead to the ground.

Catching her breath, she stood up and tried to open the front door, but it wouldn't budge. The sign on the door said "Come back at 5 P.M." No wonder the parking lot was virtually empty. She didn't need to look at her watch to know it was barely midafternoon.

But a lone car in the parking lot gave her hope that the place wasn't deserted. She pressed her face to the restaurant's frosted glass and caught a glimpse of movement.

Bingo.

She banged on the door. She'd pay double, triple, for her drinks.

She watched herself as if from a distance, knew she was acting crazy, but it didn't matter. She couldn't stop now. Not when she was so close to becoming blessedly numb.

A guy in a baseball cap opened the door. "Can I help you with something?"

"A drink," she said, surprised by how raspy her voice sounded. "I need a drink."

His tall, muscular frame took up most of the doorway

as he assessed her. Maya was suddenly aware of the way her damp tank top stuck to her skin, the fact that she hadn't bothered to put a bra underneath it that morning. It had been all she could do just to get out of bed and brush her teeth. Hell, she couldn't remember the last time she'd eaten.

Since she'd hit puberty, men had told her she was beautiful. That she had great hair. Great skin. Great eyes. A knockout body. And there'd definitely been times when she hadn't been above using her assets to get what she wanted. But nothing was normal anymore, nothing was as it should be, and she didn't have it in her to work her wiles with a stranger.

"Are you going to let me in or not?"

The corner of his rugged mouth twisted up, whether in a grin or grimace she didn't know and didn't care.

He stepped aside and she pushed past him. "Whisky, straight."

He wasn't much of a talker, thank God, not like some bartenders who would have already shot off five highly personal questions between the door and the bar stool. His hands were fast—sexy too, she was surprised to notice—as he made her drink.

He placed the glass on a napkin and before it hit the polished pine bar top, she grabbed it from his fingers, tilted her head back, and drank, shuddering as it burned going down her throat.

The first one would quench her thirst. The second

might relax her tightly fisted stomach. All the rest would help her forget, if only for a few minutes.

Alcohol had never agreed with her and she knew she'd pay the price for this tomorrow. But all that mattered was making it through the next few minutes.

She put her empty on the bar and another appeared. "Thank you," she whispered as she picked it up.

The bartender was staring at her, making her uncomfortable for all the wrong reasons. She closed her eyes as she swallowed. Ever since she'd picked up the phone three days earlier, Maya had felt dead inside. Sensation, taste, smell—it had all been wasted on her.

Until now.

Her limbs already felt loose from the whisky and she found that she could unclench her jaw for the first time in days.

"You live around here?"

She looked up at the bartender, into his dark eyes. Something about his smell was familiar to her, baking dirt in the sun, dry grass mixed with clean soap. Dark brown hair came just out from beneath his baseball cap and rough stubble covered the lower half of his face.

"No," she finally replied, the word feeling strange as it crossed her tongue.

When was the last time she'd spoken to anyone? Yesterday? Or was it the day before?

Tony's fire chief had offered to take care of the funeral arrangements. All she had to do was pick up Tony's stuff from his cabin, and she couldn't even manage that.

"What brings you to Tahoe?"

"I've got to clean out my brother's apartment."

"He's leaving town?"

She swallowed hard, staring into her glass. "He already left."

The bartender leaned back against the stainless sink behind him. "That's too bad. I can't imagine ever leaving Tahoe."

"He loved it here," she said as a sob rose up in her throat.

Oh God, she couldn't cry here, in this bar, in front of a stranger. She immediately took another slug from her glass to keep everything from spilling out.

She held her glass out. "I'll have another, thanks."

His eyes were on her and she didn't want to face the questions in them, but somehow she couldn't make herself look away.

"You sure about that?" he asked. "Maybe you should take a breather for a few minutes. Tell me more about yourself."

She blinked at him as rage and frustration and misery swirled together in her gut. She hadn't come here for a therapy session. She'd come to get blasted.

She shook the glass at him and a couple of pieces of ice sloshed over the rim onto the bar top.

Her message came across loud and clear and as he shrugged and refilled her glass, the way his thin T-shirt rode up his thick biceps made her mouth water. She didn't have to see him naked to know that his abs would be ripped.

He looked hard and beautiful.

And then it hit her: This stranger was another sign. First the bar appearing at the end of the road, and now, a fallen angel sent to help her forget.

Please, God, let me forget.

He moved forward, close enough for her to reach out and touch his face. The impulse to touch him, to kiss him happened so fast that she didn't think—she couldn't, it would kill her if she did, she just pushed herself up on the bar stool and grabbed a handful of his T-shirt in her fist. His mouth hit hers a moment before she was ready for it, knocking the breath from her lungs.

His kiss consumed her, rough and sure. She hadn't caught her breath yet, could only steal air from his lungs. She'd never been kissed like this, with an intensity that made her forget where she was, who she was, that she didn't even know his name.

His facial hair was coarse against her skin and she welcomed the violence of their kiss. Everything was purely physical now, about chasing sensation. Maya left her emotions on the bar stool. They belonged to someone she didn't want to be anymore.

He tasted like sugar, but he smelled like smoke. Her knees found the top of the bar and she crawled closer to him, using his shirt for leverage with one hand, the back of his neck with the other. His large hands circled her rib cage and he hoisted her over the bar without breaking their tongues and teeth and lips apart.

Wildness joined desperation as she pressed herself against the hard wall of his chest, running her palms and fingers over his torso. His skin was warm under the hem of his T-shirt and his tight abs jumped beneath her fingertips.

Without warning he closed the remaining distance between them, shoving his hips between her legs. His erection was hard against her lower belly and she instinctively rubbed herself into the thick length. He shoved her against the wall and cold bottles pressed into her spine.

Anguish came at her then, fierce and sudden.

Tony was dead. And she was in a bar with a stranger. What was she doing? She needed to pull herself together and get back out there to clean up his cottage—and find the person who'd lit the fire that had taken his life.

Her stomach twisted up and her skin felt cold and clammy as reality threatened to break through. But then the bartender ran his lips and teeth over her jawline, down her neck, and Maya let herself get lost again in his touch, let his kisses shroud her in temporary safety.

She arched her neck back, shivering in gratitude, losing herself in this stranger. He moved his hands over her breasts and his thumbs brushed across her hard nipples a moment before his mouth covered her, first through her tank top and then—oh God—his tongue flicked over bare skin, demanding an arousal she'd never known before.

She shifted into his mouth, wanting more friction, more heat. Her elbow caught a bottle and it crashed to the ground. The scent of bourbon pervaded everything; a fitting backdrop to their fierce, anonymous lovemaking.

The stranger gave no indication of having heard the bottle shatter and with every rasping kiss he planted on her feverish skin, reality and broken glass moved further into the distance. He stood again and captured her mouth, robbing her brain of the ability to follow the direction of his hands, to realize he'd unzipped her jeans. His fingers slid into her damp pubic hair, her wetness.

She wasn't shocked by anything but the force of her need as she bucked her hips into his hands, silently begging him to enter her. His kiss was ruthless, his mouth never leaving hers, his tongue moving in time to his fingers as they slipped and slid, in then out of her desperate body.

She'd never been this out of control, never wanted to come so bad. She clawed at his back, his hips, using all of her strength to pull him into her. He obliged and his clothed erection joined his hands between her legs, thrusting, pushing harder and harder. An orgasm took her, pulling her under wave after wave of intense pleasure.

Maya was caught in the middle of a beautiful, violent

ocean. Drowning, she cried out, begging for help, but she was too far gone.

Sudden sobs wracked her frame with as much force as her ongoing climax and she was powerless to control either of them. The only thing she could do was hold on to the man between her legs.

The weeping stopped Logan Cain dead in his tracks. This had been consensual, hadn't it? She'd grabbed his shirt, not the other way around. Still, he should have known better than to make out with a woman who looked that unhappy.

The problem was, Logan hadn't had a woman in nearly six months. And damn, did this one look good when she'd banged on the door to his friend's restaurant. She'd demanded to come in and have a drink, but he would have let her in anyway, with her long dark hair, breasts that were peaking from the cool breeze coming in off the lake, and an ass so round and sweet it could make a guy cry.

One fire after another had burned up his entire spring, summer, and most of the fall. Every fourteen days he'd gotten two days to sleep like the dead and refuel. And then it was back to the mountains—downing trees, lighting backfires, clearing fire lines, and hiking twenty miles with 150 pounds of water and chainsaws on his back.

Being a wildland firefighter was the best damn job in

the world, whether he was protecting a thousand acres of old-growth forest or saving houses at the forest's edge when the owners had already given up hope that they'd have a home to return to.

Logan never forgot for one second how lucky he was to be a hotshot. Firefighting had saved his life, had given him a way to channel his innate wildness—and his teenage anger—for something good. Fifteen years later, sleeping on rocks under a cloud of black smoke was still as good as the Ritz, but six months of near celibacy sucked. Particularly if it was a dry year and people were stupid about cigarette butts and weed-whacking.

Or, in some cases, if an arsonist had an axe to grind.

Which was why he'd been happy to let this woman think he was a real bartender, especially since his friend Eddie Myers, who owned the place, wouldn't be back for at least an hour. Hell yes, she'd seemed like the perfect way to break this summer's dry spell.

After the way she'd demanded to get inside for a drink he should have known better than to touch her golden skin, should have kept his mouth and hands off of the sexy stranger. But she'd tasted so sweet. And he'd been stunned by the instant electricity between them. He hadn't wanted a woman this much in years.

As quickly as the woman's crying started, it stopped. Her arms went slack around his chest. After aiding frantic fire survivors his entire adult life, Logan knew to move slowly, carefully.

Her pupils were huge and for a minute he didn't think she actually saw him. Suddenly, her gaze focused.

"Oh God."

He had to ask her the tough question first. "Did you want this?"

She blinked once, then twice. "No," she said. "God no."

Fuck. She was gong to turn him in for something he hadn't done. Not on his own anyway. But that didn't matter, not when the Forest Service honchos would have to pull him from his crew until they'd settled their investigation into the matter. All because of a few hot kisses.

She wasn't looking at him anymore as she jumped away. Shards of glass crunched beneath her shoes.

"I'm sorry," she whispered, almost to herself.

She was sorry? He hadn't been expecting an apology, that was for sure.

She flicked another glance at him. "I didn't mean for this to happen. For us to nearly . . ."

Her words fell away and he watched her carefully. She was skittish and unpredictable and he was long past wanting to get in her pants. Her tears put that fire out completely. Regardless, every instinct in him said she was in trouble. He put his life on the line year in and year out to protect people. Hell, when he was seventeen years old help had come his way when he most needed it. He couldn't walk away from trouble now, not even if it was the smart thing to do.

"Do you need help?"

She backed away even farther, knocking into the dark paneled wall with her shoulder. She shook her head.

"I'm sorry," she said again. "I shouldn't have come here. It was wrong."

She looked like she was going to crumple, and he took a step toward her, ready to catch her when she fell. Worrying that she thought he'd attacked her took a backseat to his concern for her health and safety. He needed to get her to a doctor to find out if there was something physically—or mentally—wrong with her that she was afraid to tell him.

But before he could put his arms back around her, she flew out of the bar, down the steps into the dining room, and was through the front door in a flash. Thirty seconds later, she disappeared behind a grove of thick trees.

CHAPTER TWO

Six months later . . .

LOGAN SWUNG his chainsaw steadily through dry brush and dead tree stumps while Sam McKenzie and Sam's younger brother, Connor, worked alongside him to clear a fire line a quarter mile from the wildfire. The three of them were working the southern edge of the fire, while other hotshots worked the east and west borders.

All morning and into the afternoon they set about clearing a four-foot path. No fuel meant no burn, so as long as sparks didn't jump the line, the wildfire would die here. Nothing fancy, just textbook wildland firefighting. Spread out, they worked in silence, their chainsaws, axes, and handsaws keeping pace to a mutually understood hard-rock beat.

Desolation Wilderness was rugged terrain, but this forest was the backyard playground for the Tahoe Pines Hotshot Crew. There was no need to call for assistance from the state's smoke jumpers or Lake Tahoe's urban crews. The hotshots easily had it covered.

In the past fifteen years, Logan had doused hundreds of blazes. Some fires scared the shit out of you. Others toyed with you a little before giving you the upper hand, like a woman playing hard to get. And some were rookie stuff. The rains had come late in the spring and it had been a slow fire season so far. This one was nothing more than a good training exercise, had only been burning for a couple of days. It was a sweet and easy burn to whet their appetites for some real action. They'd be back at the station by tonight with time for a shower and a beer.

And yet, Logan was worried. Because he had a bad feeling about this fire. About how it had started. And who had started it.

As soon as they put the fire out, he was going to head to Joseph Kellerman's cabin to have a very difficult chat—one that would hopefully ensure there were no further unexplained wildfires in Desolation Wilderness this summer.

Cutting through thick undergrowth, Logan thought about the day he'd landed on Joseph's front porch almost twenty years ago. He'd been an angry, cocky seventeen-year-old, hell-bent on destruction. He still remembered the smile the middle-aged firefighter had given him that afternoon, almost as if he was saying *This is going to be fun, you little shit*. Logan hadn't known enough to back down. He'd assumed his young muscles could beat some old guy's any day of the week. One more thing he'd been wrong about.

The two of them had gone head to head, chest to chest, toe to toe, until Logan finally realized Joseph wasn't out to get him. His rules and his tough love were his way of helping. Because he actually cared.

Joseph had been—still was—the best damn hotshot Logan had ever worked with. Before he'd retired, he'd been fearless but smart, quick with decisions but not afraid to change his mind in difficult situations. Once Logan pulled his head out of his seventeen-year-old ass and came around, he'd looked up to Joseph as a mentor, a man to emulate. Nearly two decades later, he'd filled his mentor's shoes as superintendent of the Tahoe Pines Hotshot Crew.

Logan could only pray that Joseph wasn't the one who needed saving this time around.

Realizing he was swallowing more dirt than spit, Logan pulled off his goggles to take a long swig from his water bottle, but it barely passed his lips when he saw smoke rising up in his peripheral vision.

No way. No fucking way. He'd personally scanned the area by helicopter at sunrise. The blaze had been contained to the northeast of where they were clearing a fire line.

Judging by the thick, dark plume in the sky rising just south of Sam and Connor, it definitely wasn't contained anymore.

Logan wiped the sweat out of his eyes. They were working in the worst possible place. The first rule of wildfires was a no-brainer: Missionary position would kill you. Never get on top, because fires could—and would—outrace a man uphill ninety-nine percent of the time.

Somehow, they'd ended up on top.

A series of boulders had shielded them all afternoon from the dry winds whipping up the valley. Logan quickly hiked up, cresting the rocks, and a wall of heat hit him like a baking oven.

He grabbed the radio from his back pocket and spoke into it. "I've spotted a fire rolling across the canyon a quarter mile south of the ignition point."

Even though Logan would normally trust Gary Thompson, his squad boss and second in command, with his life, Logan knew not to wait for confirmation.

It was time to get the hell out.

He scrambled down the rock and sprinted toward Sam and Connor. The tall shrubs surrounding them were a temporary cool patch, one that gave no warning to the inferno dancing up the hill. Logan wasn't afraid for himself—he'd get out of there or die trying—but his men's lives were his responsibility. He'd been proud to lead his hotshot crew for the past decade. These guys felt more like family than most blood relations had ever been. At the very least, he'd make sure the MacKenzie brothers made it out of the blowup in one piece.

Logan's radio crackled. "Logan," Gary said from the anchor point on top of the mountain, where he could watch the fire's progress, "you need to get out. Now."

In all of their years of working together, Logan had rarely heard Gary sound so concerned.

Logan knew Gary wanted to hear that he was already on his way. But he wasn't going to leave without his men. "I'm moving downhill to alert Sam and Connor and then we'll retreat."

A muffled "Fuck" was followed by a tangle of voices. Logan concentrated on his mission. Speed was essential when you were trying to outwit a fire that was starving for fresh meat.

Quickly, he scanned the surrounding hillside. A retreat along the east-flank line—the nearest clean trailhead—would be suicidal. They'd have to run west, up a nearly vertical slope.

Rather than switchback down the mountain, Logan took the fastest route, jumping and sliding down steep grades, not giving a shit about bruises and scrapes if it meant getting his men out alive. The mountain below the McKenzie brothers was quickly disappearing beneath a cloud of smoke.

Sweat poured out from beneath Logan's helmet; his heart pounded; his thigh muscles bunched and burned as he worked to stay upright on an increasingly treacherous slope.

He'd done some shit-crazy things in his life, but running straight into a blowup trumped them all. And yet, he craved this kind of adrenaline, the rush of tackling a near-impossible situation. All of them did to some extent, and it was part of the strong bonds that held his group of twenty wildland firefighters together.

Like hell if they were going to be minus three when the day was through.

Nearly upon the brothers, he didn't bother yelling. They wouldn't hear him over the chainsaws. He ran across the uneven ground, hurtling over just-cut tree stumps, waving his arms in a wide arc to get their attention.

Connor looked up first and cut his engine. Sam quickly followed suit. In the sudden silence, Logan could hear the growing roar of the hungry blaze.

"We need to get out of this canyon," Logan said, pointing to the smoke column rising up over the thick brush. "Now."

He appreciated how calm they were as they lay their tools down and took stock of the dangerous situation.

"A blowup?" Sam asked.

Logan nodded, his lungs burning from exertion and the thick, fresh smoke sucking away all of the oxygen. Enough chitchat. It was time to get the fuck out.

Moments like this reinforced how crucial their daily hard-core training routine was. Running a six-minute mile with a hundred-pound pack on your back was nothing compared to running from deadly smoke and embers through black clouds, but at least, Logan figured, they had a chance to get out alive. Just as long as no one stumbled and no one let fear get the best of them.

They took the first rise at a sprint, undeterred by the steep incline. A hundred yards ahead, the fire had overtaken the western slope. Chock-full of brush, it was the perfect midafternoon snack for the fire. Without breaking stride, Logan tossed his heavy pack several feet to the side. The wind whipped into them, driving sparks and smoke into their open mouths. It stung like a bitch and Connor coughed hard several times in a row, but barely slowed pace.

Logan had never respected his guys more. Here they were, completely screwed, moving through white ash while the fire lapped at their heels, and no one was crying like a baby, no one was pulling out a fire shelter and crawling inside.

Instead, they were running for their lives.

Sitting in her car at a stop light on Lake Tahoe Boulevard, Maya opened up her file on Logan Cain and stared at his photo. She couldn't make out many of his features beneath his helmet and sunglasses, but something about his cocky grin reached inside her and twisted her gut around.

She wanted to believe that a guy with a smile like that—and with a perfect, fifteen-year record—couldn't set a potentially deadly fire. But as an arson investigator she'd been trained to look for the worst, even when no one else could see it.

She'd worked for Cal Fire since graduating college five years earlier. When her brother had died, her boss, Albert, had told her to take off all the time she needed. But Tony's death had changed everything. Arson had become personal. Not just something horrible that happened to strangers she interviewed for her investigations. In the past six months, she'd put more arsonists in jail than any other investigator in Cal Fire history.

Nailing arsonists had become more than just a great way to utilize her Criminal Justice degree while being a part of the firefighting world she'd grown up in: It had become her mission, along with finding the person responsible for lighting the fire that had taken Tony's life.

She'd expected there to be a name and a face associated with that fire by now, someone she could pin down with her rage. But for six long months she'd followed one dead lead after another.

It wasn't technically her case—she'd been in daily contact with Cathy Hart, the state fire investigator assigned to the case—but she was just as frustrated and determined as if it were. And, if she was honest with herself, she knew Cathy wasn't thrilled with Maya dogging her every step, and likely wouldn't be overjoyed when she found out Maya had requested the Desolation Wilderness wildfire as the perfect excuse to stay in Lake Tahoe for a couple of weeks.

Maya wanted to do some digging into Tony's case in person, rather than over the phone or via e-mail. Especially since she knew Cathy was on the verge of filing the fire under "accident." Maya wouldn't sleep through the night again until she knew for sure exactly what had started the fire that took Tony's life.

But for the next week or so, she needed to focus on the current wildfire. She looked back down at Logan Cain's file. It was a shoulder-high stack of heroics. The written records of his fifteen years as a hotshot painted a picture of a protector, a natural-born hero who saved expensive real estate, people's precious belongings, and human lives. He seemed to be a man who risked his own life on a daily basis because it was the right thing to do.

At the same time, she didn't doubt that Logan was also addicted to risk. Hooked on adrenaline. That was part of the job.

If hotshots didn't want—didn't need—to kick a fire's ass, it would kick theirs.

Arsonists, on the other hand, tended to be men and women whose fascination with fire brought them back to the forest summer after summer simply for the thrill of standing in the middle of an out-of-control blaze.

But this case was different. Because this was the first time she'd ever had to assess a hotshot's guilt. If Logan Cain were a volunteer firefighter, things would be a whole lot more cut and dried. Volunteer firefighters were often desperate for glory and action. Several years ago, she'd even contributed to an FBI report on identifying and preventing firefighter arson. It wasn't just boredom that drove volunteer firefighters to start forest fires. Money was frequently a factor as well. They made more money fighting fires, often raking in overtime pay if the fire was a bad one. But hotshots got plenty of action and very rarely needed to resort to lighting their own fires.

Still, even though putting a firefighter on suspension was one of the worst parts of Maya's job, right up there with questioning survivors who had lost everything, she'd do her job, no matter how ugly it got. And she'd make sure she put another arsonist behind bars.

She shook her head, trying to make sense of what she knew about the case, given that nothing in Logan Cain's file fit the profile of a firefighter-arsonist. Nonetheless, she couldn't ignore the facts.

Two times in the past week hikers had reported strange behavior to the ranger. Evidently, the hotshot had been seen fiddling with a campfire during no-burn days. She'd interviewed both sets of hikers over the telephone and they'd told her Logan had acted strangely when they came upon him. As soon as the wildfire had been noted, the ranger had contacted the Forest Service with this damning information.

And then, just yesterday, Logan's name had been called in to an anonymous "Smoky the Bear" forest-fire tip line. Combined with his very public objections in recent weeks to reductions in pension and health care payments for veteran hotshots, her boss had assigned her to the case immediately.

With no natural lightning strikes to blame—and given that ninety percent of all forest fires were due to arson—every finger pointed straight to Logan Cain, the leader of the local hotshot crew.

She laid his file on the passenger seat, then turned her eyes back to the thick column of black smoke that rose up from the valley floor. Shifting into four-wheel drive up a narrow dirt road off Highway 50, certain that the crew would be out on the mountain fighting the fire, she bypassed the Tahoe Pines Hotshot Station and headed straight for the ridgetop.

Current Forest Service reports indicated that the fire was steadily growing, but still under control. She turned on the wipers, dousing the windshield with fluid to clean the thin layer of soot. She leaned forward, squinting up at the sky. Smoke had turned it to a gray haze. Why on earth were they under the impression that this was a controlled fire?

From her vantage point, it looked to be just the opposite. And an underestimated fire was a deadly one. Once a fire exploded it would consume everything in its path—including any firefighters currently on the mountain.

Maya was suddenly struck with a dark premonition. Burns. Fatalities. Oh God, she should never have come back here. The worst hours of her life had been spent in Lake Tahoe after Tony's death. Unlike the throngs of tourists who came to gamble and ski and backpack, when she looked around she didn't see beautiful lakes and soaring pine trees.

She saw death.

Depression.

And an unpardonable afternoon in a stranger's arms.

Slipping on her shades, she grabbed her binoculars and exited her car, hiking briskly to the anchor point at the top of the mountain. A couple of buckets of unloaded medical supplies had been dumped beneath a thick dry sagebrush.

Alarm settled in beneath her breastbone. This fire had clearly exploded, and yet there were no water trucks, no helicopters doing water drops, no additional wildland firefighting teams pitching in.

Her heart was in her throat as she moved toward a group of hotshots who were standing on the ridgetop. She scanned the hotshots' faces, counted seventeen men. Which meant there were still three hotshots in the blowup.

Was one of these men her suspect? And had he yet realized that if one of his fellow firefighters died in this blaze, the penalties would be so much worse than just millions in restitution for loss of property? He'd be charged with murder . . . and would spend a lifetime living with crushing guilt.

An older man she assumed was the squad boss spoke steadily into his radio. "Logan. Sam. Connor. Respond if you can hear me."

She squinted down the hill into the fire until she

could see three figures moving slowly toward them, their white hard hats a blessed sign of life.

The squad boss had called out her suspect's name and she briefly wondered which one of the three he was, but she couldn't hold on to the thought. Not when the only thing she wanted was for all three hotshots to make it out alive.

She couldn't bear to think of the suffering these men's families would face—of the moment when they got "the call," when their biggest fears about having a son or brother or husband who was a firefighter came true.

She'd lived it. It was horrible.

Fire was rolling over the mountain like a wave. Maya had never seen anything like this, had never wanted to. Even though her brother had dreamed of being a firefighter since he was a toddler, she'd never wanted to physically fight fire. Her father had been the one to suggest she move from criminal justice into arson investigation, and he'd been right. It was her way of quenching the fire in her blood.

Even so, ever since Tony's death, she'd avoided actual fires at all costs. Now she felt utterly unprepared to witness this one's destruction—and sure death knell—firsthand. She fought back a vision of what it must have been like for Tony before he died, of black smoke swamping his vision, the crack of a burned-out beam beneath his boots, the sure knowledge that he was going to die.

But she couldn't think of him now, couldn't keep her

lunch down if she allowed herself to go to that dark place.

A dead silence hung over the men as they watched the flames leap into the air. Once a fire exploded like this, no sane firefighter would go back in. Not without risking even more lives. Seventeen men had no choice but to watch three of their own die.

Maya watched helplessly, an unthinkable question burning into her brain: If these three men died today, how would the other hotshots erase the picture from their minds? How would she?

Because even from this distance, Maya could see that the men were about to be consumed by flames. All it would take was one hard wind and they'd be sucked into the firestorm, their skin and bones melting while they still lived. Bile rose in her throat and she swallowed it down, knowing she couldn't sidetrack any of the firefighters' attention by throwing up or fainting.

The gray-bearded man yelled into his radio, "Hit the wall. Hit the wall. Hit the goddamned wall."

Maya had been so blinded by the red-orange flames that she hadn't noticed the rock face that extended out into the canyon. If the men could make it past the rock, it might force the blowup into a different path, one that would spare their lives.

But she knew they couldn't hear the squad boss's directions. Even if they hadn't already thrown down their radios to save weight, they wouldn't be able to hear anything over the roar of the smoke and flames and the blood pounding in their ears.

Go, go, go, she silently screamed, barely keeping the words in her throat.

The fire lashed out at the small figures and Maya caught her gasp a moment too late as a wave of gas knocked over one of the men, throwing him facedown into the dirt. Putting her hand over her mouth, she inhaled her scream, the smoke searing her lungs even from this distance. She watched in horror as the two men in the lead backtracked to help the third.

A firefighter's bonds of brotherhood meant more than anything, more than even saving their own lives. The other two men were going to die helping their friend.

She prayed for them, her lips moving soundlessly. She wasn't the only one praying. The mountaintop full of hotshots had turned into a silent vigil.

And then, what felt like minutes later, but could have been seconds for all she knew, the group of three crested the rock wall. Two of them held up the third between them, and even then, they ran uphill at a pace most unburdened runners couldn't match on flat pavement.

The man with the radio turned to the crew. "There are going to be burns. Severe dehydration. Shock. We're not going to lose them now. Not a goddamned one."

Instinctively, Maya took her place in the human chain as everyone worked to quickly unload and set up the medical supplies and tents. It would take ambulances a good thirty minutes to wind their way up here.

Several firefighters carried the burned hotshot into the shade of a newly erected tent, the skin on his hands bright red and blotchy. Shaking, she made sure she wasn't going to vomit before resuming the task of bringing fresh water and bandages to his tent.

Thanking God that the young man was on the verge of going completely unconscious, she watched his fellow hotshots remove the clothes that hadn't melted in order to pour cool water over his burns.

The smell of burning flesh was inescapable.

Although she'd spent five years interviewing fire survivors and prosecuting arsonists, she'd never personally witnessed men going above and beyond human limits to outrun a deadly fire. Intellectually she knew that her father and brother's lives had been about more than simply putting out fire, but they'd always been so full of laughter and joy that she'd let herself forget the reality of what they did.

Coming face-to-face with such pain—and such incredible bravery—shook Maya to the core. Her stomach twisted with nausea, but she wouldn't let herself lose it again. She was stronger than that.

She had to be strong.

The two remaining hotshots moved into her line of vision, leaning on the wide shoulders of their fellow crew members. They were covered in dirt and soot, save the whites of their eyes. Helped into the shade of two more tents, they sucked down water. Both tall, their lean yet muscular physiques were honed for the amazing feat they'd just performed.

In the wake of such serious injuries, it was difficult to stay on task and remember that she was here on the hunt for an arsonist. But with the fire blowing up and a hotshot injured, the case had just become a thousand times more important.

Maya kept her eyes trained on the man they were calling Logan as he took off his helmet. Finally able to see his face, she stumbled back into a tree trunk.

Oh God. Him.

The bartender.

He looked exactly the same.

Hard.

Gorgeous.

And covered with sweat and ash because he'd just escaped a deadly blowup.

She closed her eyes and clung to the bark as the earth spun too fast. All this time she'd thought her biggest mistake was a bartender. A sexy guy in a baseball cap who'd made her a drink and helped her suspend time, if only for a handful of minutes.

Not a firefighter.

Not a hotshot.

And definitely not her prime arson suspect.

CHAPTER THREE

LOGAN STEPPED back into his fire-resistant pants and left the hospital examination room. He'd dealt with Dr. Caldwell and her surgical team at Tahoe General Hospital countless times over the years. Usually, she was a straight shooter with good sense. Today, she'd been a pain in his ass, wasting time he didn't have probing for signs of shock, telling him to "take it easy" and get some rest.

He wasn't going to rest a single second until he put out the fire that had nearly eaten his friend for lunch. The smell of charred flesh and the sound of Connor's raw, tortured scream as the fire slammed into him played out again and again in Logan's mind.

As if that weren't enough, he was afraid someone

he loved and respected was responsible for lighting the fire.

An ambulance driver took him where he needed to go: Joseph's cabin on the edge of Desolation Wilderness.

Logan remembered sneaking up the private road as an anger-ridden teenager, so sure he'd live forever that he'd risked his life in a hundred different ways for one stupid, seemingly important reason after another. He hadn't known the first thing about what was really important. Not until Joseph had shown him.

Joseph Kellerman had plucked Logan out of an adolescent nosedive at his mother's request after he'd fallen in with a bad crowd. It was only his mother's begging her ex-boyfriend—a seasoned hotshot—for help that got him out. Joseph was the best wildland firefighter there ever was. Hands down, Logan had never met anyone who could match his mentor's intensity. His passion.

Now he knocked, then opened, the unlocked front door. He'd grown from an out-of-control, confused teenager to a man in this log cabin beneath the pines. Every year the trees grew taller and every year he appreciated even more just how much Joseph had done for him. Not only had Joseph saved Logan's punk-ass life, but he'd given him a future.

The vaulted living room was musty and the kitchen smelled like rotting meat. As soon as this fire was wrapped up he needed to head straight back here and do some cleanup. Joseph sorely needed a regular cleaning lady, but Logan hadn't figured out how to force one on the tough old man quite yet.

He was opening drapes and windows to air out the cabin when Joseph walked in from the back.

"I thought I smelled a wildfire."

Logan noted Joseph's wrinkled, stained clothes. There had to be someone he could call to drop by and at least help out with laundry.

"We could have used you out there today."

Joseph waded through the piles of newspapers and empty soda cans and pulled a couple of Cokes out of the fridge. He tossed one to Logan.

"No way. I'd be more of a liability than a rookie." He sat down in his shredded corduroy La-Z-Boy. "Everyone make it out okay?"

Logan warred with himself for a long moment. He didn't want to lie to Joseph, but how much of the truth could he handle in his condition? Finally, he decided the best thing was to be as straight with Joseph as he could. His mentor had an uncanny nose for bullshit.

"Sam, Connor, and I got caught in a blowup."

Joseph frowned. "How the hell did you let yourself get on top of the fire?"

"Honestly," Logan admitted, "I don't know. But they're my men. I should have gotten us out sooner."

"Don't blame yourself, boy. It could have happened to anyone. Hell, it happened to me once. Wyoming, in '74. Hell of a fire. The winds changed, lightning struck, and everything went up in smoke. We nearly pissed ourselves running up the mountain." Joseph's eyes went unfocused for a moment, but thankfully his gaze was clear and direct when he spoke again. "Only thing that matters is that you're all still alive."

Logan knew Joseph was right. But he prided himself on his crew's extremely low injury rate and hated to see one of his guys in pain.

"Connor's in the hospital. His hands and arms are wrecked."

Joseph didn't waver. "Burns heal."

Logan appreciated the pep talk, but that wasn't why he was here. It was time they had a serious conversation. One he could no longer avoid.

He stood up and pulled open the back door. "Come outside for a minute. We need to talk."

Bemused, Joseph followed him onto the back deck they'd built together five summers ago. It had been a good sweaty project, full of black, fallen-off thumbnails and a dozen trips to the hardware store for extra nails and perfect, knotless strips of redwood. Dozens of barbeques and hotshot reunions had gone down on this deck. Logan remembered standing against the rail just a few months ago, drinking a beer and wondering about the girl in the bar, if he'd ever see her again.

Joseph's voice broke into his recollections. "Now I know how you felt when you were seventeen and I was riding your ass all the time, wondering what I was going to come down on you for next."

They'd never talked about that tough first year when

Logan was breaking all the rules. Logan had never told Joseph how much he appreciated everything he'd done for him. He figured Joseph already knew.

"You did what you had to do." One side of Logan's mouth cocked up as he remembered Joseph's tough lessons. "Although I was pretty pissed at you that night you cuffed me to the flagpole. I almost got it out of the ground, you know. You're lucky I didn't. I had visions of bashing your head in with it."

Joseph grinned before saying "I always worried you'd end up hating me."

But Logan had never been afraid of Joseph. Not even when things had gotten physical, when his out-of-control behavior had forced Joseph to run through every available option—even putting him in handcuffs.

"Better than ending up dead or rotting in prison," Logan said.

Which brought him right back to his reason for stopping by. Logan leveled a gaze at the man who'd been a better father than blood had ever been. It was time to spit it out.

"Are you going up in the mountains, Joseph?"

"What are you asking me that for? You know I hike."

Joseph wasn't well and Logan didn't want to trigger anything that would make Joseph worse. But he had to at least ask the question. The big one.

"Are you lighting fires?"

Surprise—then anger—crossed over Joseph's face. "Of course not."

"Are you sure?"

"Hell, boy, you don't think I know what I'm doing? Where I'm going?"

Logan clenched his jaw. He didn't want to belittle Joseph, didn't want him to think he was less of a man because age was taking its toll. But yes, that was exactly what he thought.

Over the past year, Joseph had been slowing down and forgetting things. A lot of things. Like what year it was and whether or not he'd taken a shower or eaten for several days in a row.

Logan had tried talking to Joseph's son, Dennis, about it. But Dennis and Joseph had their problems, and Dennis hadn't seemed to want to deal with the situation at all.

After everything Joseph had done for him, Logan didn't want to accuse his mentor if his behavior was simply minor symptoms of aging. Joseph was still active, still enjoyed heading up into Desolation from the trails behind his cabin to go for day hikes. Hikes that Logan feared were becoming a big problem.

Just this week alone, he'd found two campfires burning along trails with entry points in Joseph's backyard. Given his mental deterioration, it wasn't impossible that he was lighting—and forgetting about—those fires.

And now Connor was in the hospital, unconscious, about to undergo hellish skin grafts. If the nerves in his hands were fried, odds were he'd never fight fire again.

Logan couldn't imagine another life. Who knew how

Connor would deal with his injury when he came to. It was unthinkable.

Connor's injuries brought him full circle to Joseph. Somehow, he had to walk the fine line between respecting the man who'd given him so much love and dealing with his problems.

Logan simply couldn't ignore the situation anymore, not when so many lives were on the line.

"I know you don't like to talk about how you've been feeling lately," he began, and Joseph pushed away from the rail, as stubborn now as he'd always been.

No wonder he and his son, Dennis, always butted heads.

"There's nothing to talk about," Joseph insisted.

Logan tried to reason with him. "You're too close to the fire. I want you out of danger. I'm buying you a ticket to Hawaii. I'll drive you to the airport. You'll leave tonight."

"I'm not going anywhere. If there's a wildfire burning in my backyard, I've got to stay right here in case you need my help. I've never run from a fire and just because I've got a few gray hairs on my head, I'm not going to start now."

"Hell, Joseph. If you want to help me, you'll get on a goddamned plane. I can't be worrying about you. I've got to get you somewhere safe."

"What are you so worried about?"

I'm worried that you're going hiking and lighting campfires and then coming back home and forgetting all about them was on the tip of Logan's tongue. But he couldn't say it.

Damn it, he wished he could just throw the man over his shoulder and carry him to safety. But he couldn't treat him like an invalid. It wouldn't be right, not when it might destroy what was left of Joseph's strength.

Logan reluctantly accepted that he was going to have to work on Joseph a little at a time. Get him used to the idea of heading out somewhere safe.

Which also meant he'd have to work overtime to make sure Joseph didn't accidentally light any new fires in the coming days.

The situation sucked. Big-time.

"Think about my offer. A couple of weeks on the beach. Pretty girls in bikinis. Fruity drinks."

"Sounds like the ninth circle of hell," Joseph said, a stubborn old man down to his toenails.

Logan couldn't beat back a grin. It sure did. He crushed the empty aluminum can in his hand. "I gotta get back."

Joseph's short gray hair was sticking straight up and his face was riddled with uneven patches of stubble. "Come by for dinner on your next down day. And stay out of any more blowups."

"Will do."

Logan grabbed the keys to Joseph's spare truck. It was time to head back to the station. The Tahoe Pines Hotshots had a mother of a fire to put out.

Maya followed the ambulances down the mountain, her knuckles white on the steering wheel. The smell of smoke that clung to her jeans and hair kept the terrible scene she'd just witnessed fresh in her mind. She hadn't thought she was capable of wanting to avenge her brother's death any more than she already did, but after watching a firefighter emerge with severe burns—even though he still had his life intact—she couldn't stop wondering Had Tony suffered like that?

Unclenching her white-knuckled fingers from the steering wheel, she pulled into the parking lot of her motel. Cal Fire had sent her to Lake Tahoe to investigate the Desolation Wilderness fire. It was time to get a grip and focus all of her attention on the current case.

Only, now that she knew her lead suspect and the bartender from six months ago were one and the same, how could she possibly separate the two circumstances?

Logan Cain would forever be inexorably tied to Tony's death, simply because she'd made the mistake of trying to assuage her pain with his kisses. And if it turned out that Logan really was guilty of arson, she didn't know how she'd ever be able to live with herself for fooling around with an arsonist.

She checked into her room and showered off the smoke and dirt, then pulled her power suit out of her suitcase. She needed to look fierce and feel even fiercer. She was on the hunt for an arsonist, not to win a beauty contest, but there was an undeniable power in looking the part.

The first time she'd met Logan, she hadn't given a second thought to what she'd looked like. This time would be different. She would be prepared for him, using lipstick and blush and mascara like modern-day armor to protect herself from his effortless good looks.

She was thinner now than she'd been six months ago, her appetite having never quite returned full force. Sometimes when she looked in the mirror she was surprised to see her cheekbones standing out in full relief, the slightly hollow spots above her jaw. Would Logan notice that there was less of her now?

She stopped her rambling thoughts cold. What were the odds that Logan would even recognize her? He probably saw more ass than a pair of jeans. The fifteen minutes they'd shared—while she'd writhed helplessly against his long fingers, God help her—were likely nothing more than a mini-blip on his sexual radar screen. Whereas he'd been so hot—so good—she'd been unable to forget about him, particularly at night in her dreams.

After verifying via telephone that the hospital had discharged him, she entered the hotshot station, her heels clicking as rapid a beat on the cement floor as her heart did in her chest.

Twenty pairs of eyes—men only, she noted—turned

on her. They weren't stupid. They smelled an investigation.

She put her briefcase down on top of a table. "I'm Maya Jackson and I'm working with the Forest Service on the Desolation Wilderness fire."

Logan had a mass of maps spread out in front of him. She focused her attention solely on her suspect.

"Mr. Cain, could you spare a moment to speak with me?"

He didn't say anything, just laid down his pen and stood up. She waited for him to betray some sort of recognition, but his movements were easy, surprisingly sure—especially considering how close he'd come to death that morning. Clearly, a vertical slope on fire had nothing on Logan Cain.

His expression was utterly impersonal. She should have been happy that he didn't seem to recognize her as the crazy woman who'd jumped him in the bar. But she wasn't. Because the woman inside her wanted to be remembered.

How sad it was to be so easily forgotten.

And how pathetic she was for caring.

Again, she snapped herself out of it. She supposed there was a time and place for mulling over men. But not here. Not while a fire was raging.

She cleared her throat, glancing at the crowd of firefighters watching her every move. Each one was better looking than the next. Golden skin. Closely cropped hair. Incredible physiques.

And yet Logan was so striking she was left breath-less.

What was wrong with her? He was a possible arsonist and here she was in heat for the guy.

Clearing away her stray thoughts, she asked, "Is there somewhere we could speak in private?"

"Gary," he said to the gray-haired man she'd seen up on the mountain, "keep mapping routes, would you? I'll be right back."

She followed Logan into a sparse, windowless office, thinking that she'd never seen a man wear jeans and a T-shirt better, before she could push the inappropriate thought away.

Long-buried sensations rushed back at her. The feel of his lips on her breasts, the slip and slide of his fingers on her sensitive skin. He'd had the same afternoon shadow six months ago. Her cheeks had been red with burns for days from his kisses.

She took a deep breath. She'd tried not to think about that day. The hot stand-up make-out session with a stranger in a bar had been a grief-induced aberration, nothing more.

Logan offered her a chair and she noted his gentle-manly behavior. *Even if he is just a playboy firefighter,* she thought, *at least I didn't almost have sex with a complete jerk.* It was the most positive spin she could put on the situation for the time being.

He took a seat behind an old metal desk, his gaze

level. Steady. Not hard, but not open and friendly either. And full of something that looked an awful lot like lust.

Maya wanted to squirm in her seat.

No. She was in charge here.

"I'm sorry about what happened to your friend today," she said.

"The Forest Service folks are already talking about it?"

She shook her head. "I was there. On the mountain. I saw the blowup. I watched you run, watched you leave in an ambulance."

"How did you find me?"

"I followed the smoke column."

His gaze intensified. "That's not what I'm talking about."

She stared at him, mesmerized by his incredible eyes, so dark brown they were nearly black. She knew what he was asking, but she didn't want to go there.

"I've been assigned to this fire. I've read your file, knew which station you reported to. That's how I found you."

"I'd always wondered who you were," he said in a soft voice, clearly unwilling to let their past stay where it belonged, "and where you went."

There wasn't enough air in the room. Why had she thought she could do this? Why had she convinced herself he wouldn't remember her?

Of course he did. Who could forget a woman who

came all over you in a bar, then sobbed her heart out, and didn't even tell you her name before running?

"Now you know," she said in a tight voice.

"Maya. Maya Jackson." He paused, dropped his gaze to her chest for a split second, then back up to her face. "You never told me your name."

"I shouldn't have been in that bar," she said in a rush. "It was a mistake. A huge mistake. I've regretted my actions ever since."

The most handsome man she'd ever been with let her lie fall to the cement floor.

A corner of his mouth quirked up. "It wasn't all bad."

She couldn't let this conversation get any more out of control. "I'm not here to talk about that afternoon."

He looked perfectly at ease, but she knew better. A man like this, who risked his life more days than not, was on constant alert for hazards.

And she had danger written all over her.

"That's right," he said, "you're Forest Service. Here to give me some more bad news about funding, huh?"

His delivery was smooth, almost unconcerned, as if he knew that she was simply a pretty messenger.

She hated being treated like a little girl on a fool's errand. On the other hand, he'd just made her difficult job easier. Now it wouldn't be so hard to give him the bad news. Not as long as he kept acting like an asshole.

"I'm here to conduct an origin-and-cause investigation."

The half grin fell from his face. In an instant he transformed into the protector, prepared to do anything to save one of his men from unfair persecution.

"What does arson have to do with my guys?"

"Nothing," she said. "Just you."

He frowned and she knew she'd caught him utterly unaware. "How so?"

"You're our best—and only—suspect at this time."

Logan's physical response was imperceptible. She'd expected disbelief. Rage. But not this. Not a cold, black gaze.

"You think I'd light a fire that could kill my crew?"

His tone was hard, sharp, but she held her ground. "According to the ranger's reports, you were spotted putting out fires in Desolation Wilderness twice in the past week by two different sets of hikers. You should also know that your name was called in yesterday. It was an anonymous tip, but the Forest Service couldn't ignore it simply because you are one of them."

She decided not to mention that his very vocal opposition to the new retirement packages for wildland firefighters, however noble, didn't help his case one bit. Until she'd gathered more evidence, she'd keep that information in her back pocket.

Surprise registered on his face a split second before he said, "You haven't answered my question. Do you think I could have lit a fire that could kill my crew? You were up on the mountain. Did you see Connor? Did you happen to notice his hands?"

He held his out in front of her, but all she could see was the skin bubbling and oozing on the other hotshot's fingers.

"He may never fight a fire again," Logan said in a low, hard voice. "I would never take that away from one of my men. Never."

His anguish over his friend's burns was genuine—and sent strong flickers of doubt regarding his guilt through her—but none of that changed what she had to do. She laid out the facts.

"With no lightning strikes during that same time frame, all signs point to a man-made fire." She paused before slamming in the final nail. "All signs point to you."

Something flashed in Logan's eyes and her chest squeezed. She wanted to find the arsonist as quickly as possible, but she didn't want it to be a hotshot.

She didn't want the arsonist to be *him*.

"You're actually suspending me because some hikers saw me putting out a campfire? Because someone thought it would be funny to call the tip line and give them my name?"

She answered his questions with a question. "Did you put out the campfires?"

"Yes."

"Did you light the campfires?"

He looked at her hard before answering. "No. They were already burning."

She wanted to believe him, but was that because her

gut told her he was telling the truth? Or was it simply her hormones talking again?

"Okay then," she said. "If you didn't light them, who did?"

"If I knew that," he said in a hard voice, "I would have already tracked the arsonist down and turned him in. And then you wouldn't be here right now, would you?"

"The hikers wouldn't have reported you to the ranger if the situation looked normal. And as a rule, anonymous tip lines are very useful tools. But you've been in this business a long time," she added, openly challenging him, "so you already know that, don't you?"

He advanced on her. Within seconds, he had her pinned against the wall. The heat of his body scorched her even though there was a good ten inches between them. Silently, he dared her to remember all the ways he'd kissed her, touched her.

"You think these hands are capable of such destruction?"

She shivered as vivid memories came rushing back of him touching her so intimately. He had incredible hands. Big. Strong. Warm. And capable of giving exquisite pleasure.

"I saw how selfless you were today."

She hesitated for a split second, until she realized that her wavering wasn't going to get them any closer to finding the arsonist.

"You could have died saving your crew. But that

doesn't negate the evidence. Right now, all signs point to you."

She squared her shoulders and took a step forward, into his hard, well-trained body, refusing to be intimidated even as she hated her body's instinctive sensual response to his nearness.

"And until your name is cleared, I have to put you on suspension. Starting now."

CHAPTER FOUR

DISBELIEF FOUGHT with fury in Logan's gut. Tahoe Pines had been his hotshot crew for fifteen years, and after watching Connor head off in an ambulance, these guys desperately needed his leadership.

Most of his men had been fighting fire long enough to understand the risks. Injury—and death—went hand in hand with wildland firefighting. Every hotshot knew how to wall his emotions off long enough to put the fire out; forever, sometimes, if he'd lost a close friend or a buddy he'd joined up with. But sometimes it was harder to watch a live man burn than it was to mourn a dead one.

Any one of them could have been caught on the mountain this morning with nowhere left to run, surrounded by fire.

A fire this woman thought he'd started.

The same fire that he thought Joseph might have started. And if Joseph had, even if it had happened when he'd disappeared into one of his brain-fogs and had no idea what he was doing, once there were injuries—or, God forbid, deaths—he'd be in a whole hell of a lot of trouble. Joseph wasn't strong enough to withstand weeks or months of questioning, fines, or even imprisonment.

Logan's resolve hardened. He needed to protect Joseph no matter what. Even if it meant taking the heat himself.

His fists were clenched on the wall behind Maya's head as he forced himself to step away. While Superintendent McCurdy was sitting in his comfortable, air-conditioned office in the Forest Service headquarters, a beautiful woman was facing Logan down, and she was a messenger of doom who looked a hundred times hotter than he'd remembered.

Which was saying a lot, considering how good she'd looked six months ago.

Hell yes, he remembered that afternoon in Eddie's bar well. Too well. In his line of work, girlfriends came and girlfriends went, but none of the women he'd been with had stuck around in his brain like she had.

Now here she was, back in his life again from out of the blue.

No doubt about it, out of the blue was her M.O. But this time she wasn't grasping at his shirt, wasn't diving onto him, wasn't jamming her tongue down his throat.

This time around she was accusing him of arson. And she wanted to bench him while a wildfire raged.

But there was no way he could let that happen. He needed to be out there keeping an eye on his crew. Which meant getting back out on the mountain in full gear, wielding his chainsaw and Pulaski in the thick brush within the hour.

"Look, I know it's your job to track down arsonists. The Forest Service sent you here to investigate. I get that. But you and I both know I didn't light this fire. And I've got to get back out there and put it out. So why don't you run along to look for the real arsonist and let me get back to my job?"

"I'm afraid that's not possible, Mr. Cain."

Maya's expression remained neutral. She wasn't angry. Or nervous. Instead, she seemed cold. Frigid, even.

She had all the same curves in all the same places, but she sure as hell wasn't the wild woman he'd met in his friend's bar. If anything, she was standing there, her full breasts and sweet ass outlined to perfection in her goddamned suit, looking down on him for being in the wrong place at the wrong time and winding up an arson suspect in a fire that had nearly killed one of his men.

She pulled a file out of her briefcase. Quickly flipping through the pages, she handed him a single piece of paper.

His days of flipping off authority and getting away with it had come and gone a long time ago, so he took the page and read it. It didn't take long to scan the words that were as good as a death sentence: Should he disregard suspension orders to stay off the mountain, he would be banned from working with the Forest Service in any capacity, even in a city office, forever—signed his buddy Superintendent McCurdy, Tahoe Basin Forest Service.

He was about to crumple up the paper and toss it into a wastebasket in the corner when he realized why Maya's name seemed so familiar. Not because she'd introduced herself to him in the bar before wrapping her legs around his waist, but because she'd coauthored the FBI report on firefighter arsonists.

His crew had played darts with it until the pages shredded.

"It's not just me, is it? You've got something against firefighters, don't you?"

"Excuse me?"

"You're an excellent writer," he said, waiting for realization to dawn.

Her lips curved up, but she wasn't smiling. He was surprised he didn't see frost forming on the surface of her skin.

"I take it you're referring to the FBI report I contributed to."

"Hell, sweetheart"—she flinched at the endearment—"take credit where credit is due. You penned that little beauty, start to finish. Tell me, apart from one afternoon in a bar, what did a firefighter ever do to hurt you?"

Her mouth tightened and went flat. "My father was a firefighter. So was my—"

She cut herself off sharply and he noted her strange behavior. What wasn't she telling him?

"I have boundless respect for firefighters," she finally said.

"You sure have a funny way of showing it."

She narrowed her eyes, anger beginning to melt away her icy core. "I grew up surrounded by firefighters. They were some of the best men I've ever known. How dare you accuse me of being out to get them?"

Her words rang with sincerity, but he wasn't in any mood to back down. Not since she'd come between him and a wildfire, with reams of bureaucratic bullshit.

"Then why the hell did you write that report?"

"Don't tell me you've never come across a firefighter who liked to play with fire, Mr. Cain. Anyone who's worked in the Fire Service knows someone who had a problem with getting excited about fire for all the wrong reasons."

He immediately thought of Joseph and his chest grew tight. What the hell was he going to do if Joseph really was guilty?

Logan wasn't familiar with the bitter taste of fear and sure as hell didn't like swallowing it down. One thing was for sure: If Ms. Hotshot Investigator was going to keep pushing him, he hoped she was prepared for him to push back.

"Tell me something, did an investigator ever accuse your father of arson?"

Pain registered in her eyes, on the small lines around her mouth, and he knew he'd hit below the belt, but he was fighting for his life, for his fellow hotshots, for Joseph.

He'd do whatever it took to keep them all safe.

"No." She swallowed hard. "Never. My father was a hero."

"My point exactly," he said, invading her personal space one more time. He got close enough to see that her olive-tinged skin was still flawless and that her cheekbones were more pronounced than he'd remembered.

Something tugged at him, a remembered sense that she hadn't been all there six months ago, but then again, he hadn't exactly been studying her from a distance. He'd been rubbing his lips against hers while grabbing her ass with both hands.

"Hotshots don't light fires that kill their own men. Call McCurdy and tell him to pull my suspension."

"If you want a prayer of clearing your name, Mr. Cain, I suggest you stop issuing ridiculous orders and cooperate with my investigation."

Even though he was close enough now to lick her, her voice remained steady, irritatingly calm given all he'd just thrown at her. A part of him couldn't help but admire a woman this strong, even though she had his balls in a vice grip. She hadn't even tried to move away from him.

In his experience, it was a rare woman who didn't run from confrontation.

"You and I both know there's nothing to investigate," he said again. She was one tough cookie, but he was a dog with a bone, one he wasn't going to relinquish anytime soon. "You saw what happened to Connor. I need to get back to the fire to make sure the rest of my men make it out in one piece."

Her mouth tightened as she grabbed her briefcase off the table. "Again, I am very sorry about the accident today. But this suspension stands. And I encourage you to abide by Superintendent McCurdy's instructions."

Fifteen years of fighting fire had taught him to refigure his plan of attack whenever flames shifted directions. It was time to do that very thing with Maya.

"Your boss know about us yet?"

Her eyes narrowed. "There's nothing to know."

"You sure about that?" Playing off his hunch that she hadn't forgotten the way she'd responded to his mouth on her breasts, his fingers in her panties, he said, "That day in the bar, I never got a chance to tell you how pretty you were."

She held her briefcase in front of her body like a shield. "I'm not interested in talking about that day. Our previous encounter has nothing to do with this situation. Nothing at all."

He allowed his gaze to roam her body in a leisurely fashion. "The way you reached across the bar and grabbed me was something straight out of every guy's fantasies. Especially when the girl looks like you. When she's that responsive."

"Mr. Cain," she said, her tone brittle and, finally, angry, "I am long past the point of humoring you. I will contact you again for a personal interview. Until then I advise you to stay away from the fire and not bother my boss. He'll know what you're trying to do." She widened her stance. "I can guarantee he won't kick me off this case. Something that happened six months ago isn't going to alter my methodology or my assessment of the crime."

A knock sounded and Gary's voice penetrated the thick fire-resistant metal door. "Logan, we've got more trouble on the mountain."

After ten years together on the fire line, Gary knew Logan's earlier trip to the emergency room didn't mean jack and that as long as Logan could walk and use his hands, nothing would keep him away from a fire.

Nothing except a fire investigator handing him his temporary walking papers, courtesy of *numero uno* at the Forest Service.

Logan yanked opened the door and Gary shot an apologetic glance at Maya. "Sorry to interrupt your meeting."

It was pointless to waste time on pleasantries. If Gary knew why Maya was really there, he wouldn't bother being polite.

"What's going on?" Logan asked.

"The winds have shifted and the fire's headed straight

toward the new housing development on the southwest ridge."

Logan cursed. It was just the kind of bad news he didn't need right now. If the fire took out a neighborhood of multimillion-dollar houses, the insurance companies would pick up the tab. But the Tahoe Pines hotshots would shoulder the blame.

He quickly issued his instructions. "Call in several urban crews to water down the rooftops and cut fire lines in the surrounding acreage of the border properties."

"Are you going to take the mountain or the housing development?" Gary asked.

"Neither," Logan said, dropping the hugely unexpected bomb on his squad boss. "I'm out for now."

"What the hell?"

"I put out a couple of random campfires in Desolation last week and some hikers reported me to the ranger. Plus, someone called my name in to the tip line and now the Forest Service honchos think I lit this fire. I'm on suspension until they find the real arsonist."

Gary rubbed his hand over his face and when he looked back at Logan, it was as if he'd aged a decade.

"I can't believe this. You're a goddamned hero and they're trying to pin this on you?"

"It looks good on paper. I'm sure she'd be happy to tell you more." But when he turned back to the room, Maya was gone. "Shit."

He had to hand it to her, on top of being fearless, she

was wily. And quick. At this rate, she'd have the noose wrapped around his neck by nightfall.

"I still can't fucking believe this," Gary repeated.

Logan needed to get out of the station and on Maya's tail. If he were her, first place he'd go ask questions was Joseph's cabin. After all, the man had taken him in as a teenager for unspecified reasons. She wasn't stupid, she'd know there was a story there.

Only three people in Lake Tahoe knew Logan's true history: Joseph; his son, Dennis; and Logan himself. If Joseph were well, there was no way in hell that he'd give up Logan's secrets. But if Joseph's mind wandered into the darkness, even for sixty seconds, irreparable damage could be done.

Logan quickly reassured the squad boss. "You've got this under control, Gary. You don't need me out there. Put Sam at the anchor point with the radios. Take half the crew to the houses, dig a wide line along the wildland border, and keep the roofs and gardens wet."

He didn't wait for Gary's response. His squad boss and seasoned crew would deal with the fire. He had ultimate faith in them.

It was Maya Jackson he didn't trust.

CHAPTER FIVE

MAYA WHIPPED around a blind curve on the two-lane lakeside highway, desperate to put some space between herself and Logan Cain. The interruption had been her perfect chance to escape. That room had been too small. And Logan was too big, too strong, too sexy—too everything—for her to keep her head on the case.

Every time he came close she remembered the heat of his lips on hers, the rippled muscles across his stomach as she'd run her desperate fingers across his skin six months previously.

She'd caught him off guard and he'd been angry, furious at the suspension, but instinctively, she knew he'd never physically harm her. Her traitorous body would do her in all by itself.

What would she have thought of him this afternoon

had she never met him before? Would her gut still have told her he was innocent? Or would she have held on to her doubts a little longer? Their meeting had been fraught with tension, and yet, she couldn't help but feel that the Forest Service was going after the wrong man. It didn't help that no matter how she looked at the situation, it was impossible to separate their past from the present.

She'd thought he might use that one reckless, emotional afternoon in the bar against her, but she hadn't been prepared for her physical reaction to him. He was her suspect, for God's sake. She couldn't let him off the hook simply because she wanted him to take her up against the wall of the station, up against any wall, anywhere.

She used her upper teeth to pull her lower lip into her mouth, chewing as she worked things out. Without any evidence other than the ranger's reports and her tense chat with Logan at the station, she had no clear sense of the case.

Maya's GPS system beeped in warning a moment before the screen went blank. She was trying to find Joseph Kellerman's cottage, but he lived too deep in the woods for her car's mapping system to keep up. The pine trees were too mature and tall for her to get a signal. Damn it. She didn't have any time to waste. Not when she had a feeling that Logan would be trying to track her every move.

How had he become the hunter and she the prey, when he was her suspect, not the other way around?

So far she'd passed a dozen dirt roads that snaked off the highway into the forest. One of them had to lead to the cabin Logan resided in as a teenager. Eyes peeled for a sign with the name Kellerman on it, she ignored a honking minivan on her tail and slowed way down. At last, she hit the jackpot when she saw a hand-carved "Kellerman" sign nailed to a tree ten yards ahead. Maneuvering her car into the narrow lane cut out between thick tree trunks, she turned on her headlights for better visibility. The dirt driveway wound up the hill.

Several minutes later, her foot barely on the gas pedal as she inched forward, the single-lane road petered out. She parked behind a beaten-up old truck. Stepping out of her car, she was struck by the heady scent of pine trees and memories she wasn't quick enough to push away.

Her father had loved the forest and he'd taught her and Tony to love it too. She'd grown up in a pack on her father's back until she grew big enough to run along the trails, her chubby toddler legs moving as fast as they could, her hand in her father's.

Maya squeezed her eyes shut. It hurt just as much to think about her father today as it had last year right after the cancer had eaten straight through his lungs into his organs. Now that she was surrounded by hotshots again, she couldn't look at them without seeing traces of her father in all of them.

Logan's words bounced around in her brain. *Did a fire investigator ever accuse your father of arson?*

He'd been trying to get a rise out of her, but even though he nearly had, she knew that losing control of her emotions wasn't going to help her solve this case. Just the opposite, in fact.

Moving quickly through the dry pine needles and gravel, she pulled herself together as she headed for the rustic cabin. She knocked on the front door. The seconds crept by with no response, so she knocked harder. Finally, she heard footsteps.

A rumpled man with hair sticking up in a dozen directions opened the door. His wide smile took her aback, as did a clear picture of how handsome he must have been when he was Logan's age. He would have been just as much of a lady killer as his foster son.

"I haven't had a pretty girl like you on my doorstep in decades."

She smiled back despite herself. "Mr. Kellerman?"

His grin didn't waver. "Looks like you found me."

Another time—another life, long before she'd lost half her family and stupidly jumped a sexy stranger in a bar—she might have enjoyed bantering with a charming older man. Instead, she was all business.

"I'd like to ask you a few questions about Logan Cain, if you don't mind."

"Sweet Jesus. You're not pregnant, are you?"

She swallowed her shock at being asked such a ridiculously personal question by an absolute stranger. "No. Of course not."

Joseph frowned. "So you're not one of Logan's girlfriends? Although, come to think of it, he hasn't brought one around here for quite some time."

She shook her head, praying he didn't notice her blushing in the dim light filtering through the trees. "No," she said honestly, even though the truth was so much more complicated than that.

If those were Joseph's leadoff questions, how many girlfriends were there in Logan's posse? And just where had her midafternoon makeout session with him fallen on his list of sexual partners that day?

Women loved firefighters. Maya did too. How could she not? The truth was, she'd primarily dated firefighters for the past ten years, but that was before she'd finally figured out that firefighters always left, one way or another. Either they walked out on you by choosing fire first every time . . . or they died before they could.

"Who are you?"

She'd had doors slammed in her face more than once from people who were afraid of saying too much to a fire investigator. Frankly, she wasn't sure what to expect from Joseph.

"I'm from Cal Fire." She repeated the exact words she'd said to Logan. "We're working with the Forest Service to conduct an origin-and-cause investigation."

She never led with the word "arson." It scared people. Made them clam up.

Joseph's deeply lined, scruffy face went white. "Shit." He moved out of the doorway. "You'd better come in."

She followed him into the cabin, her nose wrinkling at the musty smell. A thick layer of dust covered everything. Newspapers were stacked high in corners and the kitchen was a mess of open cans and boxes and dirty plates. It was obvious that something wasn't right. How, she wondered, had Joseph's situation played into Logan's emotional state?

Joseph slid some dirty clothes off a beaten-up leather couch. He didn't seem to notice the mess. "You want a drink?"

She shook her head, idly wondering if alcoholism could be the problem. But she hadn't smelled anything on Joseph's breath, hadn't noticed beer cans and empty liquor bottles in the kitchen.

"No thanks." She pulled a small notepad and pen out of her big bag. "I'd like to ask you some questions."

He sank into an easy chair covered in shredding blue fabric. "Okay."

"Logan moved in with you as teenager, is that correct?"

"He was seventeen. A hell of a kid. Still is."

"Are you a blood relative?"

"No."

"Why wasn't he living with his parents? Or with an aunt or uncle?"

Joseph's eyes were wary. He didn't want to say too much, knew better than to say too little. "His mother asked me to take him."

This part of Logan's file hadn't added up. He'd moved from Boulder, Colorado, to California his junior year of high school. She wasn't going to leave Joseph's house until she found out why.

"Why you?"

"We dated." His eyes lost focus. "A long time ago. Before she got married and had Logan. Before I met my wife."

Maya didn't see any evidence of a wife, even though Joseph wore a dented gold wedding band. "I take it he was getting into trouble?"

Joseph's eyes were clear as they locked back onto hers. "He wasn't different from any other kid. He just didn't know what to do with all that energy." He pinned her with a knowing glance. "All that passion."

Fuck. She was blushing again. If they'd been talking about anyone else, any other man she'd made out with, she wouldn't have been the least bit bothered. But fifteen minutes in Logan's arms had been long enough to brand her. One taste of him was not enough, could never be enough.

Even though it had to be.

She cleared her throat, sweeping away the sensual images. "I'm not going to lie to you, Mr. Kellerman. The Forest Service has reason to suspect that Logan set the fire currently burning in Desolation Wilderness."

Joseph sucked in a breath. "That's bullshit."

It was never easy to hear that a loved one was potentially responsible for causing such widespread destruction. Arson tended to be a secret passion, something that usually flared up into the open when provoked by great emotions. Even then, many arsonists' first fires went undetected, staying just small enough to remain under the radar.

"Your reaction is understandable," she said in a reasonable voice.

But rather than soothe Joseph, her words provoked him. He shot out of his chair and she had another glimpse of the strong man he used to be.

"Fuck understandable."

Maya didn't move a muscle, barely blinked. When people grew agitated, they talked. And said things they would have otherwise kept hidden.

"That boy couldn't hurt a goddamned fly. Not even his shithead father, who deserves an ass kicking if anyone ever did. I don't care what Logan used to do when he was a kid, he'd never light a fire that could wipe out one of his crew. Never."

He wobbled on his feet and Maya jumped up to steady him even as she wondered, *What bad things had Logan done as a kid?*

Joseph gave her a weak smile. "I haven't gotten my heart racing like that in a while."

She helped him back into his chair. "I know I'm asking some hard questions, that they're difficult to deal with. But getting answers is the only way I can possibly clear Logan's name."

"Or convict me."

Logan's deep voice hummed up her spine, and her scalp tingled like she was a fourteen-year-old girl and the hot high school quarterback had finally noticed her.

She spun around. "I'm conducting a private interview. Please wait outside."

One side of Logan's mouth quirked up. "Like hell if I'm going to wait out on the deck while you grill him."

"Your girlfriend sure is pretty."

Maya turned back to Joseph, utterly confused by his random statement. Why on earth would he say such a ridiculous thing when he knew exactly why she was here?

"I'm not his girlfriend," Maya clarified.

Logan grabbed her elbow and hauled her into the kitchen. "Time to go."

She wrenched her arm from his warm grasp. She hated men who thought they could push her around simply because they were bigger. Even more, she hated the way her nipples immediately peaked beneath her bra at Logan's rough touch. "I'm not leaving until I'm finished with my questions."

Joseph shook his head and smiled. "She's tougher than your usual girls, Logan. And smart too, you can see it in her eyes. I wouldn't piss her off if I were you. I don't want to see you let go of a good thing. Gonna have to think about weddings and babies one day."

Joseph's eyes had become slightly unfocused and Maya

shifted her gaze to Logan. She saw worry. Fear. And then she realized what was going on: Joseph was suffering from dementia. Or, worse, undiagnosed Alzheimer's.

Logan grabbed her briefcase, his voice low so only she could hear it. "There are plenty of other people you can grill about me. Guys on my crew. Old girlfriends. People whose lives I've saved. Not a tired old man who needs to rest."

She hated the thought of walking out of Joseph's cabin without answers. But Logan was right. Joseph's health wasn't stable. She'd have to put this interview on the back burner until a time when he was, hopefully, in a more coherent state of mind.

"We're going to head out now, Joe," Logan said, patting Joseph on the shoulder.

"This is your last chance, boy. You fuck up again and you're going to lose this pretty girl." Joseph's shoulders sagged into his broad frame. "Hell, you throw a match in the wrong place and you're going to lose everything."

Logan's hand pressed into the small of Maya's back, pushing her across the room. And she let him. Perhaps another investigator would have been tougher. Meaner. But Maya believed in playing fair, and right now wasn't the time to grill Joseph, even though his mental meanderings might be full of revelations about her suspect's past and potential motivations for lighting a fast-moving wildfire.

The truth was there. She'd find it one way or another, and she'd do it without hurting anyone.

Logan pulled the door shut behind them and as she quickly moved away from his heat, she noticed that his truck was completely blocking hers on the narrow dirt driveway. Her hands fisted at her sides. Slowly uncurling her fingers one by one, she turned.

"Please move your truck."

He swung her briefcase from the tip of one finger. "You're probably going to want this too, aren't you?"

She held out one hand, making sure it didn't shake from frustration. "Yes, thank you."

He gave it to her, then strolled over to her car. "City vehicles always come with low-grade tires, don't they?"

She followed his gaze. Crap. Her front right tire was flat.

"Dry pine needles. They're hell on rubber."

His words were light, conversational. And yet, she bristled at the victory she sensed behind them. Not to mention the fact that standing in the middle of a forest with her lead suspect and a brand-new flat tire was pretty damn suspicious. But the last thing she was going to do was let him think she was scared. Especially since she didn't think he'd do anything to harm her while Joseph was just a wall away.

"I've got a spare," she said as she clicked open the trunk with her remote.

He was mistaken if he thought she was a girly girl who couldn't take care of herself. Her father had made sure she knew how to change a tire—and shoot a gun.

Logan crossed his arms over his chest, looking for all

the world like he was trying not to laugh. "Good luck getting out of this driveway with a spare. One time my buddy tried it when we were kids and we had to call a fire truck to pull him out of a mud hole. Car was stolen too, so he spent the night in jail." He headed over to his truck. "How about I give you lift? Take you wherever you need to go."

Maya couldn't believe her bad luck. Was it really coming down to this? Was she going to have to accept a ride from her primary arson suspect? She should head back inside Joseph's cabin and call AAA to come fix her flat. But that would take time. Time she didn't have anymore. Not now that the fire was out of control and had already taken down a hotshot. And if this wildfire followed typical arson patterns, there'd be new fires. Soon.

The longer it took her to nail the arsonist, the more lives and homes and land would be threatened by the wildfire. Plus, there was always Logan's lingering threat to call her boss. The story would be better coming from her mouth first, give her a chance to put a more innocent spin on things.

"Fine," she finally said, slamming the trunk shut and grabbing the rest of her investigative tools out of the backseat. "You can drop me at my motel."

She remembered seeing a rental car agency next door to the motel, which meant she'd be out on the road and back in business immediately.

She stepped up into his passenger seat. The interior smelled like leather and fresh dirt and pine needles. And

Logan. He slid in behind the wheel and her senses were overwhelmed with his smoky scent, his nearness, the way his thigh muscles pressed against the denim fabric of his jeans, the dark hair across his wrist.

She forcefully pushed aside her arousal. God, it shouldn't be so hard to remain impartial around her suspect. He started the engine and as they moved through the trees she slowly recovered her equilibrium. Instead of fighting her reaction to him, she needed to save her energy and simply accept—and ignore—the attraction so that she could get back to business. In fact, the next ten minutes of captivity in his truck were the perfect chance for another Q&A session.

"Joseph mentioned you had some problems as a teenager, that your mother asked him to take you in."

She waited for Logan to react in some way, but all he did was drive. Fine, he wanted to play hardball, she'd play hardball.

"You were obviously a problem child. What kind of problems did you have?"

"You really think I'm going to tell you?"

He took his eyes off the road for a split second and she could have sworn he was laughing at her.

"No, not really. But it doesn't matter. I'll go back to Joseph's cabin first thing tomorrow morning. I'll ask him then." Logan wasn't making it easy for her. She was happy to make it just as hard for him. "Watching his health fail must be difficult for you."

But even as she said the words, she felt herself soften. She knew how it felt to lose someone.

Logan's face shuttered closed. "You always feel this sorry for your suspects? Interesting strategy."

She clamped her lips together. Fine. She got it. He didn't want to talk about whatever Joseph was dealing with. And he was right. They weren't friends. They weren't even acquaintances. Still, from everything she'd read in Logan's file and her brief meeting with Joseph, she could see that Joseph was far more than a mentor. He was a father.

A sharp pain dug in beneath her breastbone: Logan's love for Joseph was one more potential mark against him. Had watching Joseph slip away day by day sent Logan over the edge? Had it sent him back into old patterns that had long been buried by Joseph's love? Was Logan Cain a playboy with a penchant for arson?

Or was he a true hero who'd gotten caught up in an arsonist's trap as the perfect foil?

She looked at his profile, his strong nose and chin, his full, masculine lips. Was she having a hard time imagining him committing arson because he really was a good man? Or was it simply that she'd tasted the heat of his kisses?

Logan slammed on the brakes to avoid hitting a deer running across their path. "I'm sorry," he said, surprising her with his apology. "I shouldn't have said that. All I'm asking is that you leave Joseph out of this."

Conflicting emotions tore through her. Logan had

shown her kindness in her darkest hour six months ago, but all she could give him in return was a bullet list of reasons why he was guilty of arson. She knew why he was pleading her to stop questioning Joseph, but it would be unprofessional and unethical for her to ignore an important source.

"I'm afraid I can't do that."

"You can if I give you what you're looking for."

Heat bloomed beneath Maya's skin. They were just words, not an invitation. She steadied her breathing before she replied.

"It depends on what you give me."

"Underage drinking."

She was momentarily insulted. He didn't really think that lame information was going to be enough, did he?

"What else?"

"What makes you think there's more?"

"Your parents wouldn't have sent you away because you broke into their stash a couple of times."

"Probably not," he agreed, his voice far too easy, far too calm for her to believe he was confessing much of anything to her. "I liked drugs and guns too."

She shifted in her seat, wanting to make sure he understood who he was dealing with. "If you'd lived in the city, I'd care. I might even think you'd been into gangs. But Boulder? Come on. You wore hemp and smoked pot and went hunting on the weekends."

His lips curved up in that devastating smile again, but

this time he spoke with an edge. "Okay, then, why don't you tell me the reason my mother sent me into what seemed like the middle of butt-fuck when I was seventeen and only wanted to get in trouble and get laid?" He caught her eyes before she could respond. "Fortunately, girls like a guy who knows his way around the woods."

He allowed his eyes to move down her body and land on her breasts. "And I definitely knew my way around in the dark, only using my hands to feel where I was going. Even when I was just a horny kid." He turned back to the road. "But I don't need to tell you that, do I? It's the one thing about me that you already know for sure."

Maya shifted in her seat to stare straight out the window. She hated that he knew her weaknesses, knew right where to jab for the greatest impact.

He came at her again. "Since you're all out of questions, how about I ask you a couple?"

His deep, rich voice grated on her nerves. She'd never wanted to punch and kiss someone at the same time.

"How about you don't?" She crossed her arms over her chest and pressed her lips together. She was not going to let him get to her.

"What were you doing in that bar back in November?"

"I don't go to bars." Which was entirely true, minus one stupid, grief-induced blip.

"Maybe you don't anymore, but you sure as hell did six months ago."

"You're the one who's going to be spilling secrets right

now, Mr. Cain. Not me." She wanted to shoot herself the minute the words came out of her mouth.

"Any time you want to share your secrets with me, Maya, I'm more than willing to listen."

She knew exactly how he'd "listen" to her, given the chance. But she had no intention of taking the bait. He'd never learn her secrets in a million years, never lull her into saying something stupid with his seductive kisses, his knowing hands.

Just then, Logan's radio crackled and he reached past her knee to turn up the volume. "Reporting a motel fire at 696 Lake Tahoe Boulevard, Highway 50. Station 3 and Station 4 have been dispatched to the scene."

Maya stiffened. "That's my motel. The one that's on fire."

His hands tightened on the wheel. "Who else have you pissed off today?"

Her heart pounded as the damning words left her mouth. "Only you."

Logan flattened his foot on the gas pedal. She was pushing too hard. Getting too close. Joseph was right. She was smarter than any girlfriend he'd ever had, even though she definitely wasn't standard girlfriend material. No, she was the kind of woman a guy wanted to chain to his bed until he'd had his fill, all the while knowing that day would never come.

Sentence by sentence, question by question, she was pinning him up against a wall. It wasn't fair to use their attraction against her, but he couldn't resist watching her get flustered every time he so much as danced around the subject of sex.

Six months had passed since he'd tasted her. Touched her. But now that she was sitting so close that he could reach out and pull her onto his lap, he realized he hadn't forgotten one damn thing about her. The way her tongue had slid against his. The way she'd pressed her breasts into his palms and rubbed into his calluses. The slick, wet heat between her legs.

Of all the ways he thought they'd meet again one day, he couldn't have imagined this. Anger rode him. But he couldn't let anger get the best of him, not if he wanted to see his way clear of the accusation. Which meant he needed to get a grip. Fast. Especially since they were several blocks away from her motel and he could already see flames and smell smoke through the truck's doors and windows.

Adrenaline shot through him and his thigh muscles clenched in an instinctual response to the fire. He wasn't an urban guy, this fire wasn't his domain, but he'd worked dozens of structural fires in the past whenever the stations were short-staffed due to illness or vacation or babies being born.

He looked over at Maya and saw that she'd pressed her body up against the passenger door, as far away from him as she could get. He didn't need her to tell him what she was thinking. He could read her mind. *Fuck*. She thought he'd lit this fire to scare her.

And if she found out the real reason he'd been shipped out to Tahoe as a kid, she'd think she was right.

CHAPTER SIX

MAYA'S EMOTIONS were all over the place. She'd gone from frustrated to aroused to sympathetic to angry in a matter of minutes. Right now, however, she was fighting back fear. Chances were that this fire at her motel was nothing more than a shitty coincidence. Probably just a random accident, some drunk boaters lighting up doobies and dropping them on the carpet when they passed out from too much sun and drink.

Still, she had to ask herself if Logan could be involved in some way. After all, she'd gotten a good ten minutes alone with Joseph after leaving the hotshot station, which would have been more than enough time for Logan to leave the station, set a fire in her motel, then head after her.

But no matter how she looked at it, she couldn't forget

that Logan was a hotshot. One of the elite. She wanted desperately to believe he was innocent.

What if he wasn't?

"I'll get out here, thanks," she said, pulling at the door handle to no avail, held captive by the automatic lock. Even though they were stuck at a red light a block from her motel, she wanted out of his car. Now. She had more than enough adrenaline to sprint the rest of the way.

"Hold on, we'll be there in thirty seconds" was his reply.

As they pulled into the lot she pressed every button on the door until the lock finally clicked open. Grabbing her bag and tools, she jumped out while the truck's tires were still spinning. Seconds later, Logan was out of his truck, following closely behind her.

Several red-and-yellow fire trucks blocked the motel from view and she guessed it was at least a three-alarm blaze. Maybe four. Everything closed in on her and she wished, just for a second, she could turn her back on fire. It had devastated her life, and still she walked toward it again and again.

One of the firefighters turned and saw them. "Hey, Logan, didn't expect to see you here. Not with the wildfire burning in Desolation."

"My crew's got the fire covered tonight, Bob. What's going on here?"

Maya held her breath as she waited for his answer. She needed to know if the fire was an accident.

Or if she was the target.

"We got a call twenty minutes ago that there was smoke coming out from under one of the doors."

Maya took a step closer. "Which room?"

Bob frowned at Maya's interruption. He jerked his thumb in her direction. "She with you?"

Logan nodded. "Cal Fire."

Bob's eyes widened. "Shit. If something's going down, we want to know about it."

Maya barely held back a frustrated scream. "Which room?"

The urban firefighter looked at Logan. "Should I be telling her this?"

Logan nodded. "We both need to know."

"Room 205."

She felt the blood drain from her face and her lips go numb.

Logan's hand gripped her elbow to keep her steady. "Is 205 your room?"

She was shaking. Shit, she needed to get a grip. Needed to take a step away from Logan. And then another.

Spinning away from him, she ran between engines, stopping in front of the only firefighter not geared up, the one with the radio and the clipboard. He had to be the station chief.

"I'm Maya Jackson. From 205. It's my room that's on fire. I need to know what happened."

A loud crash came from the building and she whipped

her head around just in time to witness the roof falling in on the first-floor ceiling. The firefighters calmly went about their business and Maya wished she could be more laid back about the fire's ongoing demolition. But she'd spent the bulk of her working life behind a computer, holding on to a telephone, sitting in airless rooms questioning suspects and witnesses.

She struggled to pull her gaze away from the flames. The out-and-out annihilation.

The fire chief studied her face for a long moment. "Are you related to Tony Jackson?"

Oh God, how could she have forgotten for even one second that this had been Tony's domain? He'd been Lake Tahoe Fire Department, Station 3, and his station's tanker truck was parked ten feet away. Tony should have been in the parking lot with these guys or up on the roof, checking for hot spots.

She nodded to give herself time to recover from the sudden blow. "I am."

The chief shook his head. "I'm sorry about what happened to your brother." He held out his hand. "Patrick Stevens. I'm the new chief. I apologize for not returning your last few e-mails and phone calls. I've been swamped these past couple of weeks getting up to speed. Since you're in town, would you like to arrange a time to sit down and discuss the situation?"

She blinked hard, tried to get everything untangled in her head. And heart. "Yes. Thanks. I'm in Lake Tahoe to investigate the Desolation Wilderness fire currently burning," she said, each word sounding robotic and stiff to her own ears as she tried to get herself back on track, "but as soon as I wrap this up, I'll come by your office."

He nodded. "I'm happy to help any way I can. Tony was a good one. Real good. He's been missed." He paused, clearly uncertain about whether he should continue.

Hope flared in her chest. "What is it? Have you learned something?"

He shook his head. "No. In fact, I was going to say that all signs point to the fire that took Tony's life being an accident. You know that, don't you?"

It was just what she was afraid of. They were getting ready to close Tony's case for good.

"Signs aren't good enough," Maya said. "I want facts." Even though facts wouldn't bring Tony back. Nothing would.

Just then, Logan shifted beside them and she realized he'd been standing there the entire time, listening quietly.

So much for keeping secrets from him. She hadn't wanted him to know about Tony. Too much personal information in the wrong hands was never a good thing. Who knew what he'd try to pull now that he had even more ammo to use against her?

But instead of asking about her brother, Logan pointed to the box at Patrick's feet. "Is this all you were able to recover from Room 205?"

"I'm afraid so," Patrick replied. "The rest of your luggage is gone, Ms. Jackson."

Maya squatted down to get a better look. She didn't care about losing her clothes, her makeup, or even her computer, which lay in a melted black heap in the bottom of the box.

"Did anything survive the fire?" she asked the chief, as she stood back up on shaky legs.

"Actually, yes. We did found something else in the room. Something I don't like the look of at all."

He reached into his pocket and took out a Ziploc bag.

"It's a letter with your name on it. It was in a firebox. We're going to check for prints, but I doubt we'll find anything."

Maya's entire body went still. Someone was sending her a message. From the corner of her eye, she watched Logan carefully, looking for a reaction, but he seemed as surprised as she was.

Had he done this? Or was the perpetrator someone else, someone she wouldn't suspect until it was too late?

Her instincts had always been a driving force in her investigations. But this case was different.

She'd never been intimate with her suspect before.

As she took the bag from Patrick, she kept her breathing even and steady. Freaking out wouldn't help a thing. Even if being left a personal note in a motel room on fire was definitely not a good sign.

First Logan, now this.

She pulled out a sterile pair of rubber gloves from her bag and made sure her hands were completely steady before she slipped them on.

"You don't think this was an accident, do you?" she asked the chief.

"I wish I did. But whoever lit this fire knew exactly what they were doing. Just a little smoke at first, nothing anyone would notice until it was big enough to start blowing the roof off one piece at a time."

Her heart thudded heavily beneath her breastbone as she digested his words. Hotshots possessed encyclopedic knowledge of fire behavior.

A couple of firefighters called out from the section of roof that remained, "Fire's nearly under control," and Maya looked back at the building, fighting off the sick sense that she'd fallen into a rabbit hole, one that was dropping her straight onto the day her brother had died. This motel fire was far too similar to the apartment fire that had taken Tony's life.

"Open the letter, Maya."

Logan's soft words startled her. Drowning in what-ifs and should-have-beens, she'd nearly forgotten about the letter.

Arsonists rarely got to see the fear in their victims' eyes. Did he want her to open it in front of him so that he could relish her reaction? Because if Logan was her arsonist, this moment would make his crime so much more satisfying.

The thin envelope burned a hole in her palm. She

slid one gloved finger beneath the glued flap and unfolded the single page. The note was neatly typed.

Maya, it's been six months since I've seen you and you are still so pretty. I've often dreamed of seeing your long hair on fire and watching your soft skin melt down to the bone. It won't be long now before my dreams come true.

Her fingers went cold and stiff and she almost lost her grasp on the note. Quickly reading over her shoulder, Logan put his hands on her shoulders.

"You okay?"

His strength, his touch, was almost too welcome for her to shake off, but she made herself move away from him, away from his heat.

"I'm fine," she lied as she gave the note back to Patrick. The police would want to keep it as evidence. "I need to go question witnesses."

Turning her back on Logan, she walked over to a group of women and children who were watching the action from a safe distance. The only way to keep it together was to focus her whole attention on the current situation.

"Hi," she said, forcing a smile. "I'm an arson investigator and I was wondering if I could ask you all a couple of questions."

A young mother's eyes lit up. "Wow. You sure got here fast! It really is just like those *CSI* shows on TV."

Maya was glad someone thought this was fun. Because she sure didn't.

"Did any of you happen to see someone suspicious near Room 205?"

The three women nodded their heads in the affirmative, a brunette speaking up first. "I don't know if I'd call him suspicious-looking. More like drop-dead gorgeous. He was standing outside the room for a while, like he was waiting for someone to come back."

A chill ran through Maya. "Could you be more specific? What did he look like?"

The brunette's friend giggled. "Tall. Really muscular. Brown hair. Like one of these firefighters. He had a baseball cap pulled down pretty low, though. I don't think any of us got a good look at his face."

Great. They'd just described Logan. And about half of the firefighters in Lake Tahoe, both wildland and urban.

She needed to point Logan out to these women to see if they could positively I.D. him, even without having stared into his eyes. But when she turned around to locate him, he wasn't standing with Patrick anymore and she didn't see him anywhere.

She fought a growing sense of frustration as she made her way through the rest of the onlookers. But no one else was much help, pretty much echoing the other women's statements verbatim. After finishing questioning witnesses and talking to the police, she found it impossible to ignore the grim reality of her situation: Someone was trying to scare her—or worse.

Even though her stomach was empty, she had to fight back a wave of nausea. Desperate for something to hold on to, she pulled her leather bag against her stomach. She couldn't stand in this parking lot and be the cool, unruffled fire investigator for one more second. She needed to sit down someplace where she couldn't smell smoke or see firefighters who reminded her of her brother.

Moving quickly through the parking lot, she followed a pathway that led to the lake. The sun had set and she stumbled over rocks. And then, finally, the buildings fell away and sand crunched beneath her shoes. Water lapped against the shore and she dropped to the beach, her things falling around her feet, welcoming the cool sand beneath her. Hanging her head between her legs she took several deep breaths, in through her nose, out through her mouth.

Today had been one of the worst in her life, coming in right behind the days her father and brother had died.

She lifted her head and looked up at the full moon shining on the lake, watching the water move beneath it. She wished there was someone she could call for comfort. Someone she could say "I'm scared" to. But there wasn't. Not anymore.

Her girlfriends had called and called until enough of their voice mails went unanswered that they finally got the message and left her alone. She couldn't call her mother, not when Martha was already too damaged and couldn't possibly handle the thought of another child being threatened by fire. Not when it had already taken away her husband and son.

Fire was her mother's worst enemy. Maya could see why.

She fished her cell phone out of her bag and scrolled down her address book to retrieve her boss's home number. She definitely couldn't tell Albert how shaken up she was, but at the same time she had to tell him about what had gone down at her motel—and about Logan and what had gone down between them in the bar.

She dialed his house, never having bothered him on a Friday night before. She knew how precious her boss's family time was after a long, hard week managing a dozen investigators.

He picked up on the first ring, obviously recognizing her cell number. "Maya? Is everything all right?"

Regret rose up and choked her. Albert was one of the only people who knew all about her brother, how much she missed him, how long and hard she'd searched for concrete answers. She hated to let Albert down after he'd been so supportive of her career. But if she didn't set the record straight about her past history with Logan, she had no doubt that her suspect would beat her to it.

Caught blindsided, Albert wouldn't be able to deflect the blow, and Cal Fire might lose hold of the case altogether. Worst of all, the arsonist might run free.

She wouldn't allow her shame, her embarrassment

over a reckless choice she'd made six months ago to give a potential arsonist the opening he needed to escape capture. Hopefully he hadn't beaten her to it in the past hour while she'd been questioning witnesses.

"Do you have a few minutes? There have been a couple of developments in the Lake Tahoe Desolation Wilderness case I think you should know."

Albert said something to his wife and kids, whom she could hear laughing in the background, then obviously moved to a quieter space.

"Of course I do. Shoot."

She opened her mouth, but nothing came out. She didn't know where to start. With the blowup? Or the motel fire? No, she should open with the worst. Get it out of the way.

"There's no easy way to say this, but when I informed the suspect that he was under investigation this afternoon, I realized that I'd met him before."

She could practically see Albert shaking his head across the wireless line.

"Did you know you had personal ties to the suspect when you took the case?" His tone was gentle, but his question was direct.

"No. Of course not," she said, trying not to go on the defensive. It would only make her look lamer. "His picture on file was fuzzy. With his helmet on, I didn't realize I knew him until I saw him today at the anchor point."

"I hate to ask you this, Maya"—Albert cleared his

throat uncomfortably—"but what exactly is your relationship to the suspect?"

"We met six months ago when I came to Lake Tahoe to pack up Tony's things."

She paused, hating the admission she was about to make. For the millionth time, she wished she hadn't let her grief propel her into such stupidity.

"I met Logan in a bar."

"Uh-oh."

Her boss was one of the most eloquent people she knew. She'd never heard him reduced to two syllables. She wanted to quickly spit the rest of the explanation out, before he got the wrong idea. Or the right one.

"We barely spoke." *Because our mouths were too busy doing other things.* "And I never found out his name, never saw him again until today."

Hearing the words come out of her mouth, she realized that even if her boss was likely no stranger to one-night stands before he got married, it didn't excuse the fact that she'd participated in one. With her suspect.

"But I assure you that our previous relationship is in no way affecting my investigation."

"I believe you, Maya, but it doesn't look good. Not for you. Not for me. Not for Cal Fire."

His condemning—and honest—words shot through her. Her head throbbed as he continued telling her what she didn't want to hear.

"I'm going to have to send Yeager in. First thing

Monday morning. Why don't you go ahead and return to the city. I'll assign you to another case next week."

No! Remaining in Lake Tahoe was her only chance to figure out what had really happened with Tony and move on with her life. She took a steadying breath. "I understand your concerns, but I swear to you that I can handle this case in a wholly impartial manner."

"You know I'm on your side, Maya. You're one of the best investigators we've got. I'm afraid this is a worst-case situation. My hands are tied. I've got to pull you."

But she wasn't ready to give up. "Until Yeager arrives, I'd like your okay to proceed." A couple of days could make all the difference, and if she solved the case quickly she could get back to work on Tony's investigation. "Let me work on it through the weekend."

She held her breath as Albert considered her request. "I suppose it looks better for us to have someone on the case."

"Great," she said, then made herself spit out the rest of the story. "You should also know that fifteen minutes ago when I returned to my hotel room, it was on fire."

"Jesus, Maya. You've had a hell of a Friday, haven't you?"

He didn't know the half of it. "There was a note with my name on it in a firebox."

She fought to keep her voice steady. Now that he'd agreed to let her stay through the weekend, she didn't want Albert to pull her off the case to protect her.

"What did the note say?"

Maya shut her eyes, easily remembering every creepy

word. "The arsonist said something about lighting my hair on fire and ..."

The rest of the words strangled in her throat. She couldn't say them.

"Was it a death threat?" he asked.

She swallowed hard. "I don't know. More of a scare tactic, I think."

"Get out of town, Maya. Now."

But she couldn't give up, couldn't go home now. Not when this case had become intensely personal. Someone wanted to scare her, maybe even kill her, but she refused to run. She'd been running for too long.

It was time to face her demons.

"I know this sounds crazy, but I can't. After what happened to my brother here, I've got to stay."

Albert sighed, and she hated the terrible position she'd just put him in. If she'd had another choice, she would have taken it. But she didn't.

"For the next two days," he finally said, "until Yeager comes to relieve you, assume the worst. About everyone. And until we have enough evidence to nail the sick, sorry bastard, every single person you meet is a potential arsonist. No matter how charming or helpful. If he's coming after you, you're close. Too close. Be careful. I don't want anything to happen to you, Maya."

Albert wasn't saying anything she didn't already know. Still, that didn't make it any easier to hear. His description fit Logan perfectly. Everyone thought he was the best of the best. Someone who would "never do something so horrible."

But the truth was that sometimes the guy everyone liked, the one always willing to lend a hand and help out a neighbor, couldn't keep from lighting fires that would burn down houses and kill innocent people.

She said good-bye before her boss could change his mind about letting her stay for the weekend and dropped her phone into her bag. The cool breeze coming off the lake helped clear her head and she took a moment to assess the crazy situation.

Either Logan had lit her room on fire to scare her or he was right and she'd pissed off someone else. But whom?

Whoever had written the note in the firebox knew she'd been in town six months ago. As far as she knew, the only person she'd come into contact with that day was Logan.

Her boss was right. She was too close. She never thought she'd be drawn to a man capable of such destruction.

But she was.

A wide smile gleamed in the dark. It had been the perfect little fire, timed just right. When she'd read the note it had been so satisfying to see fear on her face.

She was going to get what was coming to her soon.

Very soon.

But not too soon, not before a couple more fires were lit, not before she had to really work for it.

It was going to be so much fun to watch her go around and around in circles. And all the while, the arsonist would be right there under her nose.

Today had been a very good day.

Tomorrow would be even better.

CHAPTER SEVEN

WHAT THE hell is going on here, Logan?"

Logan knew there was no point in holding back with Patrick. No matter what he did or didn't say to his friend, news of his suspension was going to travel fast. Their community of firefighters was small and tight. No one probed where they weren't welcome, but it was impossible to keep public information a secret.

"McCurdy put me on suspension. This afternoon. He thinks I lit the Desolation fire."

"Jesus," Patrick said on a heavy exhale, looking as perplexed as Logan had ever seen him. "How are any of us supposed to do this job if we're going to be under suspicion all the time? What's next, no BBQs in our backyards because we'll get arrested for risky behavior?"

Logan appreciated his buddy's support. Even if it

didn't mean a damn thing in the grand scheme of things. But he needed to find out everything he could about this motel fire. Someone was after Maya. And he needed to find out who. And why.

Clearly, nothing had changed in the six months since he'd seen her, because he still wasn't smart enough to walk away from danger. Especially not if it meant she was a wide-open target.

"Anything else I should know about this fire?"

Patrick shrugged. "I don't know. Maybe I shouldn't tell you. After all, you are an arson suspect."

Logan didn't move a muscle, not until he was sure whether his buddy was playing with him.

Patrick punched him in the shoulder. "Just kidding. Sorry, I shouldn't be fucking with you. I don't care what those Forest Service assholes come up with, we all know you're not the one they're looking for."

Logan forced a grin. It was one thing to have a bunch of suits come after him. But once other firefighters started doubting, his career was over. The threat of arson would follow him out of the state, across the country. Not just Lake Tahoe.

"Glad to know you've got my back."

Patrick looked down at his notebook. "Thus far all we've got is a firebox and a disturbing letter. I'll give you a call if we turn up any fingerprints."

But Logan wasn't done asking questions. "Tell me about Maya's brother."

"I only met him a couple of times. He signed on last

year, before I took over, but word is he was a young, energetic guy with a great future ahead of him."

No wonder she'd bristled when he'd accused her of not respecting firefighters. Not only had her father been a hotshot, but her brother had lost his life on the job. He vaguely remembered meeting Tony Jackson one night at a bar, but last summer had been nonstop, and there were a handful of rookies he hadn't really gotten to hang with until the winter truly kicked in, in late December, and he had some downtime. Tony had already been dead by then.

"What happened?"

Patrick shook his head. "Routine apartment fire. Some kids lighting up, probably fell asleep and dropped a lit reefer onto old carpet. Tony was on the top floor making sure they'd gotten everyone out, when the beam holding up the roof collapsed."

Logan remembered hearing about an apartment building that had burned to the foundation in mid-November. Just days before Maya had walked into his friend's bar. Their short conversation came back to him. She'd told him she was in Tahoe to clear out her brother's apartment and that he was already gone. Logan had assumed a job change was the reason her brother had left town, maybe even jail, but not death.

No wonder she'd cried her eyes out in his arms.

"They couldn't get him out, could they?"

"No. He burned with the building."

She hadn't even been able to get one last look at her

her brother, to make the choice between caskets and an open- or closed-viewing vigil. She probably couldn't stand to look at a potential arsonist without wanting to plunge a knife into the guy's chest. *His* chest.

"Honestly"—Patrick rubbed one hand against his chin—"I don't know if she should be out investigating fires. Not until she gets over what happened to her brother. If she can."

Logan found himself wondering the same thing. But something told him he and Maya weren't that different. And if he was standing in her shoes, he'd be doing the same damn thing.

"She's doing what she's got to do," he said in reply. "You or I wouldn't walk away from our jobs after losing a brother. Neither will she."

Patrick grunted his agreement and Logan thanked him for the information, then grabbed a flashlight off a nearby truck, not bothering to turn it on as he headed off to locate Maya. Anger had fueled him from the moment she'd uttered the word "suspension" until they'd heard about the motel fire on his radio. But now that she'd been the target of an arsonist—and especially given what had happened to her brother—he couldn't sustain his rage.

Not even in the face of a brutal suspension.

He found her sitting in the sand, facing the lake. She looked small and forlorn, her arms wrapped around her legs.

Instinctively, he wanted to take her in his arms. She

had to be frightened. Anyone would be after reading that note. But he knew she would never accept comfort from him, not when they were still standing on opposite sides of the fire.

Somehow, he had to get them on the same side.

He clicked the flashlight on and waved it over her head in warning. She jumped up and spun around, sand flying out from beneath her feet.

Her hand flew over her chest and he instantly regretted startling her. Especially on the heels of her motel room being firebombed by someone who was into leaving threatening notes.

"Leave me alone, Mr. Cain."

"I'm sorry about your brother."

Surprise moved across her face, but she quickly shut it down.

"You always feel sorry for your investigator?" she said, twisting his earlier words around. "Interesting strategy."

Logan appreciated where she was coming from. Hell, an hour ago he was pushing her away. But knowing about what had happened to her brother had changed everything.

"That's why you were here six months ago. That's why you came to the bar." He paused, moved a step closer to her. "That's what was wrong. Why you cried."

Her head was bent and he couldn't see her face.

"I miss him so damn much. Every day. He hadn't even been in Tahoe a year."

She looked up at him and there weren't any tears on her face, but grief overwhelmed her beautiful features.

"I won't rest until I find the arsonist who killed him."

"If I were you," Logan said in a quiet voice, "I'd feel the same way. I'd be here doing the same thing, tracking down every lead."

Her mouth twisted as if she'd tasted something sour. "You were my one mistake. God, I wish I'd never met you."

"Ouch."

And yet, he got where she was coming from. No one wanted to be reminded of their fuckups. No matter how unintentional.

"Putting arsonists behind bars is the only thing that matters anymore."

He had to ask. "What about your friends? The rest of your family?"

She gave him a strange look. "What are you, some kind of mind reader?"

He took another small step toward her, wanting to get closer without scaring her away.

"No, why would you say that?"

"It's crazy, but I was just thinking about . . ." Her words fell away and she looked at him again, almost as if she were seeing him for the first time. "I can't be telling you these things. I shouldn't be talking to you at all."

But he wanted to keep their dialogue going, wanted to feel out their strange connection and see if there was something to it.

"I only met your brother once, very briefly. I wish I'd known him better. That I had stories to tell you."

"I don't want to talk about him."

But he didn't believe her. "I'd be happy to talk to the guys I know in town, find out if there was anything weird going on the night he—" He cut himself off just in time.

She stared at him in surprise. Or maybe it was anger. "I know you're not deaf. I know you heard me tell you to drop it. What the hell are you playing at?"

He held up his hands. "Nothing. I swear. I just wanted you to know that I understand how you're feeling. How hard it is to lose someone like that, so suddenly."

If looks could kill, she'd have struck him dead right then. "You don't know the first thing about me. And you don't have any idea what it's like to lose someone like that."

She was wrong. He did.

"My first year on the crew, I was partnered up with Kenny so he could show me the ropes. He'd been doing this longer than I'd been alive, had fought wildfires I couldn't even imagine and come out on the other side still grinning. And then one day, we were out cutting line on a small fire when a lightning storm kicked up. He was dead before I even realized what happened." He held her gaze. "I know I'm your lead suspect. That this is your investigation and you've got to do your job. But I still want you to know that I'm very sorry about your brother."

Maya took a deep breath then said, "Your condolences don't change the fact I didn't meet another soul in Tahoe after . . . after meeting you in the bar. And whoever wrote that note met me exactly six months ago."

"Gary and I talked for several minutes after you snuck away," he said, and her cheeks flushed as he continued. "I went straight to Joseph's cabin from the station. There's no way I could have lit your room on fire. Not without a can of lighter fluid and a match—and a key to your room."

Logan hadn't spent this much time defending himself since he was seventeen—and guilty as charged. This time things were different.

He was innocent.

"Feel free to search my truck. You and I both know you won't find anything. And I'd never scare a woman like that. Not with a fire. Not with a creepy little note. If I wanted to have it out with you, I'd do it here. Now. Face-to-face. Give you a chance to fight back."

"You don't scare me, Mr. Cain."

Her chest rose and fell quickly as she held her ground, her high cheekbones and slightly slanted eyes stunning in the moonlight.

And even though she had it in for him, he admired the way she lied to him. She was tough. Smart. And so damn sexy that even as they mentally squared off against each other, his body wouldn't let him keep a safe distance.

"Whoever wrote that note is wrong, Maya. You're not pretty."

The words found their way from his brain to his mouth before he could stop them, and her mouth opened in surprise.

"You're beautiful. I never forgot you, never forgot the way you tasted, how sexy you were."

He was close enough now for her to sway into him, and he caught her, dragging her luscious curves against him. He slid one hand into her hair, cradling her scalp. She was shaken, and although he hadn't convinced her that he was innocent, he wanted to protect her all the same.

He lowered his mouth to hers, and her lips were softer, sweeter than he remembered. He'd never met a woman with so much passion buried deep inside of her. Within seconds she proved him right, her kiss angry and hard, then seductive and teasing. He wanted to know all of the things that pleased her, uncover all of her secrets.

With nothing more than a kiss, she held him captive as no other woman had.

Six months fell away and it was as if they were back in his friend's bar with her fingers grasping his shoulders and his hands moving down past her waist to cup her incredible ass.

Only now she didn't think he was an innocent man.

"I didn't do this," he whispered against her lips. "I would never hurt you."

She pushed him away with all her might, her eyes

blazing with heat. She wanted him. He was sure of it. But she was afraid to trust him. And then she blinked, and when she looked at him again he saw ice where there had been desperate need.

"Don't touch me again." She wiped away his kiss with the back of her hand. "And you should know that I called my boss. I told him everything."

Strangely, disappointment hit him square in the chest. She'd probably be gone by tomorrow. He should be glad to see her go, but he wasn't.

"So, when's he sending in the new guy?"

"Surprise. He didn't care. You're still stuck with me. Now get out of my way before I call the cops."

Logan stepped to one side and let her go even though he wanted to grab her and kiss her over and over until she forgot about the letter, about her things going up in smoke. Until she believed him when he said he was innocent.

Instead, he was going to head back up into Desolation Wilderness on the trails behind Joseph's house and cover the same ground he'd gone over a dozen times during the past two weeks, to make sure there weren't any new fires to put out.

An hour later, Maya sat on a faded bedspread in a motel two blocks away from her old one, trying to forget Logan's kiss—and the way his gentle touch had pierced straight through her heart. Forbidden yearning tore at every last one of her principles, straining them to the breaking point.

Her years as an arson investigator should be giving her a window into Logan's life as a potential firefighter-turned-arsonist. And yet, she could only see him through a woman's eyes, as a man who knew how to give her everything she desired.

But it was more than his kisses that drew her to him. Everything he'd said about her brother had been sincere. Even his surprising offer to help her look into the apartment fire that had killed Tony.

She hadn't let anyone in that close since Tony's death. But Logan hadn't waited for her to open the door. He'd walked inside before she even realized what had happened and got her talking about her brother and how much she missed him.

A loud bang from the parking lot startled her and she jumped off the bed. Her conversation—and her kiss—with Logan had taken up so much space in her head that she'd almost forgotten not only the fire in her room, but the horrible note someone had left for her in the firebox. It hit her anew that she was in danger, and her heart raced while she prepared herself to fight an unknown predator, hands up, legs braced apart.

Seconds crept by as she waited for someone to crash through the door. But the only sounds that followed were the TV turning on next door and a toilet flushing. She sat down hard on the edge of the bed, taking a couple of deep breaths as she waited for her heartbeat to return to normal. Someone had slammed their car door or started up a rusty engine and she'd just about lost it.

That's what she got for romanticizing her suspect and taking her eye off the ball for even one second. Work. She needed to get back to work.

First, she called the rental car agency, but their outgoing message said they'd closed for the night and wouldn't reopen until 10 A.M. She was supposed to meet a helicopter pilot at the local airstrip at 6 A.M., but without a car she had no way to get there.

She fished around in her bag for the emergency contact number for the Flights of Fancy pilot. The receptionist she'd spoken to that morning had told her to call if there were any changes in her schedule. Five minutes later, she'd worked out the details with a guy named Dennis. He'd come pick her up at her motel and drop her off when they were done.

Putting down the phone, she looked up and caught a glimpse of herself in the mirror above the dresser. She lifted a hand to her disheveled hair. Her suit was sandy and covered with soot. She looked like she'd been in a war zone. She could easily buy a comb and fix her hair, but because her suitcase had been destroyed in the fire, changing into clean clothes wouldn't be quite so easy.

Again, she was struck by a deep sense of violation, even though she'd only lost one piece of luggage and her computer; and it was a strange feeling, being scared. She brushed off her clothes and shook out her hair as she stood up. She refused to let fear—or even anger—get the best of her for one more minute. She needed to get out of her room. Get something to eat. Buy some clothes to wear the next morning. Then crawl under the covers and get some rest.

She'd need to be on her toes tomorrow. Logan, she was certain, would be back on her trail. And he knew exactly how to push every one of her buttons.

Well, she'd be pushing back. Hard. And she wouldn't stop until she knew who was responsible for both the Desolation Wilderness fire and last night's structure fire and note.

She headed down to the gift shop and grabbed a couple of the least offensive T-shirts and sweatpants among the "Love Lake Tahoe" gear for sale, along with a pair of Crocs.

She'd buy proper new clothes tomorrow when regular stores were open, but she doubted the helicopter pilot would care if she was wearing sweatpants and recycled plastic shoes at 6 A.M. Heck, he probably expected people to look like shit at sunrise. The panties were the only thing that really gave her pause, the word "Lake" on one cheek, "Tahoe" on the other, capped off with a big heart over the crotch. But since no one was going to see her without clothes on, it didn't matter.

And then, just as she was about to head for the diner attached to the side of the motel, she decided to make one more phone call, to look into something that had been bothering her all day. Using the pay phone in the hotel lobby, she called the anonymous tip line.

"Hello. Lake Tahoe Crime Stoppers. How may I help you?"

Maya quickly explained that she was an arson investigator working on the Desolation Wilderness case and gave her Cal Fire employee and Social Security numbers so that the woman could log onto the system and verify her identity.

"I was hoping you could pull up the audio for a tip given on Monday afternoon."

She heard the woman click around on her computer. "Got it. Would you like to hear it now?"

"Yes, thank you."

A moment later she heard a very strange voice say, "I'm calling to tell you that someone I know has been lighting fires in Desolation Wilderness. His name is Logan Cain. And he's a hotshot."

Unease twisted Maya's stomach in knots. "Could you please repeat it for me?" she asked, but even after hearing it several times in a row, Maya couldn't tell if it was a man or woman speaking. The voice had an unreal quality to it.

"There's something strange about the voice, isn't there?"

"Now that you mention it," the woman said, "it does sound weird. Almost like it's a machine and not a person. It was a voice mail left after hours, otherwise I'd let you speak to the volunteer who took the tip."

Maya thanked the woman and headed into the diner.

Ten minutes later she stared into her chicken cranberry salad, remembering what Logan had said about someone naming him on the tip line because of a grudge. Was he right? He'd been unfailingly kind about her brother. Could Logan do anything this cruel? Again she wondered, should he even be a suspect?

Her stomach growled but she couldn't eat. She should have just gotten into bed and tried to sleep.

The waitress noticed her untouched plate as she walked by. "Everything all right, honey?"

Maya looked at the woman. The right answer was *Yes. Everything's fine,* but she'd just been through the day from hell and she didn't have the lie in her. "It's been a long day," she said softly.

The woman nodded sympathetically. "Had a few of those myself recently." She held up a finger. "Be right back with something that's bound to perk you up." Ten seconds later she slid a thick slice of chocolate cream pie in front of Maya. "This ought to help some. Sure as hell is better than a salad anyway."

It was a nice gesture from a stranger, so Maya played her part by picking up the fork and sliding it into the pie. She forced down a bite and lifted her lips in a grim approximation of a smile.

"There you go." The woman beamed. "Only thing that can cure a broken heart is chocolate pie. Works every time."

Maya managed to keep hold of the fork until the waitress passed through the swinging door into the kitchen.

It clattered to the table before she threw a twenty down, then slid from the booth and hurried out of the diner.

A broken heart. God, no, that wasn't it at all. Logan hadn't broken her heart. He couldn't have. She would never allow herself to have feelings for a suspect in a million years. No matter how well he kissed. Or how intimate he was with her body. Or how much she wanted him to put his arms around her and hold her.

But even after a long hot shower and an hour of mind-numbing reality TV, she couldn't fall asleep. Not with all the lies she'd been telling herself bumping around together in her head.

CHAPTER EIGHT

THE ALARM went off at 5:45 and it took Maya a long moment to figure out where she was. She stumbled into the bathroom, and when she saw her Love Lake Tahoe tank top in the mirror, everything came rushing back.

Recognizing Logan on the mountaintop.

Losing her breath every time he got close.

The horrible, threatening note in her burning hotel room.

Talking about Tony with the fire chief.

And worst of all, Logan's kiss on the beach.

She'd been tired and lonely and scared, all of her defenses down when he'd moved in for the kiss. For the kill. And she'd let him. She'd actually let him kiss her. Because she'd wanted it more than anything else, even though she knew she'd regret it—and she did, God, how she regretted it. She hadn't been able to push him away, hadn't been able to stop herself from reaching for him and pulling his hard body against her.

Fortunately, with the new day came clarity. And renewed confidence. She knew how to get his friends and coworkers to talk, knew she'd eventually find someone who was simply dying to dish out his secrets. And then she could make a carefully calculated decision about his guilt . . . or innocence.

She hurried through a shower, then carefully applied the makeup she kept in her bag. She hadn't slept well and needed to conceal the dark smudges under her eyes and make herself presentable for whatever the day brought her way.

A white truck pulled into the parking lot, jacked up on oversized tires. The driver rolled down the window and stuck his head out. He looked to be Logan's age and sported a goatee. There was something familiar about him, but she couldn't put her finger on it.

"You Maya Jackson?" He grinned at her as she walked down the stairs and shook his hand. "Dennis. Nice to meet you." He hooked a thumb toward the diner. "Mind if we get a quick cup of coffee before we head up? Late night last night. You know how it is."

No, she didn't. She didn't do late nights anymore, didn't want to bother acting like she was having fun with a guy when she simply didn't care. But he was the pilot, not her, so she said, "Sure, that's fine," even though every second of daylight she lost was one more opportunity for Logan to track her down and stick to her like glue.

Dennis held the door open for her and she stepped inside, waiting patiently while he ordered two coffees to go. She really didn't want one, knew the strong black brew would only make her nauseous on an empty stomach, but she took the cup from him anyway.

Country music blared from the radio as they pulled out of the parking lot. "So what brings you to town?"

Whenever possible, Maya liked to move under the radar. The less people knew about what she was doing, the more they talked. "I've heard people call Lake Tahoe the eighth wonder of the world. Thought I'd check it out for myself."

"Got any part of the lake you'd like to head toward first?"

She shook her head. "Actually, I'd like to head out over the mountains, if you don't mind."

He gave her a funny look. "That's the first time anyone's ever asked to do that. I mean, the trees are nice-looking and all, but are you sure you don't just want to head out over the lake instead? It's real pretty, especially this time of year."

"Maybe later, thanks."

He turned into the airstrip's lot and pulled up beside a helicopter. She took a deep breath. Helicopters weren't her favorite mode of transportation, especially given that it was bound to be a choppy ride over the fire as hot pockets of air flipped the small aircraft around like an ember. As always, she was struck by how small the aircraft was, even with room for three passengers and a pilot. As she climbed in, her elbows knocked into the door. The bubble front window went floor to ceiling, wrapping around them head to toe. She clipped on her seat belt and put on the headphones he handed her.

The radio was hopping with a steady stream of voices arranging for gear to be hauled in and out along with one bucket drop after another.

"I knew there was a fire going, but I didn't realize it was this far along," Dennis commented as the rotors started spinning. "You still want to head over the mountains? It might be hard to see much with all that smoke."

She nodded as they lifted into the air. "I'm sure it will be fascinating."

"Man," he said, "it looks like a mother of a fire. I know most of those guys out there, actually."

She shifted in her seat to look more carefully at him. "You do?"

"Yeah, my dad was a hotshot. You know, one of those superhero dudes who puts out deadly wildfires."

She nodded and said, "Wow, that sounds intense."

Had she hit the jackpot entirely by accident? Lord knew she desperately needed some leads, and at this point she'd take anything she could get, especially a local son of a hotshot. Maybe he'd know something about Logan.

"My dad was seriously pissed when I didn't follow his lead and join the crew." He shrugged. "What can I say?

Firefighting isn't my bag, even if everyone in town thinks those guys' shit don't stink." He shot her a grin. "I'd rather take pretty tourists up in my helicopter any day."

She made herself smile back, even though she was slightly creeped out by his compliment. The truth was that Dennis's piloting skills were in great demand by the Forest Service. He could have helped put out a lot of fires over the years. But she wasn't here to make moral judgments about other people's professions.

Directing Dennis's attention back to the fire, she asked, "Is your father down there right now?"

"No, he retired a few years ago. But my brother is. Well, my foster brother anyway."

Maya's breath caught in her throat and she found herself coughing. She'd been planning on contacting Joseph's son, Dennis Kellerman, later that morning. Instead, she'd lucked out and he'd been handed to her on a platter. Better still, he had no idea who she was—and seemed to have a very big mouth. The key was to keep him talking as long as she could.

"You okay?" he asked.

She swallowed hard. "I'm fine. Sorry about that. Anyway, I think you were saying that your foster brother is down there. Is he going to be okay?"

He shrugged. "Sure, he'll be fine. Logan knows his way around fire better than almost anyone."

Maya worked like hell not to betray any recognition at hearing Logan's name. Right now the most important thing was to keep asking innocent little questions and find out as much as she possibly could about her suspect. "What do you mean?"

"He moved in with us when he was seventeen. Man, people would never know it now, he's such a do-gooder, but he was a badass back then."

Dennis was wrong. Logan was still a badass, with a capital B. Any woman could see it. Especially her. The fact that he did good deeds on a daily basis only made him hotter. Her breath hitched as she caught herself doing it again. Allowing herself to build up Logan just because he was good-looking and his kisses made her burn with need.

Dennis continued, saying, "He was such a pyro when he came to live with us. He used to light fires all the time. That's probably why he's so good at putting them out."

Holy crap, that's what Logan had been hiding from her.

His pyromaniac past.

Maya was so stunned that she barely managed to keep up her end of the conversation. "And they let him on the hotshot crew with that background?"

Dennis snorted. "No way. No one knows about his background. No one but me and my dad." He shot her a glance. "And now you. But what the hell do you care about something a random firefighter did a zillion years ago? Don't tell anyone, okay," he joked. "I wouldn't want to get the bastard in trouble."

She manufactured another smile, even as it struck her that although Logan had moved in with Joseph as a teenager, and Dennis and Logan were practically brothers, based on everything Dennis had said to her, he obviously didn't know Logan was a suspect in the Desolation Wilderness wildfire. The two men must not be close enough for Logan to call and confide his troubles. Maya made a mental note to find out why.

But Dennis wasn't finished saying his piece quite yet. "Most girls I know love firefighters. You too?"

She paused to make it look like she was giving it some thought. "I guess so."

He snorted again. "If women had any idea how much ass these guys get they might think twice before hopping into bed with them." He seemed to realize what he was saying a moment too late. "Sorry, I didn't mean to be crude. I don't usually do the early morning flights, but I was on vacation all last week so I'm making up hours."

She waved her hand at him and said, "Don't worry about it," even though the truth was that she'd never felt cheaper.

Some silly, stupid part of her had wanted the connection she'd felt with Logan during their fifteen minutes in the bar—even last night when he'd kissed her—to mean something. But now that Dennis had confirmed she was just one of many, it was time to face the truth. Even as she continued to reel from her discovery about Logan's pyromania, she had to accept that there was no connection between her and Logan. And there never would be.

A moment later, they came up on the fire. When she

looked down through the clear glass base of the helicopter her breath went. "My God, the entire ridgeline is on fire."

Dennis pointed just to the east of the ridge. "Check that out. Those neighborhoods are about to go up in smoke."

She bit back a curse. The hotshot crew had done an amazing job of playing defense, but they couldn't keep the full-court press going forever. Houses would start burning today. One by one, innocent people would lose everything. All of their pictures. The gifts they'd been given. Mementos they'd held on to for sentimental reasons.

The sense of violation she'd felt last night after losing one suitcase and computer was nothing compared to what these people were about to go through. All they could do was gather up their kids and their dogs and cats and get the hell out, only to watch their homes burn on the news.

"I had no idea it was this bad." Dennis said. "I've definitely got to get back. I'm sure they'll be calling me any minute now to help with water drops. Sorry to cut your trip short. I'll talk to my boss to make sure he doesn't charge you for the trip."

She nodded her understanding, but needed to find out a couple of things before they turned around.

"Before we head back, can you tell from looking at the blaze where it might have originated?"

She already knew, from the obvious V-like pattern in

the hillside, and once it was safe to reenter the terrain, she'd head into the hills to get the information she'd need for a complete report. But right now she wanted to hear what Dennis had to say about it, to see if she'd get lucky again and he'd accidentally give something else away.

Dennis studied the terrain. "Might have been easier to tell you yesterday before it went crazy, but my first guess would be right there. It's pretty hard to see through the smoke," he continued, "but I fly over these mountains every day, so I can tell what's different."

She pulled out a topo map. "Could you point to that spot on my map?"

"Seriously?" he asked, frowning as he looked a little more carefully at her. "Why would you want to know this?"

Perhaps it had been a good thing that she didn't have a clean suit to put on this morning. There was no way he'd guess that she was an arson investigator in her tourist gear. Not until she told him anyway.

"For my scrapbook."

"Whatever," he said as he shifted in his seat to point to a section of the map, and she got a strong whiff of gasoline off his fingers.

She turned to look more carefully at him, studying the easy lines of his body, the careless way his hands were resting on the wheel and gearshift.

Her conversation with Albert hung heavily in her mind. She couldn't trust anyone. No matter how trustworthy they appeared, no matter how innocent they looked.

Was it at all possible that Dennis knew who she was all along and was simply feeding her information about Logan to send her off course?

And then, as she folded the map and stuck it back in her bag, he said, "Sure am glad I didn't do that hiking trip last week with Logan and my father. Otherwise we would probably have arson investigators on our asses right now. Especially since it looks like those houses are going to fry."

She spent an extra moment working the bronze clasp that held her bag shut, glad for something to do with her hands so she didn't accidentally give away her intense interest.

"Good move calling off the trip," she agreed. "Why didn't you go?" she said in a friendly, offhand tone that was utterly at odds with the significance of his reply.

"My dad wasn't up to it," he said as he spun them around and headed back toward the lake. "And I had other things to take care of."

Busy digesting everything Dennis had said during their illuminating flight, Maya looked out across the wide expanse of blue water and was momentarily stunned by the beauty all around her. Even with her brother's death inexorably connected to Lake Tahoe, she couldn't ignore the magnificence of nature at its best.

"Thanks for the ride," she said, knowing she couldn't keep him in the dark for much longer. As soon as they touched down and he'd unlocked the doors she would tell him exactly who she was, why she was in Lake Tahoe, and that she'd be back in touch with more questions in the very near future.

No doubt, Dennis would be surprised. Especially considering all he'd told her.

It had been another long night in the forest. Logan rubbed one hand across his eyes, forcing back the last vestiges of exhaustion. The fire was spreading fast. Soon it would start taking lives.

He'd run the trails, one after the other as they split off from one another like fingers from a palm. Fortunately, he hadn't found any hot spots this time, hadn't had to bury any embers. But he couldn't keep doing this every day, couldn't withstand the relentless pace for much longer.

He'd grabbed a handful of hours of sleep before the sun had risen and he'd called Dennis to give him a heads-up about the investigation. But he'd been too late: In a sick twist of fate Maya was already up in Dennis's helicopter. Mining for gold.

She'd have had to squeeze information from Joseph, but Logan wasn't so sure about Dennis. Ever since Logan had become a hotshot, their relationship had been a little strained. It was almost as if Dennis thought Logan had joined up just to kiss Joseph's ass.

Logan had stopped trying to talk his friend around

it a long time ago. Sometimes things were cool between them, sometimes they weren't. Dennis could be hypersensitive, and while conversations always started off friendly, some innocuous comment often screwed everything up.

He'd find out soon enough what kind of day this one was.

He watched the helicopter head back toward the landing pad from behind the wheel of his truck until he saw Dennis's girlfriend pull into the parking lot.

Jenny was a tall, leggy redhead who automatically made a guy's head turn to guess if her tits were real or fake. But she wasn't Logan's type, and not just because most of the guys in town had already had a ride.

Ten years ago, he'd nearly been seduced by her long legs and big green eyes. But after he'd figured out that she'd already done half the guys in turnouts, he'd let her down easy before things got out of hand. And by the time Dennis started dating her earlier this year, he'd figured his nonrelationship with her was old news, so he'd kept his mouth shut, and wished his friend well, even though she still frequently made passes at Logan when she was drunk. Frankly, she wasn't the first attached woman who came on to him, so he didn't read much into it.

"Hey, Logan." She jumped down from her truck. "I just heard about your suspension. I can't believe they're accusing you of lighting this fire."

"Word spreads fast, doesn't it?" Just as he'd thought

last night, there was nothing quite as juicy as a fallen hero.

She put her hand on his arm. "How are you doing?"

He appreciated her support, but he wasn't about to get into it with her. Or anyone else. All that mattered was clearing his name, not sitting around whining about being falsely accused of arson.

"Just working to clear my name so they can find the real arsonist and I can get back on the fire."

"Just so you know, nobody thinks you did it. And everyone's super pissed about them fingering you."

"Thanks," he said as the helicopter headed toward them. "I'm sure we'll get everything figured out soon,"

"What a shitty situation," she said, as she shook her head in commiseration. "I know you've got a lot on your mind right now, but Dennis and I are heading out for breakfast when he lands. Any chance you'd like to join us and try to relax for a little while?"

"I'll have to take a rain check," he said, "but I'm glad you're here. I've got a favor to ask."

"Whatever you need right now, I'm happy to help. Both Dennis and I are."

"Sometime today, could you check in on Joseph? He's slowing down a bit. I know he'd really appreciate some help with the cabin."

"No problem. What do you want me to do? Laundry? Cleaning?"

"You're a mind reader," he said, glad to have one less thing to worry about. "Thanks."

She made a face. "I would have helped out before, but you know how Dennis is about his dad. I don't know what his problem is. Joseph is amazing."

Logan wasn't going to go there. The damage between Dennis and Joseph wasn't any of his business. He'd spent years trying not to get in the middle of it.

A few moments later, the wind and noise from the helicopter rotors forced them back several steps. Logan reached out to steady Jenny, not letting go of her shoulders until the blades slowed. Through the glass, he could see Maya and Dennis talking. Suddenly, Dennis's face went a nasty shade of red and the next thing Logan knew, Maya was hopping out of the helicopter onto the blacktop. When she saw him her eyes widened in surprise, then quickly narrowed.

He barely had the chance to note her interesting fashion choice—even sweatpants and a T-shirt looked damn good on her—before she was in his face. Breathing fire.

"You and I need to talk. Now."

She didn't wait for him to agree before heading toward the small office on the edge of the airstrip. She clicked open her cell phone and Logan immediately wondered who she was calling and why. And how much more trouble it was going to get him in.

First, though, he needed to find out what Dennis had already told her.

"I blew it, man" were the first words Dennis said.

"Oh shit. You told her."

Dennis's hands were out in front of his body as he

defended his fuckup. "I didn't know who she was. She didn't tell me until we landed. I saw the fire and I didn't have enough caffeine in me yet and I couldn't control my mouth."

It was always excuses with Dennis. Always had been. Joseph and Dennis had taken Logan in when he didn't have anyone else and he would give up his life for his adopted family, but that didn't mean he wasn't pissed as hell right this second.

Jenny looked between the two of them. "What are you talking about, Dennis? Who is that woman? What did you tell her?"

"She's an arson investigator. She's here because of the Desolation fire." Dennis looked like he was about to cry. "I didn't mean to sell you out," he said to Logan. "I swear it, man."

Jenny looked helplessly at Logan. "He doesn't know yet. I was going to tell him when he landed." She turned to her boyfriend. "Logan has already been suspended from the fire. That's why he's standing here right now." She lowered her voice to a hiss. "*That woman* is investigating him."

Logan had never seen Dennis look more upset. Or nervous.

"Oh Jesus, I'm sorry, Logan. They've got to know you'd never do something like that, right?"

"What did you tell her about me?"

Jenny shot a questioning glance at Logan. "What are

you talking about? What dirt does he have on you? Is it something that could get you in trouble?"

A muscle jumped in Dennis's forehead. "Swear to God I told her it was just stupid kid stuff. You were never trying to hurt anyone. You were just pissed off at everything." A flurry of words were hurtling out of his mouth as he worked to clear his conscience. "I'm sorry, man. But even knowing about that stuff you used to be into, there's no way she can pin this fire on you. Everyone knows hotshots are holy men around here." Dennis glanced nervously at Jenny. "Besides, it'll be impossible to get any good evidence. It's all burning up. You're safe."

Dennis always did have a knack for saying stupid things like that. A gust of wind dusted them with ashes as Logan reminded himself that none of this was Dennis's fault. He hadn't been a pyro, Logan had.

"Don't worry about it," he said to his foster brother.

He turned and headed for the office to face down Maya. It was time to do some serious damage control.

CHAPTER NINE

A SIGN on the office window said the private airport wouldn't be staffed until later that morning, but the door would be unlocked so that people could use the bathroom. Maya locked herself in the single stall to get her thoughts in order before facing off against Logan. Again.

She gulped down some ice-cold tap water to clear her head and returned to the small room just as he let the door close behind him, his broad shoulders and six-plus feet effectively blocking all sunlight. He looked like he hadn't gotten much more sleep than she had, and still, he was so gorgeous she lost her breath just looking at him.

"You're a pyromaniac."

Logan didn't bother to deny the truth. "I used to be. A long time ago. But I'm not that kid anymore."

He couldn't think he was going to get out of it that easily, could he, that his charming good looks would make her say *Oh, okay, never mind.*

"I might have believed you yesterday when I asked you point-blank why you went to live with Joseph. But now you've forced me to reexamine things. To ask myself why you were hiding something so important from a fire investigator. To consider whether or not you're guilty, after all."

"Look," he said, "I used to light fires. I was a stupid teenage boy who didn't have a clue."

Even as he tried to talk his way out of the extremely damning evidence against him, his kiss was still imprinted on her lips. She could still smell him. Taste him.

Damn him for having such power over me!

"Why should I believe you? All I know is that you were seen putting out two fires near the ignition point— and you used to light fires for fun."

"I can see how you'd think that. But this time, it doesn't add up. You asked me about my past yesterday. Well, here it is: I lit fires when I was a kid because my dad was an asshole and it made me feel powerful. I didn't get that fires could destroy things, that they could spin out of control and kill people. I was a fucked-up kid. That's all it was. I swear to God, Maya, my past has nothing to do with these fires."

It was incredibly difficult to hold tight to her doubts in the face of his sincerity.

"How can I be absolutely sure that it really is all in the past?"

She thought back to her interview with Joseph the previous afternoon, how sad it must be for Logan to see a once-strong man fade away.

"Joseph took you in during a difficult time in your life. He was good to you, he treated you like another son, and now his health is failing. It must be incredibly hard for you to deal with. You wouldn't be the first person to act out of grief." She took a deep breath. "Like me. With you. When Tony died. You wouldn't be the first person who'd screwed up in the heat of the moment. Or the last person."

"Of course I'm worried about Joseph," Logan agreed. "I want to get him to a doctor. I want him to move in with me so that I can keep watch over him. I want to hire a cleaning crew to wash his clothes and empty out his sink and make sure that he eats. But there's a big difference between making out with a stranger and arson."

"Really?"

Her voice shook on the lone word as she thought back to that day in the bar, when it had seemed like her whole world was crashing down around her.

"Are you sure there is?" she found herself asking.

He moved closer. "It's all tied into your brother, isn't it? This case. Me being a firefighter. Being here in Lake Tahoe."

She instinctively pulled her bag up over her chest as a shield. Why did he always have to go to the one place that hurt the most? "No. Tony's case is completely separate from this one. I know what I'm doing."

At least she used to. Before everything got so damn complicated. Which was why she needed to focus on the facts at hand. And not the way her libido spiked whenever he came within five feet.

"The fact is that pyromania is a huge strike against you, Mr. Cain."

He came closer again and she felt her throat move as she swallowed, saw his eyes catch her nervous reaction to his nearness.

"Right now there's nothing to connect me to the fire other than speculation. And we both know that speculation won't hold up in court."

He was right. And she hated it, along with his ease around her, the fact that he wasn't taunting her in any way, wasn't even attacking her for coming after him.

"Some cases come together faster than others," she said, feigning tranquillity she certainly didn't feel. "I'm not going to give up."

"I know you won't, Maya," he said in the same voice he would have used to coax a frightened kitten out of a tree. "Can't you see? We're on the same team. I want to find the arsonist. I want to make sure he pays for what he's done, for dragging my name through the mud and my men with it."

His inescapable logic combined with the sensual force of his bright blue eyes, his white teeth against tanned skin, was enough to break her, to get to her agree to anything he desired. He'd had a lifetime to practice his charming lines on unsuspecting females who fell for the gorgeous picture he presented.

"I know Desolation Wilderness like the back of my hand. I can help you find the real arsonist."

Goddamn it, she hated that he was making sense. Even more, she hated how tempting his offer was. The chance to be near him tugged at her insides. *Even though he'd just admitted to having been a pyromaniac.* She was crazy to even consider his offer.

His cell phone rang and her first thought was that she'd been saved by the bell.

"Robbie? What's happened?"

She was halfway out the door when the anguish in Logan's voice stopped her midstride. A rush of words echoed in the small room, and as his face lost all color beneath his tanned skin chills ran up her spine.

A firefighter reacted like that only when something bad had happened to one of his men. Something really, really bad. And Maya knew better than anyone just how deadly fires could be.

"An explosion? Gasoline? Are you sure? I'm heading to the hospital right now." Logan pushed past her and out the door.

Maya's stomach twisted. A gasoline-fueled explosion didn't sound like another blowup. It sounded like arson at its worst. And based on nothing more than Logan's horrified reaction to the news, she knew he wasn't responsible.

She ran after him and reached his truck just as he was turning on the ignition. She yanked open the side door, barely jumping into the passenger seat before he slammed his foot on the gas pedal.

"What happened? Has there been another accident?"

A muscle jumped in his jaw and she knew that if she were in his shoes, she'd pull over on the shoulder of the freeway and kick him out the passenger door.

"I know you don't trust me, Logan, but I think you were right when you said the only way we can catch the arsonist is if we both know everything."

He didn't look away from the road at her deliberate use of the word "we," didn't outwardly react to her using his first name for the first time, but she knew he'd heard.

"I'm taking you up on your offer."

"Don't fuck with me, Maya. Not now."

She could understand his need to lash out at someone, anyone. He'd just found out horrible news about one of his men. She'd made it her mission to be a pain in his ass, and she was the only person within striking distance, so it was perfectly reasonable that he'd take his pain out on her. But an explosion that had hurt one of his men changed everything.

This was no longer the same case she'd opened Friday afternoon. The initial Desolation Wilderness wildfire had looked fairly cut and dry. But with the fire in her motel and this explosion, she was sure they were up against a dangerous serial arsonist. Again she wondered about the strange voice on the tip line. Had someone wanted to hurt Logan by framing him as an arsonist?

"If someone is setting off explosions to hurt your men, it could be the same person that lit my motel room on fire."

She'd do whatever she needed to do to catch this arsonist. Even if it meant partnering with a former pyromaniac whose mere presence played havoc with her insides.

"Logan, I need your help before they hurt anyone else. I need to know what happened."

She'd barely finished her plea when Logan slammed on the brakes at a red light. The air rushed out of her lungs as she flung toward the windshield, her seat belt locking into place just in time.

"Jesus, I shouldn't be driving this fast. Are you okay?"

"Yes. Don't worry about it. Just tell me what's happened. Please."

"Late last night the fire shifted direction toward a second housing development."

She could hear the pain in the raw timbre of his voice and when he didn't elaborate, she pushed him forward. "Given what I saw from the helicopter, it didn't look like the fire had touched any of the houses yet. Has that changed?"

"No. Not yet."

She waited silently, as patiently as she could, for him to continue. She knew what it was like to need some time to process information, to try to figure everything out in your own head before you told anyone. It was precisely why she hadn't talked with anyone about Tony since his death.

The strange thing was, she suddenly realized, Logan knew more about how she felt than anyone else. For some reason, she'd felt comfortable talking to him about Tony. Was it simply because he was a firefighter? Or was something else there that she didn't want to see?

Logan's voice brought her back to the present situation. "Gary thought he was giving Robbie one of the safer jobs. Robbie's young. Too green to be in the thick of the fire. He was lighting a backfire a quarter of a mile from the property line. It's textbook." His mouth tightened with rage. "Anyone who knows wildfire behavior would have lit it there. There's no way this explosion could have been an accident."

"Has anyone tested samples yet to make sure it's gasoline?"

Dennis and the heavy smell of fresh gasoline on his hand immediately sprang to mind. Could he have been involved with the explosion in some way?

"Robbie wouldn't be in the burn ward fighting for his life if some motherfucker hadn't gone out there and doused the entire area. He didn't stand a goddamn chance. The grass blew up in his face. Gary said he was covered in flames, head to toe, and was unconscious by the time anyone could smother the flames and get to him."

Logan's voice didn't break, his armor didn't fall, and

that was what got to Maya the most. It was his job to hold himself together even in the worst of circumstances, when the men he loved were dying.

"He's a goddamned rookie. A great kid with a pretty girlfriend in town."

"I would have given my life for my brother's," she said gently, knowing that Logan had to feel the same way, that he believed he'd personally let down Robbie by not being beside him to pull him away from the flames.

No one should go through that kind of helpless pain alone.

"We'll find out who did this to him. I promise."

Logan fishtailed into the hospital parking lot, then leapt out of the truck. She ran through the glass sliding doors a beat behind him.

For the hundredth time, Maya seriously questioned Logan's guilt. There was no way he could have poured gasoline over dry grass in the middle of the night, knowing one of his men might go up in flames. This explosion smacked of a psychotic arsonist who didn't care whom he hurt.

In five years of involved investigations, Maya had never heard the clock ticking so loudly, or so quickly. She was up against a serious threat. They all were.

Logan pushed through a glass-fronted door, and when she saw what had happened to Robbie, her spinning thoughts ground to a halt.

My God.

Tears filled her eyes and it took every ounce of will

for her to remain standing. Memories flooded into her system, rising up from the linoleum floor tiles through her feet, gunning for her heart, trying to break her again, just as they'd broken her before.

Robbie lay on the hospital bed, hooked up to a life support system, wrapped head to toe in white gauze. When he woke up—if he woke up—he would be in more pain than anyone should ever have to live through.

A pretty blonde girl who'd been weeping beside Robbie ran into Logan's arms, and he held her tight as she sobbed against him. When the girl finally stepped out of his comforting embrace a few minutes later, Maya could have sworn she'd taken some of Logan's strength with her.

The girl left the room in a daze, wiping her tears away with the back of her hand. Maya watched Logan kneel on the floor beside Robbie, his head tucked down along the side of a bandaged hand. She didn't know if he was praying or simply hiding his tears.

She'd been through hell with her brother, and still she didn't know a damn thing about dealing with it.

She blinked and wiped away the tears leaking out from beneath her lashes. When the apartment building had collapsed around Tony and his body had been pinned beneath a thick ceiling beam, the other firefighters hadn't been able to drag him out. The heat of the flames had destroyed everything. Even his bones had been reduced to ashes. She'd been so angry for so long at not even being given the chance to say good-bye to him in a hospital.

But now that she saw Robbie surrounded by machines, she wondered if Tony had been the lucky one. In all likelihood, her brother had died on impact. Whereas pain would be Robbie's constant companion for the next several years . . . if he survived.

She pushed away from the window and wiped her eyes dry. She couldn't allow long-buried grief, or its fresh counterpart, to muddy her thinking. She had to stay focused on the investigation. But it took a long moment to remember where she'd been when Logan heard the news about Robbie. She'd been standing in the airport office questioning Logan and wondering about Dennis's motives.

Intent on finding out more about Dennis, she headed to a nurses' station.

"This is going to sound like an odd request, but I really have to get online to look something up. Could I use one of your computers for thirty seconds?"

The two nurses sitting behind the counter frowned. "I'm sorry, ma'am," one of them said, "but I'm afraid we can't permit you to do that."

Maya swallowed a frustrated snarl. She wasn't simply wanting to check her e-mail to see if her nonexistent boyfriend had sent her a note. But they didn't know the severity of the situation. Somehow, she needed to walk the fine line between confidentiality and disclosure.

"I'm an arson investigator," she said quietly. "And I

desperately need to print out a document regarding the hotshot who just came in. It's a vital clue in my search for the person that did this to him."

One of the nurses leaned forward and looked both ways down the empty hall. "You can use my computer. But hurry, honey. I don't want anyone to see."

Maya slipped through the swinging door and took the woman's office chair.

"Ellen, you could get fired for doing this," the other nurse hissed.

Maya quickly pulled up a government background check on Dennis Kellerman as Ellen responded to her coworker with a snort.

"You heard her. She needs to catch an arsonist. I don't want to see another kid with third-degree burns over eighty percent of his body come in here."

Maya cringed. Eighty percent. My God, she'd known people who'd recovered from third-degree burns on one arm, and their pain had been excruciating. Her heart broke again at the thought of what Robbie would go through if he managed to pull through the initial physical shock.

With shaking hands, she printed the document and logged out. "Thank you," she said to Ellen as she retrieved the pages from the printer.

"No, honey, thank you." She patted Maya on the shoulder. "Now go find the bad people and lock them up. We're counting on you."

Feeling the weight of expectations on her shoulders—

her own the biggest of all—Maya quickly read through Dennis's short file. She sensed Logan before she saw him, and when she looked up he was looming tall and dangerous over her shoulder before she could hide the document.

"Dennis? Why are you doing a background search on him?"

Confidentiality was crucial. She shouldn't tell Logan anything, should never have let one of her suspects see a copy of another suspect's background check, even if she'd suggested they share information. She felt like her own back was against the wall.

"I have to be suspicious of everyone, Logan. It's the only way I'm going to find out who started these fires."

"There's nothing on Dennis. He's as innocent as they come. Jesus, Maya, the longer it takes us to find the real arsonist, the more people are going to get hurt." She read the grief, the anger on his face and felt them as her own. "One kid is already lying half dead in a hospital bed. We can't wait for another one of my men to end up covered in bandages."

She put her hand on his arm, then yanked it away at the surge of heat between them. "Neither of us wants that, Logan. And if I'm wrong about your foster brother, I'll back off. But if I find something there, I have to do my job and look into it."

He stood in the hospital hallway watching her, his shoulders so broad they almost looked like they were going to bump against the pale green walls.

"Tell me why Dennis is suddenly on your list."

An hour ago, she wouldn't have even considered letting Logan in on her investigation, but after having seen him with Robbie, she was absolutely certain he hadn't set off this explosion. Watching him at Robbie's bedside as much as made her decision for her: They would work together to investigate this new fire, and along the way she hoped to get some answers regarding the initial wildfire.

"I smelled gasoline on his hands."

"He's a helicopter pilot. He probably just filled the tank before your flight."

"Maybe." Maya noticed that the nurses were hanging on their every word. Either that or drooling over Logan. Probably both. "Let's go outside, where we can talk privately." They stepped under the covered entryway. "I've been thinking about some of the things Dennis said to me during our flight. Things he told me about you."

When Logan didn't respond, she asked, "Don't you want to know what he said?"

"He didn't do it."

"Humor me, okay? Would you say that you and Dennis have a good relationship?"

"Yes."

"Is your relationship with Dennis strained in any way?"

"No."

"Would he have any reason to set you up?"

"No."

All of a sudden, he was king of the one-word answer, and she felt sorry for all of the women he'd ever dated, especially the ones who'd wanted to talk things through.

"Okay, then, why don't you explain why he told a total stranger all about what a piece of work you were when you moved in with him and Joseph?"

Logan shrugged. "We were teenagers. I probably went out with some girl he liked."

She thought about it, thought about everything Dennis had said. "I don't think so. He didn't say anything about you taking away a girlfriend. It was all about his father, about how you ended up being the golden child. Instead of him. People start fires because they're angry. Or sad. Or hurt. They light fires because they want people to notice them. They harm people because they're jealous."

Maya lost the tenuous hold she had over her patience. "If you want to clear your name and get back out on the mountain, you should be happy that I'm following another lead."

"You're right. I need to be on the mountain with my men. But I'm not going to sell out my foster brother. There has to be another way to approach this."

"I've already got one," she said, knowing he wasn't going to be much happier with her next move than he was with her investigating his foster brother. "We both know that gasoline doesn't combust in open air, even if someone lights it on fire. Not without something else added to it. Which means I need you to take me to the site of the explosion and lend me some turnouts so that I can get a sample before the fire devours all of the evidence."

He looked at her like she was crazy.

Maybe she was. But she wasn't turning back.

CHAPTER TEN

LOGAN FELT like he was standing at the end of a batting cage, with baseballs hurtling straight toward his head.

He'd stared at Robbie in his hospital bed and known it could have been any of them lying there, wrapped head to toe in bandages, fighting for their lives. Sure, he and Sam and Connor had run faster than the blowup, but in so many ways getting out had been sheer luck.

The last thing Logan wanted was another reason to have to return to the hospital. Between worrying about his men and worrying about Joseph wandering onto the trails behind his house and getting too close to the fire—or lighting a new one—Logan was pulling from reserves.

And now Maya wanted to risk her life to collect evidence. During fire training, he'd been interested in every part of the fire academy, and he was fairly well versed in running an arson investigation.

To get enough solid evidence to test in a lab for flammable hydrocarbon residue, she'd need to stand on top of the explosion site.

No way.

"Using that sniffer you've been hauling around is way too dangerous right now. Forget about it."

"I'm not stupid," she said, her mouth set into a familiar stubborn line. "I know it's dangerous, but I need those samples. If you won't take me, I'll find another way to get it done."

She was the most bullheaded woman he'd ever met, which made her perfectly suited to her job.

No matter how much he got in her face, she stuck to her instincts. She followed her gut, just like he did when he was fighting fire. There was no point in arguing with her. She wasn't going to back down.

"I'll suit up and get the samples."

Her mouth opened in shock. "No way. I can't allow you to do that. You're my suspect. Not my assistant."

But Logan wasn't going to back down either. If she hadn't figured it out yet, they were well matched.

"I'm your only option, the only guy with the gear who's willing to risk his life to get you something to take to the crime lab."

She had to realize he'd never let her go in herself. He

couldn't stand the thought of seeing her wrapped up like a mummy in the hospital.

"I'm good friends with the chemist who runs the local lab. You don't want to wait out the weekend, do you?"

She sighed, knowing her hands were tied. "You know I can't wait that long."

"I'll get him to open up his lab today." Provided David wasn't sailing on the lake with his family for the weekend, of course, but there was no point in mentioning that. Not when he was using his friend as leverage.

They drove to the hotshot station to collect his gear. "You might want to stay in the car," he warned her in the station parking lot. "Odds are, you're not real popular with the guys right about now."

Ignoring his good advice, she jumped out. "Do you honestly think I care?"

Yeah, he did. But saying so would only set her off. "Don't say I didn't warn you."

He watched her square her shoulders and set her expression into an impervious mask as they headed inside. A handful of guys were gulping down a quick meal around the plastic dining table.

Logan grabbed his flame-resistant jacket, pants, boots, and helmet from his locker.

"What the fuck is she doing here?"

Even though Maya had pulled him from duty, he wasn't going to stand for the guys treating her like she was dirt. She had a job to do and she was doing it. End of story.

To her credit, she didn't appear the slightest bit bothered by their scrutiny. Logan supposed being hated by firefighters in these situations came with the territory.

"She's just doing her job, Sean," he said before turning their focus away from her. "What are conditions like on the mountain right now? How's everyone holding up?"

Sean, Zack, and Andy momentarily stopped glaring at Maya. "It's completely kicking our ass," Zack admitted. "The wind's acting all squirrelly, and with the dry shrubs, the fire's moving fast. Really fast."

Andy cut in. "I heard you went to see Robbie. How's he holding up? None of us can get out to the hospital. Not while the fire's spreading so fast."

Firefighter morale was a funny thing. Most of the time guys could block out the bad stuff until they'd finished doing their job and the fire was out. But this was a special case. His only option was to say very little about Robbie's true situation. After his brief talk with Dr. Caldwell, he wasn't at all sure Robbie was going to pull through.

Logan weighed his words carefully. "He's hanging on."

The guys nodded and ate some more, knowing better than to push for details they couldn't handle. Sean pointed to the gear in Logan's hand. "She letting you back in the game, man?"

Maya finally spoke. "Let's get going, Mr. Cain." She turned on her heel and walked back out to the car.

Andy whistled. "What a waste of a hot piece of ass."

Logan clenched his jaw, feeling more than a little proprietary about Maya's curves. "Keep your focus on the fire," he warned, knowing it was exactly what he needed to be doing himself. "I'll be back in action as soon as I can."

He headed outside and threw his gear into the back of his truck. He slid behind the wheel.

"Must be rough."

Maya didn't say anything, but her full lips were a tight line.

"Your father was a firefighter. And today you're the enemy, the one they all love to hate."

She shifted in her seat, turning away from him, her hands clasped tightly on her lap. "I don't have to investigate firefighters very often, but when I do, I don't treat their cases any differently."

"Are you sure you can do that?" Logan asked, even as he wondered why he cared so damn much. Especially when she sure as hell wasn't making it easy for him.

She was silent for a long moment. "I never expected to run into you again, let alone for you to be my lead suspect. And then after what happened at the motel, after getting that note—" She stopped, and started over. "Trying to separate this case from what happened to my brother is the hardest thing I've ever had to do. But I promise you—and your men—that this is not a witch hunt. I'm not simply looking for someone's head to jam on a stake. And I don't want any more of your men to get hurt because of a serial arsonist."

She wasn't hiding her distress from him, and he felt that maybe he was starting to gain her trust.

"Thank you for that," he said. "For your honesty. And for thinking of my men."

She twisted the sniffer in her hands. "I don't want you to get hurt either, Logan. Getting evidence is too dangerous. I can't let you do this."

But danger no longer mattered. He needed to find out who'd set up the explosion to make sure it didn't happen again and take out another one of his men.

"Robbie was my friend. He didn't deserve this. Some asshole thinks he can get away with it. He probably thinks no one will be willing to walk up to that fire and find out what caused it." His hands tightened on the steering wheel. "That asshole is wrong."

"It's too dangerous. I wish you'd reconsider."

But they both knew he wouldn't. "What do I need to know about operating the sniffer?"

"Be sure to hold the red button down for at least thirty seconds or the sample size won't be large enough to register on the meter. I'll also need a couple handfuls of dirt and grass, and anything that isn't native."

She looked like she was going to say something else.

"Go ahead. What else do you want me to know?"

She shook her head. "Nothing."

"I can take it," he said in a soft voice. He could feel her warring with herself in his passenger seat, could practically see the wheels turning in her head.

Suddenly she said, "Just be careful, okay?"

Of all the things he expected her to say, that wasn't anywhere on the list. "Nice to know you care."

"Yeah," she said, her mouth quirking up on one side, "it would suck to lose my top suspect."

He found himself grinning in the face of the hellish thing he was about to do, appreciating her quick comeback as much as her luscious curves.

"I can't believe how big these houses are," Maya marveled as he used his universal remote to open the gates to the ritzy housing development and they drove past a row of huge recently built mansions.

He knew she was trying to lighten the mood between them in the face of oncoming danger—and probably evade their growing connection while she was at it.

"They've all got killer views," he said, playing along. "I used to hike up here before the houses went in. It was a damn shame when the public lost this land."

Not to mention one more pain-in-the-ass development for his crew to protect, despite owners who went out of their way to create fire hazards. Protecting people took first priority. But saving expensive houses was a close second.

He followed the winding road up the hill to a dead end. He could feel the heat from the fire even at this distance. It was going to be hotter than hell on the other side of the wall. And a hundred times more dangerous. All it would take was one spark to land on an untouched patch of gasoline.

He jumped out of his truck and quickly suited up, but

when he came around to her side of the car Maya held tightly onto the sniffer and mason jar.

"Wait here." He dropped his keys in her lap and pried the sniffer from her fingers. "But if you see flames start to come over that wall, get away as fast as you can, then get on my radio and report it."

She curled her fingers around his keys. "I'm not leaving without you."

"No use in both of us dying," he said, then leaned in and stole a quick kiss before he walked straight into a firestorm.

CHAPTER ELEVEN

MAYA WANTED to call out Logan's name as he opened the gate, and demand that he come back. A blast of hot air knocked into the truck, pushing through the cracks in the metal, vibrating against the windshield.

He'd told her to stay put, but she couldn't just sit in his truck while he risked his life to procure evidence for her investigation, not when she could hear and smell and feel the blaze as if it were right next to the truck rather than beyond the neighborhood wall. She was the only one who could keep watch over him. She had to make sure he didn't do anything stupid.

Running up the brick walkway of the nearest house, she knocked on the front door and rang the bell several times in rapid succession before she realized no one was home. The homeowners had likely been evacuated. She ran around the side of the house, searching for a way up to the roof. Fortunately, a huge extension ladder was propped against the back wall. The owner had likely used the ladder to water down the roof until the evacuation order came.

Scrambling quickly up the two-story ladder, she steadied herself on the gray roofing tiles and pulled herself onto them. She clambered across the roof to a spot where she had a clear view of Logan. But when she caught sight of the situation, her heart nearly stopped in her chest.

While the other hotshots were keeping a safe distance from the fire, Logan was crouched down directly in front of a three-foot wall of flames, scanning the ground for the best chunk of evidence.

Oh God. She'd been so focused on getting evidence, so consumed with her vendetta against arsonists, she'd actually sent him in without really giving thought to what he would face in the site of the explosion. How could she?

She screamed, "Come back," but all yelling did was hurt her throat. It was impossible for anyone to hear her over the roar of the fire and the helicopters circling overhead. The wildfire crackled louder now, and the sun moved behind a thick mantle of ash.

The blaze had looked big and brutal from the air that morning. Now it resembled a war zone. Clouds of black smoke hung ominously in the blue sky, while men and machines scrambled to battle a wildfire that was sending dozens of fiery tentacles farther across the mountain with every passing hour.

Everything moved in slow motion as the deadly yellow-orange flames reached out toward Logan and nearly covered his head. And then, at the last possible moment, he jumped back onto a safe patch of grass. She knew the vision of Logan standing fearless among five-foot flames and a black-and-gray carpet of ash would haunt her forever.

She choked on the smoke and dust rising into the air, her heart pounding rapidly in her chest. She didn't want any more firefighters hurt. Especially not Logan.

Helplessly watching him do her dirty work, she didn't have the strength to keep denying how special he was. She watched as he squatted, his turnouts pulling tight against his muscular shoulders and narrow hips. He was the kind of man women dreamed of at night. And he willingly faced death for the greater good.

Women threw themselves at him for good reason.

He held the sniffer away from his body and stood perfectly still for sixty seconds, just as she'd instructed. Flames whipped around him and she cursed herself for telling him not to rush. There was no way for him to have any idea if and where additional gas and explosives had been strewn across the grassy hill.

At any moment, the ground he was standing on could explode.

Her legs shook at the horrifying image of Logan lying on a stretcher, covered in blisters and raw, bloody skin. Her foot slipped on a tile and she had to reach out to steady herself by grabbing an exhaust fan.

Maybe he'd been right and she should have stayed in the truck. Maybe it would have been easier than coming up here to watch him.

And no matter what side of the investigation they were on, she was stunned by his courage.

She now fully believed Logan Cain was innocent. He would protect his men with his life. She was watching him do it right now. Witnessing his superhuman nerves in action as he walked through fire to gather badly needed evidence cleared any remaining doubts from her mind.

He hadn't lit the Desolation Wilderness fire.

Which meant someone else was responsible for all of this destruction. All of this pain. All of this suffering. Someone had lit the wildfire and then left that message on the tip line with Logan's name. She was almost certain that the same arsonist had lit her motel room on fire, then tried to scare her with the note in the firebox, and then had put all the pieces in place to set off the explosion that had nearly taken Robbie's life that morning.

Finally, Logan stepped away from the flames and jogged back to his truck. How, she wondered, could he move so quickly with so much heavy equipment on his shoulders? Especially given how drained he must be from the shocking heat.

Not wanting him to find her up on the roof watching—and worrying about him—Maya started to make her way back toward the ladder, but it was harder going on the way down, and her progress was slow. She was halfway across the roof when she heard the loud clang of heavy boots on the steel rungs of the ladder. Logan's soot-covered face appeared above the gutters.

"Don't you ever listen?"

"Rarely," she replied as carelessly as she could manage, but she couldn't push away the sweet feeling of relief that he'd returned unscathed.

"I guess I should just be glad you didn't come after me to make sure I was holding down the right button."

She kept her face averted, uncertain how to respond to what sounded an awful lot like teasing. Especially coming on the heels of an adrenaline-soaked evidence run. How could he be so carefree and relaxed, while merely watching him risking his life had jumbled up her insides?

But she was so damn glad that he'd made it out in one solid, intact piece that she couldn't hold back a smile. "You can't blame me for wanting a front-row seat for the Logan Cain show, can you?"

He smiled back and it was like looking straight into the sun. "Hotshots aim to please."

She was almost to the edge of the roof and he reached out for her, setting her heart racing again. She was so afraid of what she was feeling for him, had never been more scared of anything in all her life.

Wanting to keep some much-needed distance between them, she said, "I got up here by myself and I'll get down by myself," realizing too late that she sounded like a petulant child instead of an independent woman.

He didn't move from the ladder. "I've never left a beautiful woman stranded on a rooftop and I'm not starting now."

It was the second time he'd called her beautiful. He wasn't the first man to say that to her, but it was the first time she'd really cared.

No question about it. She was in way over her head with this man.

But when he reached for her on the roof, she couldn't push him away. Not when she'd just watched him walk into fire. She wanted to assure herself that he was really here, was still solid muscles and bones and unending charm.

His large, strong hands circled her waist and she ran one finger down the side of his face, leaving a thin line of tanned skin visible through the soot. She lowered her mouth to his, could almost taste the ash on his lips— when the ladder shifted, and she stiffened.

What was wrong with her? She was up on some stranger's roof in the middle of a raging wildfire and all she could think about was kissing a hotshot. If her boss could see her now, if her father was looking down at them, they'd both be horrified by her behavior. By her utter lack of self-control.

She pulled back, working like hell to rein in her body's disappointment. She'd wanted to kiss Logan more than she'd wanted to take her next breath. But although she couldn't kiss him, she could tell him what she knew he wanted to hear.

"I believe you, Logan. I know you're innocent."

He was still holding her, his hands burning through her T-shirt, onto her back. "What made you change your mind?"

She could hardly believe they were having this conversation up on the roof. "So many things. But watching you out there risking your life . . ." She shook her head. "I don't know a single other person who would have done something like that."

He touched her cheek. "You were going to."

"Once I saw how tall the flames were, once I felt how hot it was, I would have given up. But you didn't."

Oh hell, she shouldn't kiss him again. But she was going to anyway. How could she not?

She pulled him closer and the ladder clanked hard against the gutter as she pressed her lips to his. She slipped her tongue between his teeth and moaned as he took what she was giving and gave it back tenfold.

I could love this man, she found herself thinking, and it scared her so much that she nearly fell off the roof trying to get away from him.

"I'm sorry," she said, pulling away again. "I don't want to lead you on. And you know as well as I do that we can't do this."

The look he gave her said he didn't know anything of the sort, but he was willing to wait for her to come around. He helped her climb down the ladder, and his hands steadying her body felt way too good.

When they were standing on solid ground again, he said, "Thank you for what you said up there, about me being innocent."

She felt so nervous with him all of a sudden, like a schoolgirl talking to the star quarterback. "I'm just going with my gut, but you're welcome."

She'd never been comfortable with the idea of his guilt, not for one single second. She wasn't any closer to knowing who the arsonist was, but it was a huge relief to at least feel certain it wasn't Logan. She wanted to get the okay from her superiors to take him off suspension as soon as possible, but first she needed more data. Running the evidence he'd procured from the explosion site under a microscope would help a great deal.

Wanting desperately to find some middle ground, she said, "Is the crime lab close by? I'm anxious to find out what caused the explosion."

He pulled off his turnouts and dropped them into the cab of the truck. "I'll call David right now."

He clicked open his phone just as she slid into the passenger seat. "David, I'm glad I caught you. It's Logan Cain. I need a favor. A big one."

She was relieved when he quickly got a thumbs-up on using the lab. They'd have their data—and, hopefully, some answers—soon.

"So," he said, turning his focus back to her as they

traveled down the lakeside highway, "how'd you become a fire investigator?"

His low, sexy voice and his question jostled her. She couldn't think fast enough to respond as if she had more than a handful of brain cells.

"The National Fire Academy."

"Sure," he drawled, "that's the usual way. But why?"

For the past six months, she'd avoided firefighters like the plague. She hadn't dated them or hung out with them or helped out with their fund-raising raffles beyond what she could do on the Internet in the privacy of her apartment. She hadn't needed, hadn't wanted, any more reminders of the two men she'd lost.

But now that Logan was clearly trying to get to know her—who she was, why she did what she did—making out with him almost seemed like the safer option.

Sharing their bodies was one thing. Sharing their hearts was something else entirely. Especially when she didn't know if she had a heart left to share.

Finally, she said, "I knew from the start that I didn't want to be a firefighter, but I liked certain aspects of the job. So I ended up getting a degree in Criminal Justice. When my father encouraged me to go into arson investigation, it seemed like a good path."

"You know, I was thinking that your father and Joseph must be around the same age. I wonder if they worked the same fires."

It was hard for her to talk about her dad. They'd been so close.

"Probably," she said. "He was based near Monterey, where we lived, but his crew was sent to wildfires in the Sierras lots of times."

"I probably worked some of the same fires he did. When did he retire?"

Maya stared out the window at the cars rushing in the opposite direction. "He didn't. He died of lung cancer. A year ago."

Logan's hand covered her knee, his warmth penetrating her thin cotton Lake Tahoe sweatpants. "Jesus, Maya, that's not fair."

She was glad when he didn't point out how close together her father and brother's deaths were. Most people felt compelled to say that when they found out. It didn't help.

"You must miss him."

"I do," she said, "but I also know he wouldn't have done anything differently. And I wouldn't have wanted him to."

"I'm sorry."

His two simple words pierced her heart. She didn't want to talk about herself anymore. "What about you? Why firefighting? Why hotshots?"

She wasn't asking because she was an investigator and he was a suspect. She was asking for herself now.

"Joseph is a phenomenal man. A great mentor. And he loved what he did. I wanted that life."

"It fits you."

"It's all I've ever wanted to be. The only thing I've ever wanted to do."

She had a sudden flash of insight into the gorgeous wildland firefighter sitting beside her. "It's what set you straight, isn't it? It's what made you stop lighting fires."

He took his eyes off the road for a split second and caught hers. "You're right. It is."

"And I almost took it away from you."

"You were only doing your job."

He was right. Which was why she couldn't relax and forget about the case. She had to keep asking the hard questions, even if it meant the end of their first truly pleasant conversation.

"Tell me about Dennis."

His hand tightened on the gearshift. "What do you want to know?"

"You followed Joseph into firefighting. But his own son didn't. Do you have any idea why?"

"Flying a helicopter isn't easy."

"No," she agreed. "Being the passenger isn't always easy either."

"Never would have figured a tough investigator like you would be prone to motion sickness," he teased.

She had to laugh at herself. "Trust me, it's the only thing that's ever made me reconsider my choice of career." Quickly, she got back on task. "I guess what I'm wondering is why not fly for the Forest Service? They can always use more guys on water drops and search-and-rescue."

"They can, but not everyone is cut out for firefighting," Logan said.

She'd seen enough rookies quit midway through their first year to know he was right. "That's true. But I can't help wondering if his staying away from the fire service goes deeper than that."

"Deeper how?"

"Maybe he didn't want to be in competition with you." *Because he knew he'd lose,* she added silently.

"Dennis and Joseph were good to me when no one else gave a damn. Dennis is my brother in every way that counts. Every family has its problems. They don't resolve them by setting fires and getting one another thrown into jail."

Maya wished she could let her suspicions regarding Dennis go, wished she could drop it and return to the comfortable space she and Logan had shared just minutes ago. But the more she thought about her conversation with Dennis in the helicopter, the more it seemed like Dennis had a serious grudge with not only Logan but the entire hotshot crew. Could he have been the person who set the campfires that Logan had been seen putting out? Could he have digitally disguised his voice and left the message on the tip line?

"I hear everything you're saying, but what if this is a cry for help? A way to make sure his father finally notices him? And the perfect way to make sure you take the fall?"

A muscle jumped in Logan's jaw again and she hated

having to put him in a position to defend—to doubt—his friend.

"Even if he was pissed at me for something, fire isn't Dennis's thing. Back when we were seventeen and I'd try to goad him into throwing a match into whatever fire I'd started, he never would. He wouldn't know the first thing about lighting motel rooms on fire or creating explosions on a hillside."

"Maybe he had help from someone who knows fire behavior?"

Logan shook his head. "He doesn't have a lot of fire-fighter friends. Only me."

Everywhere Maya looked, she saw brick walls. "Do you know where he was last week when he was on vacation? Did you see him at all? Talk to him?"

Logan pulled into a gravel driveway. "No, but I'm going to find out."

CHAPTER TWELVE

THE CRIME lab door was open when they arrived. Maya was used to urban steel-and-metal buildings where the chemists all looked alike in their white jackets and black-rimmed glasses. A red-and-white barn in the middle of pine trees took some getting used to, as did the spray-painted fire motif that ringed the walls. Even the chemist's arms were covered in tattoos of flames.

For a moment she wondered if she was looking at another pyromaniac—but without anything else to go on besides an abundance of fire graphics, she knew she was grasping at straws.

"David, thanks for opening up the lab on a weekend for us," Logan said when they walked in. He took in his friend's casual beach clothes and flip-flops. "Damn it, I was hoping I hadn't pulled you off the lake. Sorry about that."

The chemist waved away Logan's concern. "Don't worry about it. Kelly was dying to get me out of the boat so she could take it for a spin alone with her friends. She says I'm too much of a wimp to max out the speed-ometer."

"It's nice to meet you, Maya."

She estimated he was in his early forties, solely by the lines on his tanned face and his slightly receding hair-line. He was tanned and trim and had the physique of a much younger man. Something about the lake and the mountains and the thin air in Tahoe made all the men better-looking than they had a right to be.

It was extremely disconcerting.

"So you're investigating the wildfire?" he asked.

"Yes, but this is evidence from an explosion that took place this morning."

"We heard about that. Poor kid. We're praying that he pulls through."

She didn't need to look at Logan to know that he was still seeing Robbie wrapped up like a mummy in the hospital bed.

"I need to find out where the explosive materials came from. Once you tell me what caused the explosion, I'll have a better idea where to look for other clues."

"I'm glad I can help. Not just to clear your name," he said to Logan, "but to catch the bastard who hurt Robbie."

Logan didn't respond. His head was bent down, just as it had been in the hospital when he was kneeling beside Robbie's bed, overloaded with sorrow.

David must have sensed it too, because he efficiently took charge of them both. "No offense, you guys, but I'm not big on people hanging over my microscope. Logan, go use my shower and take whatever clothes you want."

Shooting a lopsided grin at Maya, David said, "I'm guessing either you're a really big fan of Lake Tahoe"—he gestured to her tourist duds—"or something happened to your clothes."

"No one is this big of a fan," she said, smiling back.

Logan quickly explained, "Someone lit her hotel room on fire last night."

David whistled. "Do you think it's the same person who did this?" He held up the mason jar.

Not wanting to disclose too much of what was supposed to be a confidential investigation, she said, "I'll be following up with the fire chief shortly to see if he's learned anything more. But at this moment, I don't know."

David quickly got the point and backed off. "My wife is about your size, Maya. I'm sure she wouldn't mind loaning you a few things if you're tired of being a walking Lake Tahoe billboard."

Glad for his practical suggestion, Maya followed Logan out of the barn and into David's A-frame house. The only time she'd spent in Tahoe since her brother's death was to investigate the fire that took his life. She'd always made sure to get in and out of town quickly, steeling herself against acknowledging its beauty. It had been easier to focus on the seedy aspects of Tahoe life—the drugs and the booze and the crime.

This trip was different. This time she couldn't run away, and even as she guarded herself against its charms, the beauty of the lake and the mountains and the trees seeped deeper into her pores.

Just as Logan and all his charm and good looks and heroicism pushed further past her defenses.

She turned away from the window and saw that Logan had stripped off his T-shirt. Her mouth nearly fell open at the beautiful, tanned lines of his torso. He had muscles in places she didn't know they came. And he was so much better built than any firefighter she'd ever seen.

"Since we've got to wait for David, a shower sounds good." He smiled and his flash of white teeth was utterly mesmerizing. "You want one?"

Maya instructed herself to look away from his chest. And failed.

"No," she croaked.

He let her look her fill, one corner of his mouth moving into a grin.

"Suit yourself," he said, then headed into the bedroom off the kitchen.

Maya stood in the middle of the living room and worked like hell to tamp down her stupid hormones. As soon as she heard the shower start, she stepped into the master bedroom and tried to ignore that fact that Logan was only a couple of rooms away.

And he was naked. Her mouth went dry.

Her body urged her to accept his invitation to join him in the shower.

But even though she didn't think he was guilty of arson, she still couldn't allow herself to get involved. Not while she was working on a case. And definitely not with another firefighter.

Quickly, she pulled a pair of designer jeans and a T-shirt from the dresser. She drew the line at borrowing a stranger's underwear, however. She'd just have to stick to having the words "Lake Tahoe" scrawled across her behind.

Knowing she'd do something reckless and stupid if she was still standing there when Logan walked out of the bathroom in nothing but a towel, she locked herself in the laundry room to put on the new clothes. Both the jeans and T-shirt were a bit snug, but anything was better than the pink T-shirt and sweatpants she'd bought at the tourist shop in her motel.

She waited impatiently for Logan to return to the living room, and when he finally emerged she had to work like hell not to react to how ridiculously sexy he was in low-slung surf shorts and a T-shirt. Her only chance at fighting her attraction was to stay wholly focused on the investigation.

"How much longer do you think David will be?"

When he didn't bother telling her to relax, she knew he was just as anxious for some answers.

"Let's go ask him," he replied.

David was still hard at work when they opened the lab door and stuck their heads in.

"Not done yet," he said, locking a slide into place beneath a microscope before he looked up. "I'll bet you guys haven't stopped to eat today, have you? Our fridge is pretty much empty, so how about you head down to the Bar & Grill at the end of the road and I'll meet you there when I'm done."

Maya felt Logan tense beside her. The Tahoe Pines Bar & Grill was the last place either of them wanted to go, but it would be beyond awkward to explain to David why heading to that particular establishment was a very bad idea.

And then her stomach betrayed her by growling, sealing the deal.

"You guys are hovering," David said, so they went outside, closed the door behind them, and stood looking at each other on the flagstone walkway, neither one of them saying a word.

Finally, Logan shrugged. "I'm game if you are."

"I guess I am pretty starving."

All of a sudden the idea of taking a load off for a few minutes was a good one. Even if they were about to wade into emotional quicksand.

Maya knew she needed to be on her guard at all times around Logan. He was too good at knocking through her defenses, patiently pushing them away one by one. But she was so tired. And hungry, since it had easily been twenty-four hours since she'd last eaten.

Worst of all, she was more aroused than she should be by a great-looking firefighter in surfer clothes.

Silently, they drove down the hill, parked, and walked into the crowded restaurant. Logan hadn't been back in the place since Eddie had sold it to a couple of guys from Las Vegas about a month after Maya'd come in for a drink and blown his mind.

Logan wasn't sure he liked the changes. It had always been a neighborhood hangout, somewhere his crew would go when they were streaked with dirt and sweat, to shoot some pool and forget about staring death in the face for a couple of hours. The new owners had glossed it up, making it look more like a big national chain than a neighborhood bar and grill.

Posed pictures of people having a good time on the lake studded the walls, along with new paint and windows. Even the crowd was different. Flashier, richer.

"Man, this place has sure changed," he said as they grabbed a free table by the window.

She looked around. "Has it?"

What was he thinking? She'd been so full of grief over her brother six months ago that she probably hadn't noticed anything about the place. Besides, he'd shoved her into the wall of bottles and had been all over her so fast she couldn't have seen much of anything.

"I hate to break it to you," he said, intent on changing the subject, "but you're no longer in the running for Miss Lake Tahoe. Looks like Kelly's stuff fits pretty good."

A gorgeous flush worked itself onto her cheeks. "She's a little smaller than I am."

Logan dropped his eyes to her breasts for a brief moment. "A little. But trust me, it works on you."

Dennis's girlfriend, Jenny, came around the corner carrying a heavy tray of drinks. He'd forgotten that she worked lunch and dinner all summer. She smiled widely when she saw him, but when she noticed who he was sitting with, her smile turned to confusion.

"Logan, what are you doing here?" She didn't add *with her* to the end of her sentence, but he could read her mind.

"Time for lunch," he said. "What's good today?"

She looked down at her pad. "Everyone's been ordering the grilled chicken and avocado sandwich on a French roll. We're almost out."

Logan looked at Maya and she nodded. "We'll take two if you've got 'em. And two Cokes."

Jenny wrote down their order, but didn't get the picture that now wasn't a good time to talk. Especially considering Maya's new suspicions regarding Jenny's boyfriend. Logan knew Jenny wouldn't much like hearing that. Not any more than he did.

"I went by Joseph's cabin after breakfast," she said

with a frown. "I had no idea things were getting so bad. He barely seemed to know who I was. You should have asked for my help earlier."

Up until now, Maya hadn't made the possible connection between Joseph's illness and the trails heading up from his backyard into Desolation, and Logan didn't want to give her any reason to turn her suspicions that way. Even though she'd been in Joseph's house and had talked with him, the less said about the extent of Joseph's situation, the better.

Logan's conscience knocked at him. Maya had treated him with honesty from the get-go, she'd told him precisely why she'd thought he was guilty and then admitted she was wrong as soon as she'd decided he was innocent.

He wanted to be just as straight with her, but he didn't know her well enough yet to be absolutely certain how she'd respond to his concerns about Joseph. And he couldn't let anything happen to Joseph because he'd said too much to the wrong person.

"Thanks for going by, Jenny. I really appreciate it." He didn't bother with subtlety. "I'll give you a call later and we can talk more about the situation."

Jenny shot another glance at Maya before saying "Sure thing, Logan. I'll go put your order in."

Maya gave him an amused look when Jenny rounded the corner. "Boy, does that girl have a crush on you."

"Jealous?"

She watched Jenny giggle while whispering something

to a cute busboy before walking into the kitchen. "I take it back. She flirts with everyone."

He noted that Maya didn't go anywhere near his jealous question and he grinned. She didn't need to answer. She wanted him as much as he wanted her.

Now all he needed was for her to figure it out too.

Still looking at Jenny, she suddenly frowned. "Hey, wasn't she with you at the airstrip this morning?"

"She was meeting Dennis for breakfast. They've been dating for a while."

"Dating Dennis, huh?" She looked pensive. "How does he feel about his girlfriend flirting with you?"

He'd wondered the same thing and had come to only one conclusion: "He's not the jealous type."

She raised her eyebrows. "Sure he isn't."

A couple of firefighters from the urban station walked in and headed to the bar, probably to pick up some drinks for the road, and her face fell. He knew she was thinking about Tony.

"I was serious last night when I offered to help with your brother's case."

She turned back to him, her eyes wide with surprise. "I don't get it. Why would you want to help me?"

"Why wouldn't I?"

It was clear that she didn't know how to respond. Probably for the very same reason he wasn't comfortable coming clean about Joseph yet. Despite their physical connection, she was as unsure of him as he was of her.

"Thank you," she said in a soft voice. "I really appreciate your offer. Maybe when this case is done . . ."

Her words fell away and he wanted to press her further, make her commit to seeing him again when they were on the other side of this craziness.

Right then, he saw David walk in and search through the crowd for them.

"David's here," he said, and Maya's expression became all business again.

As glad as Logan was that they were going to know what had caused the explosion, the interruption had come too soon. At last, he'd felt as if he was getting at the real Maya Jackson, the flesh-and-blood woman with insecurities and hopes and softness, not just the hard-as-nails fire investigator that she forced herself to be every minute of every day.

David pulled up a chair. His happy-go-lucky friend looked as solemn as Logan had ever seen him. "I've got it."

Before he could say more, Jenny arrived with their sandwiches. They waited in tense silence for her to put them down and go away, but she was clearly in no hurry to leave.

"Hey, David," she said, "how are you doing?"

"Fine, thanks."

"Some fire burning, huh?"

He shot a quick look at Logan. "Yup."

She looked between the three of them, finally noting

that something was up. "You guys need anything else? Ketchup? Mustard? Are you hungry, David?"

"I'm fine, thanks."

She raised her eyebrows. "Okay, then. I'll be going on a short break for the next few minutes, so just holler at Amy if you need something else."

They all nodded, the plates of food remaining untouched. Finally, Maya broke the heavy silence after Jenny left. "What have you found out?"

"I've been able to clearly identify gasoline and fertilizer."

Maya closed her eyes for a moment. "Together they explode just like a bomb. It's easy and inexpensive. Anyone could have done it. It's the perfect crime." When she opened her eyes again, Logan got the sense she wasn't really seeing them. "Gasoline and fertilizer are too common, too likely to be in anyone's garage. Finding the person who laid the groundwork for the explosion is like searching for a needle in a haystack."

During his fifteen years as a hotshot, at the first sign of trouble Logan immediately sprang into action. He used his body, his tools, and his brain to fight deadly blazes. But this time things were different. Instead of battling fire, he was up against an arsonist. One who was out for blood.

"Thanks for the help, David," Maya said, pushing back her chair without touching her food. "I need to get going, need to check a few things out."

Logan stood up and threw down forty dollars as David handed Maya a printout of his results.

"Keep the faith. You'll find out who did this. And you'll stop them before they do it again. I'll stick around the house the rest of the weekend if you need me to test something else."

Maya gave him a weak smile as she took the lab paperwork then walked beside Logan to his truck. "I appreciate you hooking me up with David," she said when they were alone again, in the front seat. "And thanks for going above and beyond the call of duty today, first with the fire, now with this." She looked him in the eye. "But you need to stop wasting your time helping me, and get a lawyer, Logan."

What the hell? She'd told him she believed him.

She put her hand on his arm. "I know you didn't do it. But this is a small town. How many gas stations are there nearby, without driving all the way downtown?"

"One."

"How many places to get fertilizer?"

"One." He knew exactly where she was going. "And if the gas and fertilizer in my garage come from the same lots as the ones David just tested and my name is already on the suspect list . . ."

She finished his sentence. "It'll look like you did it."

CHAPTER THIRTEEN

MAYA HAD come to Tahoe to prove Logan's guilt, and he'd completely turned the tables on her.

Now she was certain of not only his innocence, but his compassion and understanding as well.

He was far too perfect, and far too difficult to resist.

She looked up, suddenly, and realized she hadn't told him where she wanted him to take her. "Where are you going?"

"To my house to get those fertilizer and gasoline samples."

No. She didn't want to go there, didn't want to pick up any evidence that could possibly link Logan to the crime.

But she knew he was right. If there was a chance that they could definitively rule him out, she could call

McCurdy and get him to officially end Logan's suspension.

She needed Logan to promise her one thing first, though. "If it turns out your samples are a match, promise me you'll get a lawyer."

Stuck behind a big tour bus, he took his eyes off the road and looked her in the eye. "I'll do it, but you'll come with me."

The bus needed to get its exhaust pipe looked at. It smelled like gas was funneling straight into his truck.

She frowned. "You don't need me to find you a lawyer."

"It isn't about finding a lawyer. I'm not willing to leave you alone. Not after what happened last night. Not until we find the bastard lighting these fires."

She wanted to tell him she could take care of herself, but those words were lost amid the warmth of knowing that someone was actually looking out for her.

In recent months she'd gotten used to handling everything herself, to never asking anyone for help, but there had been a time, back before everything that had happened to her family, when her father and brother had looked out for her. They'd kept her safe, whether it was vetting out a new boyfriend or screwing her overflowing bookshelves to the wall so they wouldn't fall over in an earthquake and bury her.

She was still trying to figure out how to respond when he pulled onto a gravel road that she figured was his driveway. Much like Joseph's, it was a narrow pathway between tall pines. And then, as if by magic, there emerged a pond with bright blue water, and beyond that a beautiful meadow. The driveway meandered up the undulating hills, toward a stunning wood-framed house.

It was one of the most incredible locations she'd ever seen. And the beauty all around her spoke volumes about the man sitting beside her.

"You did this, didn't you?" she asked in a quiet voice. "You built this house."

He turned off the engine. "How'd you guess?"

"My father did the same thing when I was a little girl. It reminds me a lot of where I grew up."

She'd loved every wall of their home, the tree house in the backyard that she'd helped her father build and paint and decorate, the flowers she'd dug into the earth and carefully watered all summer long so that when her father came back in the fall there'd still be blooms for him to see.

"Sounds like he was a great dad."

Something large, yet fragile, shattered inside of her. "He was." One of the walls protecting her heart now lay in shards by her toes.

"I would have liked to have met him."

She looked down at her hands. Anywhere but at Logan. She didn't want him to see her weak like this, all because he'd expressed a sincere wish to meet a man she missed every single day.

Obviously sensing that she had one foot stuck in

quicksand, he brought things back to the situation at hand. "My workshop is through the house and out the back. The faster we get an answer from David about my samples, the better it'll be."

She got out of the truck, grateful for his understanding, but as she followed Logan up his front steps, every nerve and wire inside her was on edge. The last thing she wanted was to be alone with Logan in this beautiful home he'd built. Not when a foolish part of her brain had started spinning elaborate fairy tales as soon as she'd set eyes on the property.

What if she'd met Logan under different circumstances? What if she'd come to his house an excited, blushing date, more than halfway in love with a strong, rugged firefighter? What would have happened then? Would they have gotten into his hot tub together and kissed until they were so crazy for each other they could barely make it upstairs to his bedroom? Would she have fallen asleep in his arms after making love and woken up beside him the next morning?

She tried to tell herself that she was only having these fantasies because she was tired. But as he led the way up a paved path to his front door, not only did her mouth water for the hundredth time at his muscular, tanned arms, his wide shoulders and sexy rear end, but her heart longed for a deeper connection.

For love.

He pushed open the unlocked front door and led her into a light-filled kitchen. She'd never had much of an eye for colors and shapes, but now she knew exactly what she wanted her house to look like one day. Exposed pine beams, huge panes of glass, and counter tiles the mottled color of natural stone.

He opened the fridge and handed her a soda. Suddenly realizing how dry her mouth was, that she hadn't touched anything at the restaurant, she took a long drink from the can. And then she made the mistake of looking back at Logan, and it took superhuman strength to pull her eyes away from his fingers on the pop tab, his lips on the aluminum rim, his Adam's apple moving beneath his tanned, lightly stubbled skin.

She forced her attention back to his very impressive house. "I would have known you built this house the minute I saw your floors." She pointed to the tight-fitting inlays in the hardwood. "Most contractors won't do this kind of detail work. It isn't worth their time."

"Is your boyfriend a builder?"

Her eyes flew to his face. "No." She found herself stumbling over words, found herself wanting him to know. "I don't have a boyfriend."

Logan's answering smile knocked the wind out of her lungs and she spun away from him. She couldn't stand it when he looked at her like that, like he knew exactly what she wanted, because he wanted the very same thing.

"Good to know," he finally said. And then, "While we're here, are you sure McCurdy isn't going to insist that you rummage through my file cabinets? My bedside table, maybe?"

Great will was required to stave off the redness in her cheeks. "I've seen condoms before."

His voice was smooth and sexy as he hit her with "Even the supersized, ribbed-for-her-pleasure kind?"

Damn it. He was good.

She turned and walked out of the kitchen, keeping her reaction to herself. Because even though she knew he was just joking around, her crystal-clear memories of that afternoon six months ago—and how his big erection had pressed hard into her belly—told her he was only half kidding.

The workshop was dark and cool. She pulled out a Ziploc bag and a sterile glass jar.

"I'm surprised that thing hasn't given you a hernia yet."

She put the heavy messenger's bag down on the cement floor. "I like to be prepared."

Quickly and efficiently, she began to collect samples, using a baby wipe to clean away any petroleum on her hands before moving to collect a sample of fertilizer. Her face was as serious as it'd been at the hotshot station when she'd suspended him from duty. Just as he had then, he wanted to pull her against him and kiss the solemn expression off her face.

She looked up and caught him staring. "Stop looking at me like that."

He'd never wanted a woman as badly as this. "I wish I could," he said, his words more honest than he'd intended.

She lowered her head again to the bag of fertilizer. "I wish I didn't have to do this, Logan. I wish I didn't have to take these to David's lab for analysis."

"Stop blaming yourself, Maya. We'll figure this out."

She surprised the hell out of him by spinning around and saying "Could you stop being so fucking calm already?" Little white pellets fell out of her bag and scattered all around their feet. "Just stop being so goddamn self-sacrificing for one second!" She shook the half-full bag of fertilizer in her fury, and more tiny pellets skipped onto the ground.

"If these match the samples from the explosion you could be in serious trouble. You could go to jail for something you didn't do. If Robbie doesn't live, they'll call you a murderer. And my hand will be in it. My saying you didn't do it won't mean a damn if your supplies came from the same stores and the same lots."

He moved closer, covered her hands with his. "It's not going to come to that. And if it does, we'll find a way to fight it." He rubbed her palms lightly with his thumbs. "Together."

She stared at him like he'd lost his mind, her face awash with emotions. Lust was there, of course, it always was between them. But there was also hope. And fear.

"You're either the most optimistic person I've ever

met, or the most delusional," she said, but already he could feel her relaxing moment by moment.

And then, just as he was about to pull her into his arms, she moved out of his grasp, backing into the bags of fertilizer.

"We'd better go."

God, how he wanted to make her face up to the fact that they belonged together, naked and sweating in his bed. But she wasn't the kind of woman a guy could push around. One wrong move and she'd back so far away he'd be lucky to catch a glimpse of her across a crowded room.

He followed her sweet ass in her tight-fitting borrowed jeans back out to his driveway. When they got in his truck, she scrunched up her nose.

"It still smells like we're riding behind that tour bus."

He frowned, thinking the same thing. "Might just be all the smoke in the air."

He started the engine and began to back out, when it suddenly felt like the bottom of his seat was on fire. And then it hit him: What they were smelling had nothing to do with the exhaust from a random tour bus.

Someone had sabotaged his truck.

He shut off the engine. "Get out of the truck, Maya."

"Why? What are you talking about?"

"I think there's a bomb under my seat."

She didn't ask any more questions, just unhooked her seat belt and reached for her bag just as his ass started to smoke.

He hooked one hand around her waist and her mouth opened with surprise as he dragged her out of her seat and through the driver's-side door. A faint hissing sound pricked his ears, and it was sheer instinct that had him picking her up off the ground and throwing her away from the truck.

Her body arced through the air, her hands moving to shield her face, her knees curled to protect her stomach and groin as she hit the ground.

Logan felt the force of the explosion a split second before he landed on top of her, covering every square inch of her head and back and legs and arms from the flying shrapnel.

Where am I? And why am I lying on the ground under someone? were the first thoughts in Maya's brain as she slowly came to. Her body ached in a hundred places. She felt bruised and battered all over.

And then she realized that Logan was covering her body with his own, his hard muscles a blissful blanket of safety. His chest rapidly rose and fell against her back as he worked to catch his breath.

Oh God, his truck had blown up. And they'd almost died.

She could feel the heat from the explosion all around them. She hadn't braced herself for hitting the gravel, and her cheek was pushed painfully into the sharp gray rocks, along with the rest of her. But it didn't matter how much it hurt.

They were alive. And Logan had nearly died trying to save them both.

Violent shaking started at her chest and worked down her arms and legs, even beneath Logan's heavy weight. Her teeth chattered and sobs built up in her stomach and chest.

She heard herself moan, heard him whisper gentle, encouraging words against her hair, but the sounds came at her through a long, dark tube.

Everything faded to black and she welcomed the darkness.

He'd thrown her too hard. She hadn't had time to prepare for the landing. He was too heavy for her. He shouldn't have crushed her like that, could have broken her ribs when he'd landed on top of her.

But she was alive. And getting her out of the truck had been the only thing that mattered.

It was obvious that they were both moving targets. And odds were it was only a matter of time before the next attack. They had to figure out who was behind all this, and fast. Before they paid with their lives.

His back and legs stung like hell, but he ignored the pain as he shifted to his hands and knees. Gently, he ran his fingertips over Maya's rib cage. Thank God, everything was where it should be. Moving to his feet, he scooped her up in his arms.

Her eyelashes fluttered open, then closed. She moaned again, working to focus on his face as he carried her toward the house, and he was so damn glad to get the chance to look into her beautiful brown eyes again.

Her golden skin was ash-gray and pockmarked with indentations from the gravel. The color had fallen from her lips. No longer rosy, they were pale, sallow.

He wanted to kill the person who'd done this. Coming after him was one thing. But almost killing Maya was unforgivable.

For now, the wildfire—even the investigation—had to fade into the background. Everything else would wait while he tended to Maya.

"You saved my life."

She didn't owe him anything. He didn't want her thanks. "I'd do it again in a heartbeat."

"Someone tried to kill us," she whispered.

He hugged her closer to him, the heat of her body further reassurance the she was all right. She'd had an enormous shock. And he wasn't ready to let her go yet.

"We don't have to talk about this now."

She tried to wriggle out of his arms while he carried her to his front door and kicked it open. He'd taken care of countless survivors. Her legs would buckle when they hit the floor. Not because she was weak. But because she was human.

Still, he admired her pride. Her strength. Slowly, he

let her toes touch the ground, keeping the bulk of her weight in his arms.

She pushed back to stand on her own and her face immediately lost all its color. He pulled her close again.

"Steady, now."

She wrapped her arms around him and gasped. "Logan, you're hurt."

His back had taken the brunt of the damage from the explosion. It was going to hurt like a bitch to clean up.

"I've felt worse. I'll be fine. Right now, you need to focus on getting your equilibrium back."

"No," she said, that determined glint in her eyes, "I need to focus on helping you." Her eyelashes fluttered down. "I can never repay you for saving my life, Logan. Please, let me help you. It's the very least I can do."

He was helpless against her soft plea, against the warmth of her touch. She slowly ran her fingers over his shoulder blades, down his spine to his lower back, making contact with cuts and bruises and a couple of pebbles embedded in his skin.

He bit back a groan of pain. He didn't want her to see his wounds and feel at all responsible for what had happened.

"You're probably still in shock. Go lie down on the couch," he instructed in a rough voice. "I'll be right back."

"I need to help you," she insisted, ignoring his command as her hands found the edge of his T-shirt.

She didn't wait for him to agree as she walked around

his body. She sucked in a breath when she saw the damage his back and legs had sustained, but she didn't faint.

"Hold still."

He clenched his teeth as she pulled the sweat- and bloodstained CSI Tahoe shirt away from his battered skin.

"I hope this wasn't David's favorite shirt."

Any other woman would have been babying him, crying over his wounds, maybe even getting sick at the sight of so much blood. But not her. Instead, she was trying to make him smile, just as he had with her. She inherently understood he needed to focus on something else.

It felt like white-hot flames were dancing across his shoulders. "His wife probably staged the explosion to get rid of the damn thing," he said through clenched teeth.

Maya's hand stilled on his back. "You don't deserve this, Logan. Not any of it. I'm sorry."

"It's just a truck," he said, even though he knew she was talking about much more than that. She was apologizing for doing her job and pulling him off duty. She was apologizing for coming into his home to take back samples for the lab.

"I'm sorry about your truck too," she said in a wry tone as she lightly traced the outline of another wound with the tip of her finger. "You're a mess. A complete mess."

She'd barely walked away from an exploding truck. And she was worried about him.

"I'll heal." He looked over his shoulder at her. "The only thing that matters is finding out who did this. And staying alive."

Her eyes met his, full of resolve. "Hotshots always were some of the toughest people I'd ever met." She searched his kitchen cupboards for a dish towel. "You'd better take your pants off too."

He twitched at her words, ready for action despite everything. "I don't think that's a good idea."

She pulled a blue-and-white-striped towel out of a drawer and turned on the tap, waiting several seconds for the water to grow warm. After washing her hands, she picked up a bar of soap and moved behind him again.

"This is probably going to hurt."

He braced himself. "Go for it."

Slowly, gently, she brushed away dirt and pine needles with the pads of her fingers down the length of his back. The soap and water stung like a mother, but her touch was the perfect distraction, far better than any drugs would have been.

He could feel her breath on his spine, the heat of her body warming his back. He wanted to turn around and heal himself with her lips, her curves, her responsive moans of pleasure.

And then her hands stilled against his skin. "You could have died trying to save me." She laid her cheek against his back. "I should have known something was wrong. I should have gotten out as soon as you said the word."

"No," he said, undone by her touch.

He didn't give a crap about control anymore, not when he'd almost lost her. He turned and threaded his bloodstained hands into her hair.

"Don't you dare blame yourself. Not for a goddamned thing."

All he wanted was to forget the image of her sitting in a ticking time bomb and the utter helplessness of watching smoke rise from the engine. He had to taste her, had to confirm that she was flesh and blood and not just a figment of his desperate imagination.

"I lost you once," he said as he lowered his mouth to cover hers. "I won't lose you again."

CHAPTER FOURTEEN

LOGAN'S WORDS muddled together inside Maya's head. She tucked them away for a different time and place, when she could breathe normally, when she could think straight. Right now, all she knew was that she couldn't stop rubbing her hands over his abs, over his pecs, over every square inch of his glorious broad, tanned chest. And that she'd die if she didn't kiss him that very second.

She'd never been so close to death before. His warmth, his heartbeat thudding against hers, the desire she read in his eyes—they all meant life to her. Keeping her distance from Logan and staying safe in her little world suddenly meant nothing. Not when one malicious act had almost robbed her of her chance to feel joy, to feel anything at all. She wanted to sample life's sweetness and allow herself a taste of the pleasure she'd refused for so long.

Their mouths came together and it was a blur of heat and passion. No one was in charge. Instead, they were both taking something they desperately needed, something they could only find in each other's arms.

He backed her to the kitchen island and she opened her legs to take him in closer. He was so big, so strong, so wonderfully hot as his hips shifted into place between her thighs. Ever since she'd seen him again on top of the mountain, barely twenty-four hours earlier—no, ever since she'd kissed him six months ago—she hadn't stopped wanting him.

The floodgates flew open as she melted in his arms.

She was discovering him all over again, just as he was discovering her. Little things like his scent and the way his stubble rubbed against her cheek sent dangerous emotions slithering in between her ribs, aiming straight for her heart.

His hands were gentle as they cupped her face and she instinctively tilted her face up as his mouth moved from her lips to the concave place between her chin and shoulder bones. Her limbs felt heavy, drugged with his kisses. Her skin buzzed and her nipples were stiff and tight behind her bra as he nipped at her jaw.

Through it all, she worked to hold herself apart from him and deflect the strong emotions threatening to overtake her, the voice in her head that was whispering something about Logan being her soul mate.

No, that was crazy. He couldn't be.

But when he flicked his tongue behind her ear, then pulled at her earlobe with his teeth, her body made the decision for her.

She knew the instant he felt her capitulation, by the tender way he caressed her shoulders and back muscles with deep, soothing motions. And then his fingers moved to her waistband and he pulled at her borrowed cotton T-shirt, dirty from her face-plant into the gravel. She shifted her hips slightly to give him better access, to help him strip her down.

She knew better than to go here with him again. But knowing better didn't change anything. Knowing better couldn't possibly stop the heavy heat in her pelvis or the slick arousal that gathered between her thighs.

Not when she was already so far gone.

Not when being alive meant being with Logan.

He pulled the T-shirt slowly up her body, over her aching breasts. When it was on the floor, she pressed herself against him. The muscles on his beautiful naked chest were tight and corded, the perfect foil to her curves.

"You're beautiful," she whispered, only realizing she'd spoken when she heard the words in the room.

He looked down at her as he ran his thumb over the swell of her breasts. "No," he said, bending his head down to lick the crevasse where her breastbone was, "you're the one who's beautiful, so beautiful you take my breath away."

Her breath caught at his words, his sweet caresses. No one had ever touched her like this, like he wanted her more than he wanted to breathe. No one but Logan.

She found herself losing track of time again, six months fading to nothing since they'd last stood like this.

She tried to right her thoughts, worked to lodge herself back into the impossibilities of the here and now, but when his mouth, hot and wet, came down over her lace-clad breasts, and his hands played against the sensitive skin at the small of her back, urging her to let go, she instinctively arched into his mouth.

Goose bumps covered her skin as he softly raked his teeth over her hard nipple. Logan's fingers were warm and steady on her shoulders as he slid first one bra strap down, then the other. The heat in his eyes intensified as he stared at her naked breasts, and she was powerless to do anything but stand there and let him look his fill. Reverently, he cupped her flesh with both hands and rubbed his thumbs over her nipples.

She closed her eyes and a low moan emerged from her throat. Moment by moment, touch by touch, he was seducing her defenses away.

She grabbed at his hips to pull him in closer—oh God, she wanted him closer—to her wetness. Her hips bucked into his thick shaft and he held himself still as she rocked and rubbed and pushed against him, desperate for release.

"That's it," he said, encouraging her madness. He bent his head back down to her chest, pressing her breasts close together so that he could take both stiff peaks into his mouth at the same time.

"You taste so good. So sweet."

He lifted her into his arms, carrying her up the stairs as if she weighed nothing at all. Even as he navigated the steps and the hallway, he nipped at her lips, tasted the sensitive crevasses of her mouth with his tongue.

He was taking her to his bedroom.

To his bed.

Her sex clenched at the thought of being naked beneath Logan. She shivered as he flicked the tip of his tongue against the corner of her mouth, and he smiled against her lips.

"Do you like that?"

She was hesitant to look into his eyes, frightened to give too much of herself away if he saw how much this meant to her. At last, she found her voice.

"Yes."

He captured her mouth again, harder this time, his lips and teeth and tongue telling her just how much he desired her. He pulled back, his blue eyes dark with passion.

"And that?"

She reached a hand up to his mouth and let her thumb and fingertips graze his full, masculine lips. "Yes. So much."

More than he knew.

He sucked her index finger in between his lips and she closed her eyes and relaxed into his strong, muscular arms, drunk from his tongue on her skin. She'd never known fingers could be so sensitive; never had a man spent so much time on her. Other men were only interested in foreplay as a means to an end. With Logan, she could tell that her pleasure pleased him.

He pressed a kiss onto her palm. "Tell me everything you like. Tell me everything that makes you feel good."

She stroked his chin, his stubble deliciously rough. "I don't need to. You already know."

A low growl vibrated in his throat and she watched, mesmerized, as his Adam's apple moved in his tanned throat. She ran her hand down to his neck, then past his collarbone and over his tight band of pectoral muscles. His heartbeat was strong and fast as he continued to hold her without strain, allowing her to explore his body at her leisure.

His nipple grew hard as she leaned closer and pressed a kiss into his shoulder. His skin jumped beneath her lips and, for the first time, she realized just how badly he wanted her; that he was barely holding on to his own self-control.

She swept her tongue out along his collarbone and tasted a faint sheen of clean sweat on his skin. His erection swelled against the side of her hip and his passionate reaction emboldened her further. She grazed a stiff tendon with her teeth, loving the taste of him, his masculine scent. He was just as beautiful beneath her lips as he was to her eyes.

He carried her across the room, laying her beneath

him on his bed. "I've wanted to do this for so long." He bent his head down to one breast and suckled her. "And this," he said as he laved the other.

She gasped with pleasure and arched into his mouth. Back and forth, he swirled his tongue on her breasts, kissing her flesh, softly nipping her sensitive skin. Every move he made aroused her, made her grow increasingly damp and desperate to feel the hot, hard length of him pressing into her sex.

"Please," she said, and a moment later his hands were on the waistband of her jeans and he was undoing the zipper and pulling them down her thighs.

"So beautiful," he said in a low voice as he slid her shoes and jeans to the floor. "So damn beautiful."

She waited with delirious anticipation to feel his fingers—or possibly, if she was really lucky, his erection—between her legs, and was utterly unprepared for warm breath on her heated skin. Her hips bucked into his mouth of their own volition, as utterly out of control as she'd ever been.

She was frightened by this intimacy, yet she craved it too badly to possibly make him stop.

And then his mouth came down fully over her cotton-covered mound and she stopped thinking altogether. She cried out his name as she moved against his lips, his teeth. His tongue found her clitoris through the fabric and waves of satisfaction moved through her, over her.

His touch was turning her inside out, but right now,

right in this moment, losing control felt right. Because she felt safe with Logan.

His fingers grazed her hipbones, then stalled. She instantly knew what he was asking. His erection pressed hard against her—he was as crazed with lust as she was—but even then, he waited for her to lead him forward.

She whispered "Yes" to tell him it was all right to continue, that she wanted him to remove her panties, that she was desperate to drop all the remaining barriers between them.

He pressed a kiss to her stomach, just below her belly button, and she sucked in a breath, waiting. And then, slowly, much too slowly, he slid her Love Lake Tahoe panties off her hips.

"I can't wait another second to taste you."

The fabric was still at her thighs and she should have been prepared for the slide of his tongue on her clitoris, for the muscles at the base of her stomach to clench and pull, but she wasn't.

Nothing could have prepared her for Logan.

Slow warmth moved through her as his tongue slipped and slid over her heated flesh. He cupped her butt cheeks to shift her mound higher, closer to his mouth. She wanted to watch this beautiful man touch her so intimately, but her eyes closed as she arched her neck, her body straining toward him. Alternately he sucked at her clit, pulling and dragging on her arousal, then swept his tongue down the slick length of her labia.

Her muscles clenched with need. She wanted all of

him, wanted to be filled with his huge, hard shaft. She opened her mouth to beg, to plead, but before she could utter a word, he slipped one thick digit inside of her.

Her breath stopped as she clamped around his finger. With painstaking slowness, he slid it in to the knuckle. She pushed against his hand, trying to take more of him inside. All the while, his tongue kept a steady beat on her clit. He added another finger to his sensual onslaught and she rode his fingers, pressed into his tongue. But instead of letting her crest the peak, he forced her to ride the ridge of pleasure, backing off when she got too close. He slid his fingers in, then out of her slick passage.

Higher and higher she flew, her muscles tightening one by one until she thought she might shatter.

"Please, Logan," she finally begged, even though she was a woman who'd never begged anyone for anything, ever.

He grasped a thigh in each hand and dragged her legs wider. Just the simple act of repositioning her and the feel of his hair brushing against her belly was enough to send her crashing over the edge. He thrust his tongue inside her and her muscles clenched and convulsed around him.

And then he was focusing every ounce of his attention on her. Licking. Sucking. Pulling at her until she wanted to scream with joy.

She'd never known it was possible to feel like this, like she was dying and coming to life all at the same time. He didn't stop licking her until her final tremor. She'd never known orgasms could be all-consuming, had never been limp and shattered afterward.

At last, she collapsed back onto the bed, gasping for air. Logan shifted his weight from between her legs and brought his mouth back to her breasts, tenderly nuzzling the undersides. Unlike other men who went straight for the nipple, he acted as if he had all the time in the world, and she found herself blossoming again beneath his mouth. She ached to feel his entire weight over her, and now that she'd found her breath again, all she wanted was to feel him sliding into her heat.

He lifted his head, a half smile on his beautiful lips. Lips that had brought her pleasure she'd never imagined possible.

"Soon," he promised, "but not quite yet."

She shifted and her foot grazed something hot and smooth. He immediately went stiff beneath her and, suddenly, she wanted him to know the torture of being teased—of being made to wait for something that was long past due.

She flexed her ankle and arched her foot, then pointed it and slid her toes slowly down his long length. Two could play the same game of anticipation and boundless desire.

Logan was levered above her on his forearms, his biceps and triceps shaking beneath her fingertips. And then the thick head of his erection was pressing into her heat.

The words "You win" came from his mouth a moment before he imprisoned her lips beneath his.

She bucked her hips into his hard heat, even though she knew better than to make love without protection. She was that far gone.

He allowed the head of his penis to slide into her, to stretch her wide, far wider than any other man before him. His eyes were blue-black with desire as he pushed inside another inch, and then another.

Her muscles gripped him tightly to pull him in farther. All the way in.

But Logan was a master of control, and her body ached for him as he pulled out and reached into his bedside table for one of the aforementioned condoms. He sheathed himself without her help—Lord knew her trembling hands would have been no use at all—and repositioned himself between her legs. He cupped her face and kissed her long and sweet.

She slid her hands against the great wall of his chest, then over his rib cage to hold on to his outspread lats. She shuddered as her forbidden dreams of making love to her mystery man from so many months ago came true.

"You're mine, Maya."

His passionate words rocked her to the core and she opened wide for him, moisture flooding her canal to ease his passage. Again and again, he thrust his hard, thick length into her. His heavy weight pressed her into the bed and his skin grew slick beneath her hands. Sweat beaded between her breasts and he bent his head to lick it from her skin without missing a beat, the steady propulsion of his hips driving her back up to what should have been an unattainable peak.

She'd never come more than once a night, not even hours apart. But here, beneath Logan's mouth and hands and erection, she was heading straight for another explosion, one that promised to be at least as powerful as her first.

He lifted his head again and locked his eyes on hers, knowing what was coming. And then his hands were in her hair and his mouth was on hers and she was wrapping her legs around his waist and rocking into him.

A cry of ecstasy tore from her throat and merged with his growl of pleasure as spasms wracked her body, starting from her heated core and working their way out to her skin, to the tips of her toes and fingernails and each hair on her head. She rode the length of his shaft again and again, her orgasm breaking her completely. She didn't know how long they lay together afterward, his wonderfully heavy weight pressing into her. It could have been seconds. Minutes. Maybe even hours.

Maya had known from previous experience that Logan could play her body like a fiddle . . . but she'd had no idea it would be a symphony.

Being with him felt—just as it had six months ago—so incredibly right, even though it was wrong for a million different reasons, more so now than it had been six months ago. Back then, she supposed she could claim the disorientation of grief for her impulsive actions. But now, minutes after begging Logan to take her hard and fast, her excuses fell flat.

Yes, she'd almost died.

Yes, she'd needed to feel alive.

But those were simply excuses for taking exactly what she wanted.

And she'd wanted him fiercely. Even though being with Logan—wanting Logan with every fiber of her being—spoke to her deepest fears.

Her mother had barely spoken at her father's funeral. But the one thing she'd said to Maya was forever etched into her brain.

Don't let yourself love a firefighter. It will only break your heart.

She hadn't had to say it again at Tony's funeral. It had been understood.

Now Maya was in a hotshot's bed, in a hotshot's arms. Logan was everything she'd ever wanted. Strong, courageous, willing to help people in need regardless of the risk to himself.

But all those pluses were minuses too.

The very things she admired about him, all of the things that made him so attractive, were the same things that made what he did on a daily basis so dangerous. She wished she could keep this contentment of being in his arms, hide inside of it.

But she couldn't allow herself to love—and lose—another man like him.

CHAPTER FIFTEEN

MAYA STIFFENED and unwrapped her trembling legs from around his hips. She pushed against his chest, and in the aftermath of the most powerful lovemaking of his life, when all he wanted was for Maya to stay cradled and warm against his chest, Logan had no choice but to release his hold on her, to give her the space she demanded.

He'd been desperate to claim Maya as his own. She was so damn beautiful—and so incredibly responsive, even more responsive than he'd remembered. She'd seemed equally as possessed, and he'd wanted to be gentle with her, wanted to erase the threat of death that hung over her. And he hadn't been able to resist the sweet pull of her body, her slick heat.

"We shouldn't have done that." Her voice was raw. Unsteady.

"We both took what we wanted, what we needed," he said, tipping her chin up with his fingertips to force her to look him in the eye. He wouldn't let her talk her way out of what had just happened. "There's nothing wrong with that."

A faint haze of satisfaction still covered her features, even as he watched her recoil from her loss of control. She was the most frustrating—and most seductive—woman he'd ever known.

She shifted away from him. "I shouldn't be here with you. Naked. In your bed."

He sat up, unconcerned with his own nakedness. "Don't ask me to apologize for what just happened. Because I won't." He dropped his eyes to her bare breasts, her soft skin red from his rough handling. "Not this time. Or the next."

She pulled the sheets up to tangle over her hips and thighs, before covering her chest with her arms and looking away, her mouth pinched tight even though her cheeks were still flushed from satisfaction.

"No matter how hard you fight it," he said, "no matter how much you wish we didn't have this connection, we do. This isn't over between us."

"It has to be, Logan. It's not even the fact that I'm here to investigate you. I can't date a firefighter. I just can't."

All at once, it was clear to him what was going on

in her head. She thought that hiding herself away from everyone and everything that reminded her of her father and brother would keep her safe.

"Only once have I had to tell a woman that she was a widow."

Her eyes flew to meet his. "Kenny? You had to tell his wife? But you were just a rookie."

"The superintendent wanted to make sure I had it in me to make it back from the edge." He thought back to that shitty afternoon, in the blazing sun, watching his awful words make a pretty woman cry. "I'm not going to lie to you. It was one of the worst things I've ever had to do." He touched her hand. "But the next day I was back out there on the mountain. To quit then would have made Kenny's death even more pointless."

She didn't say anything, but he hoped she was hearing what he was saying.

"You're incredibly strong, Maya. You're one of the strongest people I've ever met."

"I want you to understand," she said in a very serious voice. "You're wonderful, Logan. Anyone can see that. And you're right, our connection is . . ."

She didn't finish her sentence, but the rosy color splashed across her cheeks and her plump lips, reddened from their kisses, spoke volumes.

"I can't do what my mother did. I can't spend the next five, ten, fifteen years sitting at home waiting for the phone to ring."

He wanted to argue with her, but he couldn't. Not

when she'd been through hell already. How could he blame her for wanting to protect herself from more unbearable pain? He should have been happy to just be with her, naked in his bed. But he wasn't.

He wanted more.

Out on the mountain, when he was facing a fire, he knew to move slowly. Patiently making his way closer, inch by inch if that's all he could get. Rushing the flames never worked. Only a slow assault would get him closer to the flames, to the point where he could overtake them.

Yet again, he needed to take a page from his hotshot experience. He was moving too fast with Maya. He needed to back off and give her time. Otherwise, he'd lose her.

"I don't want to pressure you into anything."

She smiled a crooked little smile. "You're not. I just want you to know where I'm coming from. What just happened was great, but I don't want to lead you on. It wouldn't be fair."

She was the most honest, straightforward woman he'd ever known. His own conscience kicked into overtime.

"You've been completely honest with me," he said, knowing for certain that he could trust her. "Now it's time for me to come clean with you."

Surprise whiplashed across her face. "I'm not going to like this, am I?"

"Probably not," he admitted.

"I'm listening."

"You know that trails lead into Desolation from behind Joseph's house, don't you?"

Her brows furrowed. "I saw that on the topo map, but I hadn't thought . . ." She quickly worked out what he was getting at. "You think he's involved in the fire in some way?"

Logan shifted uncomfortably on the bed. "I sure as hell hope not. But with his memory failing, I can't stop thinking that anything is possible."

Maya sat up quickly, the sheet falling off her breasts to her hips. Logan fought to keep his attention on what she was saying, rather than on her spectacular curves.

"Including the possibility that he started the wildfire?"

This time he wasn't going to leave anything out, not even the most incriminating details. The only way she could help Joseph was if she knew the full, unvarnished truth.

"A couple of weeks ago, I dropped by to check on him just as he was coming back from a hike. I noticed ash on his treads, but when I asked him what he'd been doing, he couldn't tell me. He didn't know. Two miles up the trail I found a fire burning in a circle of rocks to the side of the footpath."

"I don't get it. Why would he have lit a campfire in the middle of the day during a short hike?"

"I've been trying to figure that out, and the only thing I can come up with is that the fog was pretty heavy, so maybe he got cold. Or maybe he got hungry and was cooking something to eat." He let her digest what he'd said, practically able to hear the gears churning in her head.

"Okay, so that could possibly explain what started the wildfire, but what about everything else? The anonymous tip? The fire in my motel room? The explosion? The bomb in your car? Who hates me and you and all of the hotshots enough to try to kill us all? Because there's no way Joseph could be involved with any of that."

Thank God, she wasn't blaming Joseph for everything, wasn't leaping out of bed and calling the police to go after an old man who wasn't hurting anyone.

"Someone is obviously watching us. Following our every move. We need to find out when that bomb was put in your truck. In your driveway? Or was it earlier?"

He went to the window to look down at the smoking vehicle. He wasn't worried about it sparking a fire on the wide swatch of gravel. But there was no way they were going to be able to sort through the wreckage until it cooled down.

"It'll be hours, at least, before we can get close to the truck."

She stood up, letting the sheet fall away completely. *God,* he thought as his chest constricted just looking at her, *she is absolutely beautiful.* The most beautiful woman he'd ever seen.

Taking her once wasn't enough. Not nearly. Where Maya was concerned, he was insatiable.

Their relationship wasn't going to end with the resolution of this case. He wanted to be with her, and not just because of the hot sex. How could he let go of a woman this fearless, this resilient in the face of daunting odds and death threats?

"I can't just sit here and wait for the truck to cool down."

She reached for her underwear and pulled it on before jamming her legs into the severely beaten-up borrowed jeans. And then, suddenly, she looked up at him, a strange look on her face.

"You need to get back to the fire."

He heard the words coming out of her mouth, but he could hardly believe they were real.

"Say that again?"

"You've told me absolutely everything. I know about your pyromania. About Joseph. Even about your relationship with Dennis. I also know you didn't light any fires. You didn't put a bomb on the hillside or in your own truck. You're completely innocent. I'm not going to wait another second to take you off suspension."

Holy crap. She'd just offered him the one thing he'd wanted most—and hadn't expected: The chance to get back to his crew, to keep his men safe, and to make sure they put the fire out in the most expedient way possible, before it struck down anyone else.

And yet, how could he go? The last thing he wanted to do was leave Maya alone. Especially after their near escape from the truck.

He couldn't let anything happen to her.

"I appreciate the offer, but I'm not going anywhere."

Maya stared at Logan in utter confusion. Why wasn't he already halfway out the door? He'd said his men needed him to put out the fire. What the hell was going on?

"If you're worried about that letter from McCurdy, I'll make sure he knows this is entirely my decision. I've never met him in person, but from everything I've heard he's a fair man. And he wouldn't want an innocent hot-shot sitting around twiddling his thumbs while a fire is raging."

Logan was across the room in a heartbeat, his hands on her rib cage. His strength and warmth were far too welcome, his faint five o'clock shadow making him look far sexier than any man had a right to be.

"Thank you for your willingness to go to bat for me, but there's no way I'm leaving you alone."

She shivered, even though his gaze was hot. Possessive. No man had ever looked at her like that. She hadn't known how much she'd like it. But she did know that she couldn't possibly allow herself to get used to it.

"I don't need you to protect me," she said softly, even though until she nailed the arsonist, potential danger lurked around every corner.

"Some point or another, we all need help," he said. "Even a tough arson investigator like you. I don't want to see you get hurt. I couldn't live with that."

His reaction to her declaration of independence was not what she'd expected. She'd gambled on stubborn, not protective. She wasn't at all certain how to respond, could barely wrap her head around the idea that he was more concerned for her safety than his job and his responsibilities to his men.

"None of this makes any sense, Maya. Hell, I wish it did. Everything would be different if your life weren't in danger. But someone set your hotel room on fire. Someone wants to hurt you. It'll be harder for anyone to get to you if I'm there too." His eyes were dark and impassioned. "I won't let anyone harm you. No matter what."

She should have pushed him away, but she couldn't stop herself from running her hands down his back. He winced and she couldn't believe she'd forgotten for one second about the beating he'd taken to protect her from the explosion.

"You're bleeding again," she said. "You should have told me to stop, you know, earlier."

His answering grin took her breath away. "I wouldn't have even if I'd noticed. Which I didn't."

"Where's your first aid kit?"

He stepped away from her and pulled it out from a bottom dresser drawer.

"Sit down," she said, and when he sat on the edge of the bed she pulled out what she needed. "This is going to sting," she warned, but he barely reacted as she gently swabbed his back with alcohol.

As she worked, she grew more convinced that Logan needed to return to his crew. Not only to fight the fire, but because someone was trying to kill him. She hoped that putting him back in action would get him out of harm's way.

According to the note she'd been left at the motel, this was personal. What had she and Logan both done six months ago to piss off an arsonist? And could it have something to do with her brother, with something—or someone—he'd been involved in before he'd died?

Logan looked at her over his shoulder. "I'm not going to like what you're thinking, am I?"

No. He wouldn't be happy to hear that she had no plans to hide away from the arsonist, to run scared.

In fact, the more she thought about it, the less afraid she became of dealing with the crazy bastard herself. One on one, no more bullshit, no more bombs in cars and setting hillsides on fire.

"Your crew needs you out there, Logan. Especially after what happened to Robbie. Please, go."

He was silent for a long moment, his eyes searching hers. "You're putting your job on the line by letting me off suspension without getting the thumbs-up first, Maya."

"If they want to fire me, fine. I'll find another job."

He shifted on the bed and put his hands on either side of her face, kissing her so sweetly, so tenderly that tears suddenly threatened.

His mouth still against hers, he asked, "Now tell me what you're planning."

"First promise me that you'll go back to your crew."

She had to hold firm, had to make sure she had his word. More lives than hers were at stake here. They needed to split up, attack the fire from both ends. He'd put it out and she'd make sure she caught the person responsible for the continued destruction.

"Promise me, Logan, that you'll report back to the station immediately."

She could feel the tension radiating from him as he struggled to make the difficult decision. At his core, Logan was a protector. If he could, he'd watch over them all. But there was more at stake here than her personal safety. So many lives. Houses. Slow-growth forests. All of his men.

He stroked her cheek with his thumb. "How can I do that when I know you're planning to dig deeper into danger without thinking about yourself?"

She smiled at him. "You do the same exact thing every single day. You're dedicated to your mission and always put others first, even when you're personally at risk by doing so."

"We're a lot alike, aren't we?"

Yes, they were both committed to their goals, no matter the sacrifice. Which was why she'd given up everything else in her life after her brother had died. She couldn't afford to lose focus. Not when time was running out on stopping Tony's case from being labeled "cold."

He threaded his hands through her hair. "Tell me what you're planning."

She simply repeated her request. "Promise me."

His mouth found hers again and when she'd almost forgotten everything but the slide of his tongue, the tingles that moved through her when he nibbled at that sensitive spot in the middle of her lower lip, he whispered, "I promise."

Relief washed over her and she let herself relax into his arms—one last time. "Someone wants to scare us, doesn't mind killing us if we don't react fast enough. It's a game I'm done playing. I'm sick of being taken by surprise."

She got up off his lap, forcing herself to ignore the sure pleasure that awaited her if she remained.

"Until this weekend, you and I only met each other once. And yet, we both seem to be targets. Is there anyone you can think of who could have seen us together six months ago?"

"I suppose there's a chance that my friend who owned the place came back early."

"And if he had and he saw us together, I'm sure he wouldn't have wanted to say anything to embarrass you."

"Maybe," Logan agreed, "but why the hell would Eddie want to harm you? Or me? He sold the place a month later, moved out of town, and has been living with his new girlfriend in the city ever since."

She couldn't see a good connection. It was one more puzzle piece that either fit—or didn't.

"I'd like to ask him some questions, just to make sure he didn't come back early and see someone outside."

Logan scribbled his friend's name and telephone number on an old receipt on his dresser. "Go easy on him, okay?"

"I promise to be nice," she said with a small smile. "Do you have a spare car we could use to get out of here?"

"A motorcycle," he replied. "Do you know how to ride?"

She tried to pretend she didn't hear the double entendre, but she blushed nonetheless. "My father had a bike. He taught me how."

She needed to step away from him, away from his heat, the endless power he had over her.

"My T-shirt is downstairs. Why don't you get dressed and I'll meet you in the kitchen. I'll drop you off at the hotshot station, and if you don't mind, I'll keep the bike for a while."

His eyes were dark, unreadable. "I don't care about the bike, Maya. I care about you."

Afraid of what else he was about to say, she quickly moved out of the bedroom before she could find out. Downstairs, as she bent over to pick up her bra and T-shirt from the kitchen floor, she ignored the throbbing in her skull, the flash of pain and breathlessness that told her she'd barely left Logan's truck alive. She was able to continue her investigation only because of his daring rescue.

She owed Logan more than she could ever repay.

A handful of minutes later, she was following him out his front door into a separate building when a soft snapping sound to her left surprised her and she instantly came to a standstill. Her heart pounded and the tiny hairs on the back of her neck rose in alarm.

Someone was watching them. The same person who had nearly killed them an hour ago.

"Did you hear that?" she asked.

"Hear what?" Logan looked all around them, into the trees, the sky, back at his house.

But as the seconds crept by, no one launched themselves out of the trees at her. The only sounds were the monotonous peep-peep-peep of a nuthatch and the rustling of pine needles in the late afternoon breeze.

With the slowing of her heart rate came an acute feeling of foolishness.

"Never mind. It was nothing," she said, hating that she'd given him any reason to doubt she could take care of herself.

Logan's eyes were dark and his jaw was jumping. She knew he was thinking of a hundred reasons he needed to stay with her.

She needed five minutes alone to get a grip. Fortunately, she suddenly remembered that her samples from his garage had gone up in flames in the front seat of the truck.

"I need to get those samples again."

She hurried back toward his garage. Thankfully, he didn't follow, and even though she felt naked without her leather bag of tricks, she shook some nails out of a couple of small glass jars and used them to collect what she needed.

When she returned with the full jars, he said, "I still don't like this."

She tried to resist, tried to cut herself off cold, but she couldn't help planting a quick kiss on his beautiful mouth. "I know you don't. And it means a lot to me that you're trusting my decisions."

Soon they were sitting astride his Ducati 695, a motorcycle people went to crazy lengths to own and ride. She dropped the sample jars into the center console and slipped on the helmet Logan handed her. His clean scent assaulted her senses. She was acutely aware that her underwear was still damp from the pleasure he'd given her . . . and that she'd been inexcusably alive in his arms not fifteen minutes earlier.

She wrapped her arms around his waist, letting herself enjoy his heat one last time as he revved the engine and drove out of the barn.

His motorcycle was a perfect part of the Lake Tahoe lifestyle. Too bad it was a life that didn't belong to her.

And never would.

Rage sounded in the silent forest.

They were still alive.

It had been an ideal setup. A tiny heat-activated bomb beneath the driver's seat that would randomly explode should have been the perfect way to kill them, perfectly untraceable as it melted inside the burning engine.

Revenge without penalties.

Setting the wildfire in Desolation had been a fun way to watch Logan boil in hot water, a sweet taste of revenge for what he'd done. But that bitch, the pretty little investigator with the big tits, had gotten in the way. And Logan couldn't resist playing hero again.

Risking his life so he could get in her tight pants.

Lighting her hotel room on fire with a bag of potato chips and a match should have been enough to make her run. But no. She was still here. Ruining everything.

Logan could wait.

The bitch had to die.

CHAPTER SIXTEEN

PRAYING IT wasn't the last time she'd see Logan, Maya concentrated on the road as she left the hotshot station, working to retrace her path to David's lab from memory. She could see why people came to Lake Tahoe for a vacation and never left. The beauty was staggering. Not just the lake, but the mountains, the trees.

And especially the hotshots.

Which was why she needed to solve this case and get out of Lake Tahoe, ASAP. She was no match for Logan. Everything he was pulled at her heart and made her want to give in to loving him. It wasn't just the way he touched her, wasn't simply the fact that she'd never come apart like that in anyone's arms but his.

At last David's house came into view and a pretty middle-aged blonde walked out onto the porch. "Hi. I'm

Kelly, David's wife. I'm assuming you're Maya and that you need to talk to him again?"

Maya stood awkwardly on the driveway next to the motorcycle, holding her containers of evidence from Logan's garage. "I do."

She tried to smile, wanted to be friendly, but her thoughts were such a tangled mess of desires and re-criminations she failed at both.

"Come on in," the woman said, holding open the door. "David just went out for a six-pack. He'll be back soon."

Maya didn't have time to sit around and wait for David to come back from his drink run. She stepped inside and set the bottles on the table.

"Could you give these to your husband?"

Kelly's eyes were startlingly blue and full of kindness. "Sure. I take it you need him to examine them quickly?"

Maya stared at the samples, wishing she didn't have to test them.

"I do," she finally said, belatedly realizing she was wearing her host's clothes. "David told me to borrow these. I hope that was okay."

Kelly wore an odd expression as she scanned Maya's clothes, and when Maya finally looked down at the T-shirt and jeans, she saw that they were filthy, covered in a myriad of rips and tears.

"I'm so sorry. I didn't realize . . ."

"Don't worry about it. It's been a rough day, hasn't it?"

Kelly's eyes saw far more than Maya wanted her to.

God, how Maya wanted to sit down and tell this stranger everything. But no amount of pouring out her soul over coffee would fix a goddamned thing.

Saying as little as possible had been her M.O. for a long time. No point in changing things now.

Fortunately, Kelly didn't seem to be the kind of woman who took silences personally. "Why don't you go ahead and grab something else out of my closet?"

Maya shook her head again. "I'm fine. Thanks."

If she got a chance she'd have the motel charge more "I Love Lake Tahoe" gear to her room.

Kelly filled a glass with purified water, then leveled Maya with a steely glance. "Drink this. I'll be right back."

It wasn't until Maya gulped down the water that she realized how thirsty she was. Kelly returned with what looked to be a very expensive pair of designer jeans and another cute T-shirt.

"I really don't think I should take those from you," Maya said. "The way things have been going, they'll probably be shredded in an hour."

Kelly dropped them on the counter beside Maya. "You need them more than I do." And then, after a beat, "How's Logan handling the investigation? I'm worried about him."

Maya's heart ached for the trouble she'd brought to Logan's door with his suspension, for his fears regarding Joseph, for his crew members who were in the hospital. And then there was the bomb someone had planted in his truck. Her knees started shaking again as she thought about just how close they'd both been to dying.

She swallowed hard, tried to find appropriate words. "He's been working with me to try to figure out who set these fires."

Kelly cocked her head to the side. "Isn't it kind of hard to do that when he's a suspect?"

"I've just released him from suspension. He's heading back onto the mountain as we speak."

The smile Kelly gave Maya said she knew this was more than an objective professional decision.

"I'm very glad to hear that," Kelly said. "How about you give me your cell phone number and I'll have David call you with the results."

Maya shook her head. "My cell phone blew up."

For the first time, Kelly looked scared. "What do you mean it blew up?"

Maya had said too much. She held up the neatly folded clothes. "Thanks for these."

Kelly reached into a purse on the counter and held out a wad of twenties. "Here. Buy a new phone at the convenience store in town, then call me with the new number."

Maya hesitated for a second, even though Kelly was right, then shoved the bills in her pocket.

"Thank you. I'll pay you back soon."

"No rush, okay?" she said as she walked Maya out to the front porch. "And take care of yourself. I'd like to see you again. Have you over for dinner. Under better circumstances, of course."

Maya kept her head down as she swung a leg over the bike, not wanting Kelly to see how much she wanted the very same thing.

The fifteen-minute ride into town to buy a cell phone should have been exhilarating, the perfect way to blow off some steam. Instead, her muscles were tight, her thoughts racing because the last time she'd driven into downtown Lake Tahoe on a motorcycle had been with her brother on his birthday at the end of last summer. Tony had wanted to show her his new firehouse and she'd been thrilled for him, thrilled that he was finally getting to live his dream. His new job was just different enough from what her father did in the mountains for it to be something Tony could claim as all his own.

Memories kept coming at her, one after another, of how he'd been on her to move to Tahoe too, to set her up with one of the guys from his station.

No, damn it, she didn't have time for this. She had too much to do in the here and now to get caught up in the past again. She owed it to this case—and to Logan—to keep moving forward. She couldn't afford to miss a thing.

Parking the bike in front of a 7-Eleven at the edge of the Nevada border where the casinos took over, she quickly purchased a disposable cell phone, then headed into a Starbucks to charge the phone in a free outlet and force herself to eat and drink something while she waited. She'd never felt less like eating, but she needed to be smart and keep her strength up.

She grabbed a seat in the back corner of the coffee shop, a spot she'd specifically chosen to make sure she could see everyone who entered the store. She couldn't forget that her life was in danger.

Thirty minutes later she hadn't seen anyone she recognized, let alone anyone who looked remotely shady. When the phone was ready to go, she pulled the telephone number Logan had given her for his friend Eddie Myers, who used to own the Bar & Grill, out of her pocket.

When he didn't pick up, she left a concise message that she was an arson investigator working with the state and she had some questions regarding his old restaurant. She called information next and had them connect her with the urban fire chief, Patrick Stevens.

"Patrick Stevens's office," his secretary said, "how may I help you?"

Maya had spoken with Cammie a handful of times during the past few months. "Cammie, it's Maya Jackson."

"Hi, Maya. Has the new chief gotten back to you yet about your brother's case?"

"Actually, I'm calling about yesterday's fire at the motel. It was in my room."

Cammie made a soothing sound. "I'm sorry, honey. I saw that note. You must be so scared."

No question about it, the note that had been left

for her in a firebox had been incredibly creepy. But she wasn't about to admit fear to anyone. Not even herself.

"I'm fine," she insisted. She'd been repeating the words all day, saying she was fine, when she wasn't. Maybe if she said it enough times she'd start to believe it. "Is Chief Stevens in? I'd like to see if he's learned anything more about the fire."

"I'm afraid he's at another fire right now, but I'll be sure to tell him to call you the minute he walks in." After she wrote down Maya's new cell number, she said, "I sure hope we find out who did that to you."

Maya managed a soft "Thank you," then hung up and called information and had them connect her to the Flights of Fancy office. Finally, good news. Dennis was due to return from doing water drops in the next half hour or so.

She was going to be lying in wait for him when he arrived.

Dennis lived in a new tract house not far from the Starbucks. His smooth white stucco walls struck Maya as the polar opposite of Joseph's rustic cabin. But unlike the other, picture-perfect properties, Dennis's landscaping was nonexistent, his lawn a sickly yellow.

Shortly after she arrived, Dennis pulled into his driveway. Stepping out of his truck, he looked thoroughly confused.

"Maya? What are you doing here?" He took a step

back. "Oh shit, you want to ask me more questions about Logan, don't you?"

"Actually," she said in a slow, steady voice, "I'd like to conduct a property search. Of your house."

He frowned. "I don't get it."

"There was an explosion today near one of the housing developments. I'd appreciate it if you'd let me into your garage."

"I still don't get why you're here. I'm not a suspect, Logan is."

"No," she said, "he isn't. Not any longer."

At that, Dennis's face went beet red, as if a hand were squeezing him tightly around the neck. "Are you fucking kidding me? What the hell are you looking at me for? I haven't done anything! He told you I did this, didn't he, so that you'd stop accusing him?"

"You've got it backwards," she said firmly. "He's been defending you up and down all day long to me."

But Dennis's anger continued to grow. "All my life I've treated him like a brother. I should have known that this is how he'd repay me. I hope they pin this on him and he rots in prison. I'm sure the other inmates would love to feel up a hotshot."

"Dennis," she said again, in the level, reasonable tone she often used to speak to frightened fire victims, "he didn't sell you out."

"Like hell he didn't! He wrapped my dad around his little finger, just like he's done with you. Once he moved in with us I became invisible. The only time my father bothered speaking to me was when he wanted to brag about something Logan did. I got so fucking sick of hearing his name. I'm not telling you a goddamned thing, and you're not getting into my garage. Not without a warrant. I watch TV. I know you can't take any of that without a search warrant. Now get the fuck off of my property."

Quietly, she corrected him. "In arson cases, a warrant is not necessary. And I'm afraid I do need to ask you some questions before I leave, Dennis."

Nearly apoplectic, he said, "You think you're so smart. So important. But you're just like the rest of them. I'll bet you don't have any idea how many chicks he's banged. You're just another stupid slut who wants to fuck a hotshot."

Maya took a step toward Dennis, her expression menacing. "You need to calm down, Mr. Kellerman, and answer my questions: Where were you last weekend and the following Monday through Friday? Who were you with? And why did you bail out of the camping trip with Logan and your father?"

All at once, Dennis deflated like an emptying balloon. "Jesus, is that what this is about?"

She frowned. "Where were you? What were you doing?"

He slumped down on the edge of the curb, his head in his hands. When he looked up at her his eyes were bleak.

"I was driving all over the state talking to doctors."

"Are you sick, Dennis?"

"No. My dad is."

Dennis's answer completely blindsided her. She knew how devastating it was to lose a family member.

Dennis hadn't been lighting fires. He'd been trying to help his father.

"I met Joseph yesterday."

He looked up at her in surprise. "You did?"

"He seems like a wonderful man. I'm sorry about his illness."

"All I want is to find some pill or doctor who can operate on his brain to keep him from getting worse."

She had to ask. "Have you talked to Logan about this?"

He almost looked embarrassed. "I know this sounds stupid, but I wanted to be the hero this time. Just once. When it really counted. Instead, everything's fucked up and you think I lit the fire. I didn't do it. I swear to you."

She couldn't help but believe him, not when he was so upset, so genuinely concerned about his father's well-being, but she still needed to confirm his story before crossing him off her list. "I'd appreciate it if you'd give me the names and phone numbers of some of the doctors you've visited, so I can verify your whereabouts."

He didn't argue with her this time, and ten minutes later she'd confirmed his story.

She'd crashed into another dead end.

CHAPTER SEVENTEEN

MAYA DROVE away from Dennis's house and headed toward the fire. Maybe if she watched it burn long enough, she'd figure out what the hell to do next. Something was niggling at her, had been digging into her gut for the past few hours, a voice that told her she already knew more than she thought she did. If only she could figure out what it was.

Pulling off the lakeside freeway at a state park, she wound past a Smoky the Bear sign that said "Extreme Fire Danger" and continued up the packed-dirt road until she got to the peak. Taking off her helmet, she shook her tangled hair out before looking down at the smoke and flames.

Had Joseph lit the first fire that started this enormous firestorm? she wondered. Possibly.

But even as she took in the newly charred hillsides where tall pines had stood only days before, the truly important question remained: Who was responsible for everything that had happened since the Desolation Wilderness fire began?

The only thing she knew for sure was that the attacks were personal. Someone wanted to hurt her and Logan, maybe even kill them.

The obvious plan was also the most dangerous. The best way to smoke out the arsonist would be to become an open target, to put herself out in clear sight, some-place the arsonist would feel safe coming after her.

I have to do it, Logan, she thought silently. *It's the only way. I'm sorry.*

She could still feel his touch on her skin, his lips in the hollow of her neck. And she could see his beautiful face in her mind's eye, could imagine him fighting her tooth and nail over her plan to catch the serial arsonist. But she couldn't let the arsonist hurt anyone else. Not if there was a way she could stop the attacks. Even if it meant putting her own life on the line.

And yet, even though it had been a rough twenty-four hours and danger was following her through Lake Tahoe, she couldn't help but relive those sweet moments in Logan's arms over and over again. Being with him, in his bed, wrapped up in his strength, had been some of the most powerful, most wonderful moments of her life. Just as she'd known it would be from their first kiss.

High in the hills, with black smoke swirling all around

her, it was impossible to keeping hiding from the truth: She'd allowed herself to get in too deep. Way too deep. Especially since Logan was as stubborn, as bullheaded as she was. She strongly suspected that he wasn't going to let her just walk out of his life.

He was going to fight for her every step of the way.

And even though she'd been honest with him and told him why she couldn't let him get any closer, the truth was that they were just words. What she felt way down deep inside was exactly the opposite.

Every cell, every nerve, every part of her wanted to be with Logan . . . and he was a man who could die at any moment, who could be dying right now, for all she knew.

Staring into the raging fire, she couldn't stop seeing Logan running as flames chased at his back. Yesterday it had been horrible to watch him run from death, but he'd been a stranger. If she had to watch the same scene again now, it would destroy her.

She'd never be able to protect herself with a false sense of security like so many firefighters' wives and girlfriends did. One day there'd be a fire he couldn't run from and he'd leave a wife and kids behind.

Maya didn't want that wife, that mother, to be her.

The cell phone buzzed in her pocket and she was glad for the interruption, for any opportunity to stop thinking about her pointless feelings for Logan.

"Maya, it's Patrick Stevens."

"Have you learned anything new?" Her stomach

churned as she waited for the fire chief's reply. He knew there had been a man knocking on her door, waiting outside her room before it was set on fire.

He cleared his throat, obviously uncomfortable with what he was about to reveal. "Before I reveal the man's identity, I want you to know that I'm absolutely certain he had a good reason for wanting to speak with you. And that he did not light the fire that burned your room."

Alarm hit her squarely in the chest. *Please,* she prayed, *don't say Logan's name. Don't tell me someone saw him on the premises that afternoon.* She couldn't be wrong about him. She couldn't be. Not when she'd willingly—desperately— taken him inside her body.

Not when she'd practically admitted to herself that she was in love with him.

Her heart raced as she made her lips form the words "Who was it?"

"A hotshot."

No.

"His name is Sam MacKenzie. He's one of the best."

It took a long moment for relief to register. Chief Stevens hadn't said Logan's name. Thank God.

"Wasn't Sam MacKenzie one of the other hotshots who was out on the mountain during the blowup with Logan yesterday afternoon? Wasn't his brother badly burned?" Patrick confirmed this, and she said, "I was there at the anchor point. I saw Logan and Sam save him. They almost died."

"Sam's a good guy and everyone respects him," Patrick said, before clearing his throat again.

Uh-oh. "There's more, isn't there?"

"I'm afraid there is. A couple of witnesses said he slipped something under your door. It must have burned up before we got there. I've called the station several times today, but he's been out on the fire and I haven't been able to discuss the situation with him yet."

She thanked Chief Stevens for his help and was about to hang up, but he kept her on the line a moment longer. "I want you to know that I've been asking around about your brother."

She nearly lost her balance on the motorcycle. "Thank you. But you and I haven't even sat down and talked yet."

"Logan called me an hour ago. He asked me to look into the case for you, to call in some favors. From everything I've read it looks like an accident, not arson, but I lost a brother too. I know how hard it is. I won't let the case drop until we're absolutely certain that there are no further leads."

"I don't know how to thank you, Patrick."

Or how to thank Logan for spearheading the renewed effort on her behalf. He was such an amazing man. Even when his head was on the chopping block, even when he was about to walk into an out-of-control fire, he was thinking about her. Helping her.

"After reading the note that the arsonist left you yesterday," Patrick continued, "I can't help but wonder if the motel fire had something to do with Tony."

She'd been wondering the very same thing, but she'd been trying to keep her focus on the current case. Yet it was an incredible feeling to know that other people were out there supporting her quest.

"I'll let you know if anything turns up," he said, then disconnected.

Two beeps sounded in her ear. A call had gone to voice mail while she was talking to Patrick. It was David, and she braced herself for bad news as she dialed his number. She turned away from the fire to look out at the lake, and the setting sun nearly blinded her as she waited for him to pick up.

"It's Maya." She got right to the point. "Have you tested the new samples?"

"Where did you get these?"

"Logan's garage." The lump in her throat grew bigger. "They match the evidence from the explosion, don't they?"

David was silent for a long moment. "They do, but there's no way Logan did this. This is a small town. Anyone could have a match in their garage. Just to check the theory, I grabbed samples from my garage; they were a match too."

Her hands shook on the receiver. "You shouldn't have done that," she said in a low voice, even though she was glad that he had. With David's help she hoped to show that the evidence against Logan wasn't remotely strong enough to even charge him with the crime, let alone convict him.

"Logan is not only my friend, he's one of the best men I know. I'll do whatever it takes to keep him safe. Hell, I'll test samples from every garage on this side of the lake if I have to."

A bright orange, red, and yellow ball of fire slowly disappeared into bright blue water as she thanked David and hung up. It had to be one of the most spectacular sunsets she'd ever witnessed. But the beauty was entirely wasted on her.

Logan's radio crackled with voices as he suited up and jumped into one of the station trucks to head out to the anchor point. He quickly learned that the suburban subdivision next to that morning's explosion was engulfed in flames. Shit. It hadn't taken long for the fire to jump out of the mountains and onto rooftops. Just hours ago, he and Maya had been up on one of those rooftops.

A knife lodged in the pit of his stomach.

Maya.

Ever since joining the Tahoe Pines Hotshot Crew fifteen years earlier, his decisions had been clear-cut. He put out fires. He supported his men. No woman had ever come between him and what he knew to be the right course of action.

Until now.

Until Maya.

Everything in him wanted to keep her safe. He'd never forgive himself if something happened to her.

But the same was true for his crew. He already felt responsible for what had happened to Connor and Robbie. He couldn't let another one of his men end up in the burn ward.

No matter what he did, no matter which choice he made, he was screwed.

But years of dealing with that split second between life and death had taught him to make the hard decisions, and to make them fast, before indecision compounded the problem. And the fact was, no matter how compelled he was to protect Maya, she was tough. And smart. She understood the danger she was in, that conducting this investigation put her life at risk. Whereas, his men were trying to stay one step ahead of a complex and deadly fire. Logan couldn't let them continue that battle without his support.

Late-afternoon tourist traffic crawled on the lone highway that ringed the lake. Large sunburned families were crowded into cars after a happy day at the beach, intent on their fun even though the sky was hazy and the air quality was terrible. Logan wove through lanes as safely as he could manage, to speed up his trip into the housing development. He was running behind a ticking clock, one he was afraid he might never catch up with.

He parked in front of a manicured front lawn and moved quickly past the fire trucks, toward his squad boss.

Gary's expression was grim. "Tell me you've found the asswipe who did all this."

"Not yet," Logan said, "but as of fifteen minutes ago I've been taken off suspension."

"Thank God for that," Gary said.

Logan scanned the scene. The few men the hotshots could spare to work on saving the houses had been joined by the urban teams. From where he was standing, the fire looked to be raging completely out of control.

Gary confirmed his assessment, saying "Zero percent containment. We're fucked."

Gary's cell phone rang and Logan watched his squad boss's face go ash gray as he listened to the caller.

He clicked his phone shut. "That was the hospital."

Logan braced himself. "Connor?"

Gary shook his head. "No. He's fine. In pain, but he'll heal. It's Robbie."

All day he'd thought about Robbie, pictured him unconscious in the hospital bed, every inch of his skin covered in bandages.

"He's not doing well. His blood pressure is low. His heart rate is all over the place. They're not sure he's going to make it."

"Jesus," Logan said in a low voice. "He's all alone."

"I'll keep holding down the fort. You go help Robbie fight like hell for his life. And whatever you do, Logan, bring him back alive."

CHAPTER EIGHTEEN

THE MOON hung low over the hotshot station when Maya walked in and saw that it was nearly empty, except for a lone, dark-haired man sitting at the dining table, his head bent down over maps and charts. With a fire like this, hotshot crews worked as long and hard as was humanly possible, only taking short breaks to refuel and snatch an hour or two of sleep to recharge.

She hated bothering firefighters in the middle of a blaze when they were exhausted and desperately needed downtime. But the longer it took her to find the arsonist, the more potential danger the firefighters faced. And so she'd forge ahead with her investigation and continue asking hard questions.

"Excuse me, I'm looking for Sam MacKenzie."

The man looked up at her and she was momentarily

startled by his looks. His eyes were a penetrating blue, his hair jet black, his jaw was actually chiseled, and his forearms were sinew and muscle.

"Ma'am."

She swallowed uncomfortably, hating what had to be said.

"You're Mr. MacKenzie?"

He nodded, pushed back his chair, and stood up. Tall with broad shoulders, he gave off the impression of great strength. "Ms. Jackson, you are just the woman I wanted to talk to."

"Chief Stevens informed me that several witnesses saw a man bearing your description standing outside my hotel room yesterday afternoon."

"That's right."

Hotshots never backed down from a challenge. Well, neither did she. She looked him directly in the eye. "I need to know why."

He crossed his arms over his chest. "I came to talk some sense into you."

The tiny hairs on the back of her neck stood up. "Excuse me?"

"You've got the wrong suspect."

She couldn't stand to add another hotshot to her list. But Sam seemed intent on writing his own name down for her. "Are you telling me you know who the right one is?"

"No, ma'am, I don't."

For a minute there, she'd been afraid he was going to say *You're looking at him.*

She breathed a small sigh of relief before saying "Witnesses said you slipped a note under my door."

"I wanted you to know I'd been there. That we needed to talk about Logan. We depend on him. Hell, he nearly died yesterday trying to save my brother in a blowup."

Softly, she said, "I was there. I saw what he did. What you did."

But Sam wasn't impressed by her admiration. "You sent him into the site of the explosion with that damn sniffer, didn't you?"

"He offered."

"And you were more than happy to let him risk his life for you, weren't you? After all, if he'd died, he would have just been another casualty on your spreadsheet."

Maya's hands fisted at her sides. "How dare you accuse me of something like that? I didn't want him going anywhere near that fire." She stopped herself from admitting that her heart had nearly stopped a dozen times while she stood on the roof and watched Logan collect the data.

Sam was unrelenting. "All I know is that he could have died getting your damn data. Two dead hotshots in two days, is that what you want?"

Her heart stopped beating. "Two?" She must have heard him wrong. "Robbie's in the hospital. He's alive."

For the first time, Sam's expression softened. "The call just came in from the hospital. Robbie's gone."

———

Logan raced to Tahoe General in record time, but he was too late. Standing in the hallway, staring at Robbie's empty bed, images flashed by, one after the other, of Robbie's antics, his practical jokes on the other hotshots, how much he'd sucked at cleaning the burned chili out of the bottom of the aluminum pot. He'd been no more than a kid, but they all knew he'd grow into a hell of a firefighter one day.

Now he was gone.

Logan's legs were stiff as he followed the nurse to Connor's room. She opened the door and put her hand on his arm as he walked past her.

"I'm sorry," she whispered, her eyes soft and sympathetic. "I'll leave you alone with your friend."

Logan watched Connor's chest steadily rise and fall as he moved toward the bed. Even though Connor was heavily drugged for pain, every few breaths he grimaced. Logan stared at his friend's face, remembering too well the agony etched across it as they'd outrun the fire.

He owed it to his men—especially to Robbie and his family—to find the arsonist soon, before anyone else got caught in his flaming trap.

Quietly, he left Connor's room. Out in the hallway, he called his squad boss. "He's dead, Gary."

Because wildland firefighting was one of the most dangerous professions in the world, clinical psychologists spent a couple of days with the crew every year forcing them to talk things through. Hotshots understood that even when they did everything right, death was sometimes an inevitable outcome.

But everything was different this time. Robbie hadn't been killed out on the mountain, wielding a Pulaski. He'd been caught in a madman's web.

Gary's sound of anguish mirrored what was in Logan's heart. "He was just a kid."

"I'll be back at the station in fifteen," Logan said. For Robbie's sake, if nothing else, he needed to take down the fire while Maya continued to track the arsonist.

The killer.

But Gary wasn't on board with that plan. "The winds are too squirrelly for any of us to be out there. Everyone on crew is already on their way back in. I'm not authorizing anyone to fight fire again until morning. Not even you."

Futility tore through Logan. "Shit. I should have been there."

"None of this is your fault," Gary said. "None of it. Go home, Logan. Try to get some sleep."

The signal went dead before Logan could pull rank. He wanted to be in Desolation Wilderness fighting the goddamned fire. But Gary was right about one thing—he couldn't let his men see him like this. It was his job to keep it together no matter what. His crew looked to him for strength and he wouldn't disappoint.

He drove home on autopilot while Robbie's favorite Bruce Springsteen song played on the radio.

Maya wasted a precious hour driving first to the hospital and then to the station. The nurse said she'd missed Logan by a matter of minutes and Gary hadn't said much of anything at all, just that he was glad she'd finally come to her senses and taken Logan off suspension. The fact that she'd felt like a fly buzzing around a swatter was irrelevant. All that mattered right now was finding Logan and making sure he didn't blame himself for Robbie's death.

She breathed out a deep sigh of relief when she pulled into Logan's driveway and saw moonlight glinting off the bumper of a station truck.

Her heart thumped hard in her chest as she climbed the same front steps he'd carried her up after the explosion that afternoon. Although they'd made love only a handful of hours ago, it seemed like a lifetime had passed since then.

She knocked on his door, then rang the doorbell, but there was no reply. Taking the chance that it would be unlocked—she'd grown up in a house where no one had needed a key—she turned the knob, and the door swung open. She stepped inside, scanning the empty foyer for sign of Logan.

He emerged silently. On the surface, he didn't look any different. The same dark shadow covered his jaw, and he stood with his usual self-confidence. But she'd been trained to look deeper than that and instantly noted grief in the tightness around his mouth, frustration in his eyes.

"I heard about Robbie," she said softly. She wanted to reach out for him, wanted him to know she understood what he was going through. "I'm so sorry, Logan."

His big, strong hands pulled her toward him and she was momentarily shocked by the enormous hard-on she felt against her belly, but only for a short moment. After all, hadn't she dealt with her loss in exactly the same way? Hadn't she used Logan's body to try to forget her sadness?

She owed him this. And she would gladly give him a piece of herself if it would help deal with his loss in some small way.

She pressed herself into him and rubbed her breasts against the wall of his chest, and a growled curse was on his lips as he captured her mouth in a hard kiss. Mindful of his cuts, she gently wrapped her arms around his wide back and opened her legs to bring him closer. His hands moved from her hips to her hair, then back again.

Somewhere in the background, she heard fabric ripping, realizing he'd ripped her T-shirt off her body only when the ruined cotton fell to the floor. Her bra came off just as quickly, and then his mouth was on her skin, hot and insistent as he sucked her nipples in between his teeth, cupping her breasts so that he could lave them both at the same time.

A moan sounded, maybe hers, maybe his. She arched into his mouth and pushed her hands into the back pockets of his jeans, his tight muscles jumping against her fingers. He barely took the time to undo her zipper before yanking her pants and underwear off, and when his fingers found her she was already wet and swollen, desperate for more. His cock came free from his jeans and boxers and he lifted her off the ground, forcing her thighs around his hips.

Instinctively, she wrapped her legs around him and when he pushed into her, high and hard, she gasped with pleasure. His erection tightly sheathed within her, her elbows locked around his neck, she buried her head against his shoulder and rocked up and down on his shaft.

She'd come to help him, but there was no denying her own release, or even to slow it down. Her muscles began to dance around him and when he pushed in deeper, she lost what was left of her control and tumbled into a stunningly powerful climax.

Logan rode her steadily through her waves of pleasure, and it was only as she was coming down from her orgasm that he pulled out and came warm against her belly.

She couldn't take in air fast enough as she clung to him, her skin damp with sweat and semen. She hadn't planned on this, couldn't have made a rational case for what had just happened between them, but deep within she knew it had been exactly right.

Logan set her away from him, lines of remorse joining those of sorrow. "Jesus, Maya, I attacked you."

Recrimination underlay every word.

Ignoring her nakedness, she reached for his hand. "Six months ago I did the very same thing to you. It's all right. I understand exactly how you're feeling."

His eyes briefly met hers, just long enough that she could tell he was still blaming himself for everything, including their quickie. Refusing to release his hands, she led him up the stairs and into his bathroom. She turned the shower on and stepped under the water, pulling him in with her.

"Let's clean up," she said softly, "and then I want to share something with you. Something I hope will help."

Exhaustion mingled with confusion on his heart-stoppingly beautiful face. When, she wondered, was the last time he'd slept? She wanted to pull him against her and stroke his hair like he was a little boy, until he finally got some rest.

She ran a bar of soap over his chest, trying to keep her attention on simply bathing, but it was difficult. Very difficult. She sucked her lower lip in between her teeth as she ran bubbles across his pecs and down his washboard stomach.

He covered her hand with his own before she got any closer to his budding erection. "I can't control myself around you."

She looked up at him and admitted the truth. "I know. I feel the same way."

The bar of soap dropped to the tiled floor as his mouth came down on hers. But before she could kiss him back, he turned off the water and wrapped her in a towel.

"I'm a monster tonight, Maya. I don't want to hurt you again."

"You've never hurt me, Logan. Never." She walked over to his bed and sat down against a pillow, curling her ankles beneath her thighs. "Please, come and listen to what I have to say. And then if you want me to leave, I'll go."

He looked at her for a long moment, just long enough for her to wonder if he was going to refuse her request. Finally, he wrapped a towel around his waist and moved to the bed.

She clasped and unclasped her hands on her lap, staring at her reddening knuckles. She'd never talked to anyone about the night she'd lost her brother. Not her friends. Not her mother. Not even the therapist who'd tried repeatedly to get it out of her. It had been none of the woman's business. Now here she was, sitting on Logan's bed, wrapped in a towel, ready to talk.

"I was sitting in the kitchen paying bills when I got the call. I still dream about it, about hearing 'Tony's dead' and dropping the phone. It broke on the tile floor, actually. Shattered into a hundred pieces. I remember feeling like I was that phone, like I'd never be whole again."

It was the strangest thing, but as Logan held her, she wasn't fighting back tears. For once, she'd thought of Tony—actually talked about him—and wasn't going to cry. Maybe she was all cried out. Or maybe it was simply that being with Logan and sharing with him had sped up the healing process.

Feeling much stronger than she had in a very long while, she leaned back against the headboard and stroked the top of his large hands lightly with her thumbs.

"His landlord needed his place cleared out, but I just couldn't do it. Not without a drink to make me numb. Which is how I found you."

He squeezed her hands. "I'm glad you did. I'm glad it was me."

"Me too," she whispered, coming up on her knees in front of him to kiss him gently. "And I'm glad I can be here for you."

"I'll be all right, Maya," he said, and she believed him. He was an incredibly strong man. But it was like he'd said once to her, even strong people needed help sometimes.

"Ever since Tony died I've been consumed by the fact that a murderer is walking around out there, just waiting for his next chance to kill somebody's brother, or sister, or best friend. Thank you for asking Patrick to look into Tony's case. You'll never know how much it means to me."

"I want to help, Maya. Anything I can do, I'll do."

She didn't want to get distracted by his kisses, by his touch, before she said what she'd come to say, but she couldn't resist pressing her lips to his to silently let him know how much his concern meant to her.

Forcing herself to pull away from his heat, she took

a deep breath and tried to put all of her feelings into words. "I don't want you to fall into the same trap I've been stuck in, living only for revenge."

"Is that what you've been doing?"

She closed her eyes, finally accepting the truth she'd tried to hide from for so long. "Yes, that's exactly what I've been doing."

He dragged her body into his and as she rested her head against the hard wall of his chest, she almost forgot who was comforting whom.

She didn't unwrap her arms from his warmth as she said, "What happened to Robbie isn't your fault, Logan."

She felt him tense. "I wasn't there to save Robbie. Now he's dead."

He tried to pull back, but she refused to let him go. Not when he needed her so desperately, as much as she had needed him six months ago.

"You're one of the best men I've ever known. You lead your men with honesty and integrity. You've earned their trust. And mine. Forever." She looked at him and allowed her deeply buried feelings to shine through. "Let me love you, Logan. Let me help you heal."

CHAPTER NINETEEN

LOGAN CRADLED Maya on his lap, overwhelmed by the depth of his feelings for her. He tucked her head under his chin and stroked her soft hair in long strokes as it fell over her shoulders and down her back.

"You don't have to do this, Maya."

She shifted on his thighs and looked up at him. "I want to."

She brushed his lower lip with the pad of her thumb and he bit back a groan as she bent over his torso and the tips of her hair swept across his skin. His abdominal muscles twitched and tightened in anticipation of her mouth. He barely felt the tip of her tongue at first as it slid into the deep ridges of his stomach.

He was already perilously close to the edge. His hands fisted at his sides as he reached deep for control.

His abs had served him well for hoisting and twisting and carrying, never for foreplay.

The towel fell from her breasts and her soft, round flesh brushed against his cock. He wasn't even sure she knew what her beauty was doing to him. Maya wasn't just some fire groupie who wanted to bag another fireman. Instead, her emotions ran deep and pure.

It made him want her even more, and he wanted to drag her up his body and bury himself in her heat. But this lovemaking, with her at the helm, was meant to heal them both. Somehow, he'd find a way to keep his hands off her and let her continue her tongue's path down his body.

A moment later, she unhooked the towel from his waist, and as she peeled back the thick white cotton, cool air suddenly rushed across his cock a moment before Maya wrapped one hand around his shaft and went still.

He worked to find his voice, to give the impression that he wasn't about to explode in her hand. "You act like you've never seen it before."

She sucked her lower lip under her front teeth. "I've only felt it," she said, tightening her grip on his cock and slowly sliding her hand down. "This is the first time I've got to really look at you. You're beautiful, Logan. Absolutely perfect."

She bent her head and dropped a kiss onto his engorged head, then licked away the answering drop of arousal.

He was this close to rolling her over flat on her back and taking her even harder and faster than he had by his front door. And then her mouth came down over him, sheathing him in warm, wet heat, and the only thing he could do was bury his hands in her hair and buck his hips up into her mouth. As her tongue swept up and down the length of him and she squeezed the base of his erection with one hand, his cock pulsed and thickened in her mouth.

He was all for letting her explore his body, but he wasn't going to come in her mouth. Not this time, at least. It was a torture to pull out from between her soft, slick lips.

And then, a moment later, she was lying on her back, her towel on the floor, her thighs spread open beneath him.

"I wasn't done," she said.

He silenced her protest with a long, slow kiss. From his very first taste of her, she'd remained the benchmark by which he'd judged every other kiss.

He found the word "love" sitting on the tip of his tongue and it shocked the hell out of him. He levered up on his arms, nearly locking his elbows to create some space between them, to recover his grip on reality.

Her eyes filled with concern. "Logan? Are you all right?"

She reached for him, and he knew she thought he was pulling away because of Robbie. But while Robbie's loss would always haunt him, would hit him hard at times when he least expected it, like Sunday afternoon cleanup and grocery runs, right now he was thinking about Maya. And whether there was a chance in hell that she felt the same way he did.

Because even though she'd just shared so much with him, he knew she was still holding back, was still afraid to let herself love another firefighter.

She'd given him her body, but he was going to have to fight like hell to capture her heart.

He let her pull him back down over her, let her gently rain kisses over his face, his neck, before he turned his focus to her pleasure, to cupping a breast in each hand and lightly rolling her nipples between his thumbs and forefingers before he settled his mouth over one stiff peak.

With every stroke of his tongue against her breasts, he concentrated on slipping his fingers between her wet, slick labia, slipping one, then two fingers into her, all while laving her nipples with his tongue, until she was writhing beneath him, silently begging him to take her again.

She reached for his shaft, but he knew he couldn't last much longer, so he dodged her hand and found a condom in his bedside table. He ripped open the package and was about to slide it on, when she held out her hand.

"I'd like to do the honors."

He handed her the condom and held his breath as he watched her put the rubber on his thick head and slowly roll it down.

"It barely fits," she whispered when it was halfway on. "You really do need the extra-large ones," she said with a small smile.

He clenched his teeth, finding it impossible to joke around when her hands were on him and he was this close to losing it.

"You have five more seconds to get it on," he warned.

"Or else?"

"Or else this," he said, covering her hand with his own and sliding the condom the rest of the way before grasping her thighs in his hands and spreading her legs open wide for him.

The soft "Mmm" sound she made sent him over the edge and he thrust all the way inside.

Her hands clutched at his shoulders and even though he took her mouth as roughly as he did the rest of her, she was right there with him, driving him higher, wilder. He heard her gasp and call out his name and then everything went black as he spiraled into his own climax, his hips moving of their own will. Her inner muscles clenched and pulled around him, drawing out his orgasm.

He rolled them over so that she was nestled in the crook of his arm, and his lungs burned from exertion.

As he stroked her hair, he knew there was no point in thinking she was just an exceptional screw. She was all that and more. Much more.

He loved her.

He looked down at her face and saw that her eyes

were closed, dark circles of exhaustion beneath them in sharp relief to her beautiful honey-tinged skin. She'd been through hell in the past couple of days. They both had.

Exhaustion pulled at Logan. With Maya safe in his arms, he gave in and slept.

Hours later, as night fell away and daylight returned, jealousy burned in the woods surrounding Logan's house.

She was there with him. Fucking him.

Goddamn it. Even after everything that had happened, they were still doing it like bunnies. Nothing was stopping them, not explosions or bombs or even deaths.

This time they'd finally pay.

And so would everyone they loved.

CHAPTER TWENTY

LOGAN FELT Maya stir, one of her thighs sliding against his. Sunlight streamed into the room and he was already rock hard, ready to take her again. He shifted their positions so that she was lying flat on the pillow and he was leaning on one elbow, looking down at her. Her eyelids fluttered as she awakened and he took a long moment to appreciate her high cheekbones, her lush mouth, the curve of her jaw, and her long, smooth neck.

She was the most beautiful woman he'd ever seen, the only one he wanted in his bed for the rest of his life.

Her eyes opened and she smiled at him, stretching her arm up to press her palm flat against his chest. "Hi."

He smiled back, relishing her touch, loving that she

was in his bed and not looking for an excuse to leave. "Did I wake you up?"

She rubbed her hip against his erection. "Something did."

"I want you again, Maya. Badly."

"Then take me. Now."

Women had frequently praised him for his smooth moves, for his control. Their pleasure came first, no matter what. But he'd never been this tempted, this desperate.

"You make me lose control," he said as he pushed her thighs open with his knees.

"Good."

She pulled his head down and kissed him just as she lifted her hips and took him inside her soft heat. He hadn't touched her in hours, but she was as ready for him as he was for her.

He kissed her hard, holding himself rigid and unmoving within her. More than anything, he wanted to thrust once, twice, three times, and come with her squeezing him tightly, no rubber barrier between them. But it was too soon. She wasn't ready to commit to a lifetime with him. Yet.

He forced himself to slide all the way out, even when the small sounds of disappointment coming from her throat clouded his thinking, and had a condom on in less than thirty seconds, rolling over so that she was straddling him. She smiled again, a seductive grin that made him even harder, and then her quadriceps tightened as she shifted into place above his shaft. Balancing her hands on his chest, she slowly lowered herself down onto him, one inch at a time.

It killed Logan not to thrust high and hard into her slick heat. Finally—Lord, it couldn't have been soon enough—she settled down onto his base, her soft, round butt cheeks pressing into the tendons across his hips. And then she was lifting herself nearly all the way, only to come crashing back down, over and over, harder, faster each time.

She threw her head back and arched her spine as she rode him, her breasts bouncing in rhythm to her thrusts. He slid one hand to her ass, the other to her tits, and stroked her, groaning his encouragement. He was unable to hold back his orgasm until she'd found her own pleasure.

Gripping Maya's hips hard with both hands, he held her hard against him as his shaft twitched and jumped within her tight canal. She ground her hips against his groin as she cried out his name, her inner muscles squeezing him.

She collapsed onto his chest and he wrapped his arms around her rib cage and waist. They were still catching their breath when he said, "I don't want there to be any secrets between us anymore, Maya. I want to tell you about the reasons I used to play with fire." He hoped that if he opened up completely, she would too.

Maya shifted slightly to look at him. "I'm listening," she said, her eyes soft, already filled with understanding.

"I was ten years old the first time I lit a fire." He remembered that hot summer afternoon well, when a pile of leaves and a match became an epiphany. "My father was a difficult man to be around. A grade-A asshole, actually."

"I can't imagine that. It must have been hard for you."

"Harder for my mother. She cried a lot. I figured out pretty early on that sticking up for her only made things worse. I was hiding from them, kicking through piles of dry leaves, when I found a box of matches on the ground. I'm not going to lie to you. That first fire was awesome. Dangerous. I felt like a goddamned superhero."

"Any boy would have."

Her insight, the fact that she wasn't judging him for what he'd done, meant the world to him. "That first fire didn't last long. Thirty seconds, maybe a minute. But it was just enough smoke and flame to make me excited. And a little nervous."

"What if your father had found out? What would he have done?"

Logan hadn't spoken to his father in over a decade, not since he'd convinced his mother to get the hell out. "Beaten me to within an inch of my life. But he didn't find out. And when I got away with it, I did it again."

"Risk was the reward, wasn't it?"

Logan nodded. "Exactly. How long could I let them

burn? How big could they get? It didn't take long for things to escalate. I hung out with the older kids in town, the ones who didn't give a shit what happened to them because their lives were already crap. They liked having a guy like me around who wasn't afraid to create diversions with fire. They stole stuff, then I lit fires in Dumpsters and garbage cans. Guess what got more attention?"

"I imagine store owners thought it was better to lose a couple of things off the shelves to pickpockets than watch their businesses go up in flames. How old were you when you finally got caught?"

"Barely seventeen. I was stunned. Couldn't believe it, even when I was in handcuffs. In my head, I was completely invincible."

She gave him a crooked smile. "Some things don't change much, do they?"

He covered her hand with his own. "It might look like I take crazy risks, but I know damn well that I'm not invincible. My crew isn't invincible, either. I've relearned that lesson every single day on the mountain, every time I have to go to the hospital to visit one of my men."

She brought his hand to her lips and pressed a kiss onto his knuckles. "That didn't come out right. I meant it as a compliment. I think you're incredibly brave. In fact, I think you're just plain incredible."

He brushed his fingers against her lips. "Joseph taught me about bravery. He showed me that an arrogant seventeen-year-old kid was pretty much worthless unless he did something good for someone else. I owe him everything."

"I know he feels the same way about you. I didn't talk to him for very long on Friday, but he couldn't stop talking about how great you are. How proud he is to know you."

"He liked you, too. Quite a bit."

She brushed aside his compliment. "He only met me once."

"Doesn't mean you didn't make a hell of an impression."

Maya grinned, obviously pleased by Joseph's assessment. "I liked him too. Does he have a girlfriend? A wife?"

"No. He always said his wife was the only woman he'd ever love. She passed away the year before I came to live with them."

She frowned. "It must be hard for him to live alone. I don't know many older men who know how to keep up a house by themselves. They came of age in a different time." She tightened her grip on his hand. "Has he seen a doctor?"

"I can't even get him to talk to me about it. There's no way he's going to walk into his doctor's office and tell them he's losing his mind."

Maya covered his hands with her own. "My best friend's father went through this. I have some idea what kind of specialists Joseph needs to see, the questions that need to be asked. I'd like to help you, Logan. Joseph is a fine man. He deserves to live a long, healthy life."

Logan placed his hands on either side of her face and simply held her. She covered his hands with her own. He was about to kiss her again, taste some more of her sweetness, when a flash of color outside the bedroom window caught his attention.

He jumped from the bed, his chest clenching with dread and foreboding. "Quick, get dressed."

Maya obeyed his sudden order without a word, her movements efficient as she found one of his T-shirts and put it on, along with her jeans.

"There's a fire extinguisher on the wall next to the door in each bedroom. Grab them all, then wait at the top of the stairs for me."

He took the stairs three at a time and what he saw out the windows on the main floor of his house confirmed his worst suspicions. Smoke was streaming in under the doors, and the redwood decks surrounding his house were completely engulfed in flames.

There was nothing wild about the fire surrounding his house. The blaze had been set deliberately to make sure they couldn't get out easily—if at all.

He ran back up the stairs and found Maya standing by a window, surrounded by fire extinguishers, her expression fierce.

"Your beautiful house," she hissed in anger. "I'm going to make the arsonist pay for this."

Most women would be worrying about saving their own lives right now. Not Maya. If he hadn't already figured out that he loved her, he'd have known it now as she faced the deadly danger utterly unafraid.

From what he could tell, the fire was moving fast around the base of the house and up the surrounding trees. They didn't have much time to get out. He cupped his hands and held them out. "We've got to go through the attic to the roof. Hop on and I'll hoist you up."

Her natural athleticism showed as she easily pushed the cover off the ceiling and pulled herself up into his attic. He grabbed an axe from a closet then jumped and grabbed on to the edge of the two-by-four with his fingertips, lifting his body up into the peaked, unfinished space.

"Move back," he said, then swung the axe over his shoulder into the roof. He closed his eyes as shards of wood splattered. "Cover your face with your hands."

Her voice was muffled as she said, "Anyone ever tell you you're kind of bossy? And that it's pretty hot?"

Rather than replying—but appreciating her good humor in a supremely shitty situation—he swung again at the wood, finally seeing a patch of blue sky. It didn't take many more hits to open up a big enough hole in the roof for them to squeeze through. He shoved a metal storage trunk under the opening.

"Time to go."

She hurried over, and before he could warn her to be

careful on the steep pitch of his roof, she was gone. He held on to the axe as he followed her out. She was walking along the slate tiles as if she'd been born balancing in precarious situations. Still, Logan held his breath until she made it to the more level section, over his kitchen.

From the roof, they could see the carnage all around them. Logan's barn and garage were heading the way of the house, as was his truck. Everywhere they looked, they saw fire.

They stood beside a skylight and weighed their options, which were getting slimmer by the second. Logan walked the perimeter of his roof, looking for an escape route. While he hunted for a way out, he talked to keep Maya calm.

"One time, Dennis dared me to jump off Joseph's roof."

"Teenage boys are so stupid."

She didn't sound worried about the fact that they were stuck on his roof, surrounded by a ring of deadly fire, even though he knew she had to be.

"Who broke what?"

He found himself grinning amidst the danger. "A finger for me. An arm for Dennis."

She grabbed his arm. "I can't believe I forgot to tell you. I talked to Dennis."

Shit, he'd wanted to get to Dennis first. "He can be a loose cannon," he said, and when she nodded her agreement he asked, "What did he tell you?"

"He was visiting doctors last week. For Joseph."

"Why the hell didn't he tell me? I would have gone with him."

She squeezed his hand. "He wanted to do this on his own. To give his father a reason to be proud of him." She pressed her lips together. "You were right all along about Dennis. I don't think he did it."

A loud crack sounded from the first floor and Logan pulled her to the other side of the roof. They'd have to finish this conversation later.

"We need to get out of here. Fast. And it looks like there's only one way out." He pointed at the swimming pool off of what used to be his back deck. "We're going to need to jump into the water."

She took a deep breath. "Okay."

He put down the axe and squeezed her hand. "We'll go together."

She looked up at him, trust blazing from the depths of her eyes. "Let's do this."

Maya was the equal of any man on his crew. She didn't let fear stop her. Even when it was a life-or-death situation. And she was right. It was better to act first, before thinking—and fear—got them in trouble.

"On three. One, two, three."

Even one moment of hesitation would have been deadly as they sprinted across his roof and leapt into the air. Releasing each other's hands and curling into balls, they hit the water in a perfect bull's-eye.

The force of hitting the water temporarily knocked

the air from his lungs. He smashed his knees into the cement bottom of the pool and the water swallowed his roar of pain. His legs and tailbone hurt like hell. But he was alive.

An instant later he was able to open his eyes and look for Maya in the churning water. She wasn't moving, she was simply floating facedown in the middle of his pool, her limbs limp.

He prayed that she'd simply been knocked unconscious when she hit the water. What would he do without her?

Logan swam to her side and yanked her unmoving form out of the water. As soon as her head was above the surface, he confirmed her pulse, then hit the heel of his palm between her shoulder blades in a steady motion.

Her sudden coughing was the most beautiful sound he'd ever heard. He held her close in the water, rubbing her back, whispering "It's all right. We made it. Long, slow breaths." Her inhalations slowed and he murmured, "That's it. Just like that."

She clung to his neck, her legs wrapped around his waist.

"Do you think you broke anything?"

"No," she rasped out, then coughed hard several times in rapid succession. "We're not dead, are we?"

"Not yet."

She pulled back slightly to look at him and he was so

happy to see her eyes open and bright with life that he kissed her hard, then soft and slow.

"See," she said, "what did I tell you? Invincible."

He hugged her tightly, then said, "We've got to figure out who the next target is going to be. Who else could the arsonist want to destroy?" One name immediately popped into his head, and when Maya looked at him, he knew she was thinking the same thing.

"Joseph."

He nodded. "For some reason, he and I were both set up to look guilty. Now that the arsonist thinks he's got you and me, I'm afraid he'll go after Joseph."

Maya started to swim for the edge of the pool. "We've got to get him out of his house, move him somewhere safe." But when she saw that the shrubs all around his pool were encased in flames, which rose to twice the height of the plants, she stopped midstroke. "Oh God," she said, "we're trapped in here."

They were surrounded by a five-foot wall of flames on all sides. It didn't help any that the morning was breezy and the flames reached out in all directions. There wasn't a single safe place to exit.

Logan moved to her side and pulled her close, needing to reassure himself yet again that she was okay. "We'll have to wait it out in the water."

Of all the things he thought he'd be doing in a pool with a beautiful woman, he'd never thought it'd be watching the house he'd built burn down.

"This really sucks," Maya said, putting his thoughts into words. "I wish we could do something to save your house."

"The arsonist can have my house. But he can't have the woman I love."

CHAPTER TWENTY-ONE

MAYA WHIPPED her head around and stared at Logan.

He loved her.

She'd been a constant thorn in his side, an utter pain in the butt, and more prickly than a porcupine.

But he loved her anyway.

He put a finger on her lips, then kissed her gently. "Let's get out of this alive. Then we can talk."

Neither of them spoke again as they waited for the flames to die down. Fifteen long minutes passed before the fire pushed away from his pool and met up with the fiery ball of what had once been his home.

Logan was so strong, amazingly stoic as he watched his beautiful home burn down. Yet again she understood exactly why he was such a phenomenal leader: No matter how bad things got, he was a lone spot of calm in the midst of the storm.

They swam to the edge of the pool and Logan pulled himself out first, giving her a hand up, lifting her into his arms.

"I'm okay," she protested. "I can walk."

"The soil's too hot. The soles of your shoes could melt into your skin."

He didn't put her down until they were at least a hundred yards away from the flames, even though his own feet had to be burning up. She didn't protest—she was enjoying the strength and comfort of his touch too much. When he finally released her, she had to work like hell to ignore the aches and pains that accompanied standing.

She was alive, none of her bones was broken, and she was with Logan. Which meant she didn't have a single thing to complain about.

"What's the fastest way to Joseph's house on foot?"

"The deer trails behind my house."

Maya didn't hesitate. "Let's go."

"It's hilly terrain," he warned. "We'll go at a pace you're comfortable with."

"You lead and I'll keep up."

Thirty minutes later, Maya's calves burned, her quads felt like jelly, and although the hot summer sun had quickly dried her clothes from the unexpected dip in Logan's pool, she was soaking wet from head to toe with sweat. She'd thought an hour at the gym four days a week kept her in good shape. She was wrong.

Even though they were jogging up steep, rocky slopes, Logan was barely exerting himself. Considering he wasn't wearing 150 pounds of equipment, this was probably the equivalent of a stroll in the park for him.

Without her, he could have gone at least twice as fast. But she knew he wouldn't leave her, so she saved what little was left of her breath.

Finally, the deer trail they'd been following connected with a Forest Service–maintained trail. Logan waited for her to catch up.

"We can slow down now. We're almost there."

She managed to get the words "Which way?" out between gasps.

He pointed down the hill and she didn't waste another second before running toward Joseph's house. A handful of minutes later, she saw the roof. Logan sprinted past her and was already inside by the time she caught her breath. She wiped the sweat out of her eyes and stepped inside the cabin.

It was much tidier than on her previous visit. Almost eerily so.

Logan walked into Joseph's bedroom, concern etched into his face. "Where the hell is he?"

"Could he have gone on a trip without telling you?" Maya asked, working to mask her own concern.

"No way. I offered to send him to Hawaii but he refused to leave."

"Are you sure he didn't decide go stay with someone until the fire stops spreading?" Lord knew, that would have been the smartest thing to do.

He opened closet doors, one after the other. "All of his things are here." And then Logan's tanned face went white as he stepped away from a freestanding armoire. "He's out there."

Maya hurried across the room, saying "Where?" even though she was afraid she already knew the answer.

"His gear is gone."

"He's trying to fight the fire, isn't he?"

Logan nodded. "It's possible that he forgot he retired. He probably heard the wildfire was spreading."

"And he decided to go help fight it."

She'd never seen Logan's eyes look so bleak, even in the hospital with Robbie. She knew how horrible it was to lose a father. She didn't want that to happen to him.

"Go find him," she said. "Go bring him back."

"I can't leave you alone. You've got to come with me."

"I'll only slow you down. I can take care of myself until you get back. You can't be in two places at once. Joseph needs your help more than I do." She wrapped her arms around him. "I promise I'll be waiting for you when you both return."

Going on her tippy-toes, she kissed him with all of the love she felt but couldn't say aloud. He kissed her back, hard and sure, and then he was gone.

She wouldn't let herself go to the window and watch him disappear into the hills. That was the kind of a thing a desperate, clingy girlfriend or wife did. Even after everything, she still didn't know what to do. Yes, she loved him. But was love enough? Would love prepare her for a dreaded phone call, for word from the Forest Service that Logan had been injured or, worse, that he was gone forever?

Again, it struck her that Joseph's cabin was oddly quiet. Goose bumps dotted her arms. The room was warm, but there was a chill lingering in the air.

She left the bedroom and poked her head into a second bedroom, down the hall. Two twin beds were on opposite walls, a *Top Gun* poster beside one of the beds, a Guns N' Roses poster over the other. It wasn't too hard to figure out which was which—Logan had definitely been in full-on badass mode as a teen. She smiled. He never would have gone for the regimented feel of the Tom Cruise hit.

It didn't look like the room had changed much in the past twenty years. Without a woman around to spearhead a house-wide cleanup, Joseph certainly didn't seem to be the kind of man who cared about updating his surroundings.

She opened the dusty dresser under the window and sneezed as she pulled out a pile of papers and photos. On top was a picture of Logan and Dennis jumping off a rock into a lake in cutoff shorts. She couldn't imagine having been a teenage girl and seeing such beauty. The years had given Logan a rugged, hard beauty, but even at seventeen, she could see the man he'd become.

She tucked the photo into her jeans and continued flipping through the stack of photos, until one of them made her stop and do a double take.

It was a fairly recent picture of Logan sandwiched between two women. And Maya was nearly certain that one of the women was Dennis's girlfriend, Jenny.

Maya studied the photo, taking in the fact that Jenny was looking at Logan with naked adoration, and all at once, that niggling feeling that had been dogging her heels all day clicked into place.

"Have you been under my nose the whole time?" she asked herself, her brain flying through the possibilities, through everything that had happened.

Her cell phone buzzed in her pocket and she was just reaching for it when the front door creaked open. Her heart pounded hard beneath her breastbone.

From the phone, she heard Chief Stevens tell her, "Tony dated someone named Jenny," and she whispered, "I'm in Joseph's cabin. Help," then closed the phone and slipped it into her pocket, along with a pen she found on top of an old wooden table in the hallway.

Slowly, making sure she was as calm as she could possibly be, she rounded the corner. Jenny was standing in the middle of the kitchen.

"Hey there, Jenny," she said in an easy voice, even as the smell of gasoline permeated the cabin. Maya swallowed the bile that rose up in her throat.

"It's so nice to see you again, Maya," Jenny said, as if

they were two girlfriends simply getting ready to go out and grab something to eat. "Do you remember me?"

Maya forced a smile. "Sure. We met a couple of times yesterday."

"Oh no, I've seen you before. Six months ago, actually."

Maya's heart pounded hard. "Are you sure about that?"

Jenny's mouth twisted. "I've never been more sure of anything."

CHAPTER TWENTY-TWO

LOGAN RAN up the trail at a fierce pace, his lungs burning, sweat pouring into his eyes and down his chest. Smoke and ash fell from the sky, blanketing his clothes and skin in a dark, sooty layer of burned-up brush.

On the run from his house, with Maya following bravely behind him, he'd noted the astonishing growth of the wildfire. There must have been a thousand acres between these trails and the original burning point, and yet they were close enough now, he could see new smoke columns rising.

The fire was moving closer with every minute that ticked by. Time was not on his side. He didn't have the leisure of running every trail split to locate Joseph. He had to guess right the first time and pray he wasn't already too late.

It was not yet noon, and the wind had picked up speed, blowing more powerfully than usual for midday. Another strike against Joseph, against each and every one of the hotshots on this mountain working to put the wildfire out. If the winds kept up, they would send the flames straight into town, which was crammed full of tourists for the summer. Wildfire always looked for a way down to the flatlands, to the houses and cars and campgrounds, which were full of fuel. With only two main highways snaking out of town, the enormous traffic jams would make casualties inevitable.

Hitting a Y in the trail, Logan made a split-second decision to take the right fork north, even though Joseph tended to favor the other direction when hiking. If Joseph had suited up, it was because he intended to fight the fire. This trail would lead directly to it.

A quarter mile later, a fire whirl lifted off the hillside below him. Logan jumped back against a rock and watched the fire and ash rush up the hillside.

Barely breaking stride at the close call, he continued up the trail until he saw that the small meadow up ahead was burning. Without gear—without even so much as a fire shelter clamped onto his belt—he couldn't go much farther. He prayed that Joseph had realized the trouble and was turning back as well.

A familiar sound buzzed through the sound of crackling flames. Moving closer to the fire, he scanned the area for a sign of life.

A bright yellow body moved in front of the orange

wall of flames and Logan shouted, "Joseph," only once, knowing better than to waste any more breath trying to be heard over the imploding gases.

Without any protective gear, it was borderline crazy for Logan to go in and pull Joseph out. But had their positions been reversed, he was certain that Joseph would have risked his life in the same way.

Logan sprinted off-trail, making a beeline for the man to whom he owed his life. His debt would never be repaid, not even if he got Joseph off the mountain today in one piece.

Fully intent on wielding his chainsaw, Joseph didn't notice when Logan ran up behind him. Knowing better than to tap on the arm a man holding heavy, deadly machinery, Logan picked up a rock and threw it at Joseph's leg.

Joseph's head whipped around, his mask covered in black ash, and seconds later he'd moved far enough away from the flames to put down his chainsaw and flip up his mask.

"Logan, what the hell are you doing out here? This fire's a killer. It's no place for a kid. Get back to the cabin."

Logan instantly understood that Joseph had traveled back to a time when he was lead hotshot and Logan was a teenage kid acting stupid. This wasn't the place to try to talk Joseph back to the present, not while a killer was on the loose.

First, Logan had to get him to safety. Then they'd

work on putting the pieces together and figuring out what had happened today.

"You've got to follow me out of here, Joseph. Now. It's not safe."

Joseph had never once backed down from a fire. He had the scars from second-degree burns to prove it. But Logan couldn't wait for his agreement. He moved behind Joseph and put his hands on his shoulders, scorching his palms on the heat of the thick fire-resistant fabric, pushing Joseph in the direction of the trail, off the meadow.

Joseph struggled over the rocky hillside under the weight of his gear.

"Give me your pack," Logan said.

Joseph growled, "Like hell if I'm letting you carry my gear."

The wind howled across the mountain, taking the smoke—and flames—with it. In an instant, Logan had Joseph's pack off and in the dirt. Squatting down, he reached in and pulled out the fire shelter, praying it wasn't too old to be useful.

Heat singed his shin and he grabbed Joseph in a bear hug and pushed him to the ground, struggling to deploy the shelter over both of them in the whipping wind, his feet to the fire, his boots jammed into the straps at the foot of the shelter. It took every bit of his strength to hold it down as flames and wind rushed over the aluminum and fiberglass tent.

Joseph's breathing was ragged beneath him, and Logan hoped he hadn't caused the man any broken bones or other injuries that would prolong their hike back to the cabin.

Logan had only deployed his shelter once before in all the years he'd been a hotshot. It wasn't something a guy wanted to repeat. The sensation of being microwaved alive was even worse with two men under the silver aluminum and fiberglass cover. Radiant heat was one thing, but direct flames could burn right through to their skin.

Still, Logan knew damn well that the most likely cause of death for a firefighter was getting scared and throwing off a shelter.

He held fast to the hand-and-foot holds even as the temperature soared. The nickname "shake'n'bake" was well deserved.

And then, as quickly as they came, the flames rushed over and off them, the wind taking them up the hill. Logan held fast in case another fireball was about to roll across the trail. He lay over Joseph for several minutes, until he was certain the fire had jumped them for good.

Slowly, he pushed back the shelter, closing his eyes against the ash raining from the charred trees surrounding the meadow. He held out a hand to Joseph and pulled him up. In one glance, he could see Joseph's mental fog had cleared.

"What the hell just happened?"

"I'll tell you soon. Do you think you can run?"

Joseph looked at him like he'd lost his mind. "Of course I can."

"Good. Head back down to the cabin as fast as you can. I'll follow behind."

Joseph shot downhill through the meadow back to the trail at a pace that belied his years and mental wanderings. It was five minutes of good, hard running before Logan felt safe enough to slow their pace. Moving alongside Joseph, he put his hand on his arm.

"We can slow down now."

Testament to all his years as an elite firefighter, Joseph only took it down to a very fast hike. He was winded but determined.

Logan didn't want to blame his mentor for what had happened, not when he probably couldn't have done anything about it. But it was time to make some command decisions. Screw Joseph's independence. He was coming to live with him. It was the only way Logan could make sure something like this didn't happen again.

A sudden vision of his house on fire backhanded Logan. He'd been so worried about Joseph that he'd temporarily forgotten that his house was gone.

Fine. He'd move in with Joseph while he rebuilt. Although maybe this time around, he hoped he'd have to plan enough space for a wife. And children.

"What the hell happened?" Joseph asked again.

Logan weighed his words carefully. "I'm not completely sure. Maya and I went to the cabin and saw that you were gone."

Joseph rubbed his chin as he tried to work out what had happened. "All I remember was waking up from a nap and seeing Dennis's girlfriend in my living room, holding up my gear. She said she wanted to see what I looked like in it. She helped me put everything on."

Jenny? "Is that the first time she's done that?"

Joseph nodded. "I haven't put these on in years. Not until she mentioned it."

Logan's mind reeled with the implications. Was it possible that Jenny was responsible for the Desolation Wilderness fire? For the motel fire? For Robbie's explosion and the car bomb too? Had she been laughing inside as he'd practically begged her to spend time with Joseph, to "take care of him"?

She'd taken care of him, all right. She'd tried to send him straight to his death.

But why?

"Did she send you out here with a chainsaw? Was this her idea for you to come out and fight the fire?"

Joseph's thick gray brows furrowed over his eyes. "I don't know. I can't remember much of anything else." He shot Logan an apologetic glance. "You were right. I should have gotten on that plane to Hawaii. I almost killed us both out here."

"Forget about it. We made it out alive," Logan said gruffly.

But Maya was still in the cabin. And Logan had never been so scared in all his life. Because if Jenny had written the letter in the firebox in Maya's hotel room, her intent was clear: *I've often dreamed of seeing your long hair on fire and watching your soft skin melt down to the bone.*

"Maya's in your cabin, Joseph. She's waiting for us. I left her all alone. She could be in trouble."

For all he knew, Jenny had been waiting in the wings to see if they'd made it out of his house alive.

Joseph picked up the pace. "Let's go get your girl."

CHAPTER TWENTY-THREE

MAYA QUICKLY assessed her surroundings, looking for something she could use in self-defense, and decided the fireplace poker was her best bet.

"Actually," she said in a perfectly calm voice as she slowly made her way toward the fireplace, "I'm glad you're here. I've been wanting to talk with you."

Jenny frowned. "With me? About what?"

Maya forced herself to sit down on the arm of the couch beside the stone fireplace. "I'm worried about Dennis. About some of the things he's told me." If she could convince Jenny that she thought Dennis was the guilty one, maybe she could escape.

"What kind of things?"

Maya waved one hand in the air. "You know, about his

relationship with his dad and Logan. And the competition between them."

Jenny smiled viciously. "Dennis hates Logan."

"Really? Why?"

"He's jealous. After all, Logan's so much better-looking. So much better at everything. Everybody loves him."

Maya's heart thudded as Jenny moved toward her. The poker was almost within reach. She'd never hurt anyone before, but she'd do whatever she needed to do to make sure this terrible woman sat behind bars for the rest of her worthless life.

Jenny got a dreamy look on her face. "I love him too, you know."

"Of course you love Dennis," Maya said, purposefully misunderstanding Jenny's intent. "He seems like a great guy. And very devoted to you."

"Not Dennis, you idiot. I'm talking about Logan. I love Logan. We were meant to be together."

Maya edged closer to the fireplace. "Does Logan know you feel this way about him?"

"We would have been together if it weren't for you. I was there. I saw you six months ago."

"Where did you see us?"

"When you and Logan started your fuck-fest. I walked in and heard you talking."

"The bar was empty," Maya stated, but now that she thought about it, she'd been so upset about everything that she supposed she could have gone past a crowd of people and been blind to every last one of them.

"I forgot my wallet after the lunch shift and when I came back I walked in on you. Not that either of you noticed. You were too busy sucking face. And after that he didn't want anything to do with other girls anymore. He was under your goddamned spell. What did you do to him?"

"I didn't do anything," Maya said honestly. He'd rocked her world and she'd left him stone cold.

"Like hell you didn't," Jenny spat. "He hasn't touched another woman since you left."

He hadn't touched another woman.

Had their stolen kisses meant as much to him as they had to her? Maya was deeply moved by Logan's behavior, even as she continued to face Jenny.

Jenny's rant continued, unrelenting in its fury. "He stopped coming into the bar. I hardly saw him anymore. He was supposed to be mine."

Maya swallowed. "I'm sorry." She forced the words out between her lips, hoping they sounded somewhat sincere.

"No you're not. You're fucking him again, aren't you?"

Maya jumped to her feet. "No."

"Don't lie to me."

Maya followed Jenny's eyes to the corner of the folded photo sticking out of her pocket. Just as Jenny grabbed it, Maya's cell phone fell to the ground, and Jenny stomped it hard with her boots.

Maya stared at the busted phone and tried not to

focus on how much trouble she was in. Hopefully Chief Stevens had heard her whisper and was on his way.

Jenny shook the photo in Maya's face. "You're in love with him, aren't you? And he probably said he loves you, hasn't he?"

Maya hesitated a moment too long and Jenny crumpled up the photo and threw it on the floor.

"He did. I can tell. He thinks you're his soul mate. He wants you to have his babies."

Maya shook her head back and forth, saying "No" again as she inched toward the poker. She nearly had her hand around it when Jenny pulled a handgun from her pocket. Maya went completely still.

"Whatever," the crazy woman said in a dull tone as she waved the gun in Maya's face. "Everything will be better once you're gone. Once all of you are dead. You should have died yesterday, in the truck. Then I wouldn't have to do this."

"You still don't have to do it, Jenny," Maya said. "I can help you. I can tell my boss the fire was an accident. I can tell the Forest Service it's impossible to determine how it started. I'll give you money, enough to get you out of the country and make sure you never need to work again."

"You could do all that for me?"

Hope flared in Maya's chest. "Give me five minutes on the phone. That's all I need."

Jenny chewed on her lower lip. "Um, no thanks. I think it'll be more fun to kill you instead."

Maya shivered at the delight in the woman's voice. At

this point, a mental institution was a far likelier future home for Jenny than a prison.

"But before I do, I need you to help me with something," Jenny said. "Out on the back deck. I've got two dozen containers of gasoline waiting." She shoved the butt of the gun into Maya's spine. "Go."

Maya slipped her hand in her pocket, grabbed the ballpoint pen, and spun around, lashing her weapon at Jenny's eyes. The tip of the point struck Jenny in the neck, just below her ear.

Jenny screamed, "You're going to pay for that, you little bitch," and as Maya lunged for the fireplace poker, Jenny threw herself on Maya's back, scratching at her hair.

Tears of pain filled Maya's eyes as Jenny ripped a thick wad of hair from her scalp and dug her gun in deep between Maya's ribs.

"Maybe I should just kill you now," Jenny hissed.

No. Maya had promised Logan she'd be here waiting for him when he returned. He'd be back soon with Joseph in tow and together they'd find a way to thwart Jenny.

She needed to hold out—and stay alive—until then.

"I'm sorry," she ground out. "I'll do whatever you want. Tell me what you want me to do."

Jenny lay across Maya for a long moment, long enough for Maya to wonder if the last thing she was going to hear was the gun's release. But then Jenny shifted her weight off to the side. Pushing Maya into a standing position with her gun, Jenny shoved her out the door.

A row of gas cans was waiting for them. "Start on that side and work your way back to me." She massaged one bicep with her free hand. "Lighting Logan's house on fire was hard work. I should probably go to the gym more often."

Maya saw red. This bitch had killed a hotshot and all she cared about was lifting weights? "How could you do it?" she asked in a low voice.

She wanted to launch herself at Jenny and wrap her hands around her throat, but a moment's satisfaction wasn't worth a bullet in her chest. She wanted to be alive to witness Jenny's life sentence, to watch the handcuffs clip into place over her bony wrists.

Jenny didn't reply as she shoved the gun into Maya's breastbone. "Get to it, already. I'm working the afternoon shift and I don't want to be late." She shoved Maya back to work with the gun's cold metal barrel.

After everything she'd done—after everything she was about to do—Jenny was worried about clocking in late to work? But then, hadn't she served them their sandwiches yesterday, knowing that Robbie was in critical condition in the hospital, knowing she'd likely killed him with the explosion?

Maya's hands were numb as she picked up a heavy gas can and hefted it over to the far corner of the house.

"Don't try to run," Jenny warned. "I'm a great shot."

After everything Jenny had done so far, Maya didn't doubt it. She possessed a strange group of talents for a waitress, and clearly could have done so much more with her life if she weren't so deranged.

Maya's heart clenched as she uncapped the can and started pouring fuel onto the redwood decking and shrubs surrounding Joseph's cabin. Logan had grown to manhood here, had started his life anew in this house. It wasn't enough for him to lose one home today, Jenny had to take everything from him in one fell swoop.

"Feels good, doesn't it?" Jenny's words were carefree and happy as she watched Maya do her sick bidding, liberally sprinkling fertilizer pellets in her wake.

"No," Maya said. "This is a horrible thing to do."

"Actually, if anyone ever asks, I'm going to tell them that I tried to stop you from setting dear Joseph's house on fire. He was such a sweet man, after all."

Maya was this close to throwing the empty red gas can at her. Silently, she completed the atrocious task, her shoulder and arm muscles burning from picking up so many cans of gas. All that mattered now was staying alive as long as possible. She prayed Logan was on his way back.

"Now for the really fun part," Jenny said when Maya was done. "Here's a box of matches. Start lighting."

Maya's eyes widened. With this much fuel on the dry grass, and with the wind blowing a gale, even one match could instantly combust and burn her. "You're crazy."

Jenny raised an eyebrow. "Guys sometimes say that, but it's just because they can't handle a girl like me." She jammed the gun into Maya's skull, making her wince. "Start lighting."

Maya's hands trembled as she lit the first match. Silently asking for forgiveness, she threw the match against the house. A path of fire lifted off the grass and goose bumps of horror covered her flesh, head to toe.

"I can't do this," she said, backing away from the house.

She heard Jenny cock the gun. "Sure you can. Especially since it doesn't look like lover boy's coming back any time soon to save you. He and Joseph are probably already dead."

No, Jenny was wrong. Logan was alive. She'd know if he was dead, would feel it deep in her bones, in the center of her heart.

Temporarily out of options, she dropped one lit match after another against Joseph's cabin, and then, suddenly, Jenny's cold hands were on Maya's wrists and she was duct-taping them together behind her back.

Maya clasped the half-full box of matches tightly in her palm. They were all she had, her only potential weapon.

"Good job," Jenny praised. "Now let's go for a hike." Jenny pushed her forward with the gun, then picked up a chainsaw. "Move it."

Maya felt her eyes go wide as she looked at the machine and forced herself to speak calmly. "You don't want to do this, Jenny."

"Sure I do. I couldn't believe how lucky I was when you showed up to investigate. Here I thought I was only going to fuck with Logan's life by lighting the wildfire and calling the tip line, but now I get to take you down too. This is going to be superfun."

Fumbling with the matchbox at Jenny's straightforward admission of guilt, Maya forced herself to calm down so that she could slide it open and slip out a match. She let it fall to the ground for Logan to find.

"If you get caught for starting a wildfire and burning buildings, you won't be in jail too long," she lied. "But if you murder people—"

"Too late," Jenny said cheerfully. "That young hotshot is already dead. Which is really too bad, because he was kind of cute. You know what's really sad, though? I hadn't gotten around to fucking him yet. The young ones are always so energetic and eager to please."

Maya stumbled over a rock, stunned by the woman's cruelty. She dropped another match to the ground, praying her trail of bread crumbs wouldn't catch fire and disappear before Logan found them.

"How many hotshots have you slept with?"

She'd need to know these things when she got away, when she was testifying against Jenny in court, even though she couldn't stand the thought of Logan or any of his men in bed with this horrible woman.

"Not as many hotshots as I'd like. It's a pain that they're gone for so many months every year. But most of the guys in town."

Maya's skin went cold and clammy, even though they moved closer to the heat of the fire with every step up the trail. Ignoring the push of metal against her ribs, she spun around.

"Did you know Tony Jackson?"

Jenny's lips curved up. "Oh yeah, I knew Tony."

Her words snaked around Maya's heart like a huge, deadly anaconda. "Did you sleep with him?"

"Of course I did. He was one of the best I ever had. Too bad he had to die." Jenny poked her head closer to Maya's and asked, "Why, did you know him or something?"

CHAPTER TWENTY-FOUR

HOLY SHIT."

Logan nearly barreled into Joseph, who'd cursed and then gone dead silent as he stood in the center of the trail. What now? Logan moved out of the shade of a baby oak and that's when he saw that Joseph's cabin was engulfed in flames. His heart stopped cold.

"Maya's inside."

Joseph grabbed Logan's shoulders as if he were still seventeen years old. "Goddamn it, go save her!"

Logan sprinted downhill. All he'd been doing for the past two days was running up and down this god-damned mountain. First to save Connor. Then Joseph. And now Maya.

His house was gone. Joseph's cabin would be nothing but ashes very soon. But Robbie was dead. *Dead*.

Someone had killed him. And if it turned out to be Jenny, Logan hoped she'd burn in hell for what she'd done.

He was long past the point of pain as he sprinted onto Joseph's property. Flames leapt ten feet in the air and the stench of gasoline filled his lungs.

"Maya," he roared into the smoke-filled sky, yelling her name over and over, praying she'd answer.

A quick check of the property's perimeter confirmed what he'd already guessed: Maya was gone. She'd promised to be here waiting for him, but she hadn't bet on Jenny. Neither of them had.

Logan had never been this scared and knew it would be nearly impossible to treat this situation like any one of the hundreds of emergencies he'd worked. But he wouldn't be worth shit if he didn't calm down. He unclenched his fists and forcibly slowed his heart rate.

Maya was one of the smartest women he knew. She wasn't going to let someone haul her off without leaving a clue as to her whereabouts. And Jenny's truck was parked between two pine trees. Which meant they couldn't have gone far.

He quickly ruled out the driveway. If they'd been headed to the road, Jenny would have taken her truck. Which meant they had to be back up in the mountains, on a different fork of the trail than he and Joseph had taken.

He looked down and saw a match on the ground,

and then another, heading toward the trailhead. Logan sprinted back toward the mountain, passing Joseph, who was on his way down.

"You didn't find her?"

"No. But I will. She left me a trail of matches."

"Smart girl." Joseph stripped off his fire-resistant jacket. "Put this on. It'll buy you some time if you need it. I'll run out to the freeway and get some help."

Joseph didn't tell him to be careful. Not when he already seemed to know that Logan would do whatever it took—and risk everything—to ensure Maya's safety.

Logan put the jacket on as he ran uphill, not giving the burning cabin another glance. It was just another building, wood and nails, not flesh and blood.

Maya was all that mattered now.

"Did I know him?" Intense, unending rage raced through Maya, from head to toe and back again as she launched herself at Jenny, swinging her bound arms around in an arc, knocking the woman into the mountain, screaming "You fucking bitch, he was my brother!"

She spun around, wanting to hit Jenny harder, faster this time. But before she could make contact, a sharp blade whacked against her skull and knocked her back into a tree trunk. She felt something warm and wet trickle through her hair.

Jenny threw the bloodstained chainsaw down into the

dirt. Taking advantage of Maya's momentary shock, she quickly rolled duct tape around her body. Maya kicked and yelled, but without the use of her hands, she was soon imprisoned against the tree.

"I was planning on killing you," Jenny said viciously, "but now I'm thinking I should just leave you here to burn. It'll hurt so much more that way, take so much longer for you to die."

Somewhere in the back of her mind, Maya registered Jenny's crazy threats. But she needed to know for certain what happened to her brother.

"Did you light that apartment on fire?"

Jenny put the roll of duct tape next to the chainsaw and her gun. "Oh, you mean the fire that killed Tony?" She almost looked bored, as if one rookie firefighter mattered so little. She fluffed her sweat-dampened hair. "Um, yeah. But he'd really pissed me off."

"How?" The word left Maya's lips like a bullet. Like the one she wanted to put between Jenny's eyebrows.

"Do you really want to know?" Jenny rolled her eyes. "I mean, he's been dead for months. Don't you think you should get over it already?"

Maya tried to wrench herself away from the tree, but the duct tape around her chest and legs held her firmly in place.

"Tell me why."

Jenny continued taping her up as she said, "We went

out a couple of times. And then he told me I was acting all weird and he thought we should cool it. Piece of shit rookie was lucky to score me in the first place. He hadn't seen weird yet. The things I could have made him do." Her eyes went slightly unfocused. Glazed. "I knew his shifts. Thought it would be fun to see how he did in a big fire. It was just pure luck that he died. Served the bastard right."

"Bitch!"

Maya's scream reverberated through her entire body and still it wasn't enough. She wanted to rip Jenny limb from limb for taking her brother away without even the slightest bit of remorse.

Jenny's face contorted in anger and she grabbed the chainsaw from the dirt and forced the blade up under Maya's chin.

"No, you're the bitch. The shady bitch who stole my man."

Maya's eyes teared from the saw's jagged teeth and chain digging into her neck and jaw, but she refused to show any fear. There was no point in playing nice anymore, no reason to keep her mouth shut.

"You're disgusting. No wonder Logan wouldn't go near you."

Jenny jammed the chainsaw harder into Maya's neck. "You're wrong. He would have fallen in love with me, and I'd be carrying his baby instead of Dennis's, if it weren't for you."

Maya was amazed she could register one more shock at this point. "You're pregnant?"

"Aren't you going to congratulate me? Because I'm going to tell everyone Logan's the father."

Jenny's sick words lanced Maya's heart like knives. Oh God, even after they were all dead, it wouldn't end. A child would have to live with this insanity every single day.

"No one will believe you," she choked out from beneath the pressure of the chainsaw. "They'll all know what filth you are. They'll all know you're lying."

Jenny snarled and pulled the chainsaw away from her neck, looking for the start cord, then pulling it hard. Maya gasped in a breath, one that looked like it was going to be her last.

Her nemesis lifted the grinding chainsaw, aiming right for Maya's heart. "I've changed my mind. I think I'll kill you instead of letting you burn. And I know exactly what I'm going to cut off first. Your precious tits. Logan would be so sad if he knew what I was about to do to your boobies. Tell me, how did it feel when Logan sucked them? When he squeezed them?"

Maya shot a quick barb at her killer: "Amazing."

Jenny's cheeks went red, as if Maya had slapped them. "I wish he could find you like this, see your charred tits on the ground. But if he's not already dead, I'm going to have to take care of him too. I hope you fucked him good and hard this morning, because it was good-bye."

Maya pinched her eyes shut as Jenny moved closer. Back when she'd lost her father and brother, she'd wanted to die. But now she wanted to live, if only to see Logan's face one more time, to feel his heart beating steady and strong beneath her cheek.

A roar sounded to her left and she opened her eyes just in time to see Logan flying through the air, his hands clamping around Jenny's waist as he dragged her to the ground.

Maya's heart was in her throat as she watched the man she loved knock the roaring chainsaw off the side of the trail and wrestle Jenny into a prone position beneath him.

"Stop it, Logan. I love you," Jenny cried.

He shifted his weight slightly in shock. "Did you start this wildfire to get back at me for not going out with you?"

Maya watched a tear seep out from beneath Jenny's lashes as she said, "Dennis told me about Joseph's problems. I knew you'd think he lit the fires. And I knew someone would see you putting them out." Her tears stopped falling and she smiled a sick, twisted smile. "It was so easy to set you up. But I wasn't going to kill you, Logan. I was going to comfort you." Her smile turned to a scowl. "If *she* hadn't shown up, that's what I would have done." She craned her neck up from the dirt to yell, "But you did, you stupid cunt. Because you wanted to fuck him too bad, couldn't wait to drop to your knees and suck his dick, could you? That's when I knew I needed to kill both of you."

Logan's low, hard voice interrupted the woman's angry ramblings. "I could kill you for touching her."

Spit flew from her mouth and slid down his cheek. "Fuck you, asshole."

His hand went around Jenny's throat and even though Maya hated her more than anyone on earth, she couldn't let Logan kill her. Not for her. Or Robbie. Or Tony. Or Connor.

No matter how much Jenny deserved it, Logan would be haunted by her death for the rest of his life. Maya couldn't let it be one more thing Jenny took from him.

"Logan, please. Don't. Let go of her." She wasn't sure if he could hear her, but she kept talking anyway. "I know she deserves to die, but not like this. She'll get what she deserves. I promise. She'll rot in prison for the rest of her life."

She held her breath as she waited for him to decide. And then she realized he must have let up his grip, because Jenny started coughing.

He didn't turn his face away from his unwilling hostage. "Are you all right? Did she hurt you?"

Maya'd certainly felt better, but she was alive. Thank God.

"I'm fine."

She was about to tell him the duct tape was by his left foot so that he could restrain Jenny, when her shoulders and her hair suddenly felt like they were about to ignite.

She looked up into the branches above her head and worked to contain her fear.

"Logan, this tree is on fire."

He shifted his weight to look at her, and Jenny took advantage of his split-second distraction to wriggle away. She ran up the hill, as fast and nimble as a rabbit.

Logan squatted at her feet, ripping at Maya's duct tape with his teeth and hands.

Seconds later he'd removed enough tape to set her free. Grabbing her hand, he pulled her out from beneath the tree, just before a loud crack sounded and it split in half.

"The fire will take care of her," he said, and even as the fire threatened to overtake Maya, she shivered at the picture his words painted.

He pulled her down the trail; the smoke was so thick she couldn't see farther than her elbow. She tripped and fell to her knees, and the next thing she knew, Logan's arms were around her and he was carrying her through the smoke. She clung to his neck, knowing if she let go and they were separated, she'd be toast. She tried to take a breath, and choked on the thick haze of smoke.

"We're going to get out of this," he promised her in a low voice, and she believed him, even though all signs pointed to the opposite outcome.

Suddenly, another blaze appeared, a fireball rolling up the hill, straight toward them. Maya heard a squeak of fear emerge from her lips as the blaze illuminated their circle of hell. She tried to get closer to Logan, her heart racing.

"Hold on tight."

He dropped down and pressed her into an indentation in the rock, pulling his fire-resistant jacket over his head and fanning it out to cover them both completely. It would buy them fifteen seconds, maybe twenty, in a flame front.

Her nose was jammed into his breastbone, and even though she could hardly breathe, even though she'd nearly been massacred by a madwoman with a chainsaw, she felt strangely safe.

Flames rolled over the trail and he said, "Scream," so she started yelling. It was the only way to keep the fiery gases from scorching her lungs, but she would have screamed anyway, as she felt a sphere of fire roll straight toward them.

She braced for impact, tried to somehow prepare herself to be burned alive, when the fireball rammed into the rock and exploded. She didn't know how long Logan held her as her entire body shook. Of everything that had happened so far, this was by far the scariest. Jenny's bombs and house fires were crazy, but nature was wholly unpredictable.

Logan pulled her against him and she'd never been happier to feel his strong arms circle her body. She scrunched his sweat-soaked shirt in her hands, burrowed her face into the hard wall of his chest.

"Thank you," she finally said, the words "I love you" still stuck on the tip of her tongue.

God, why couldn't she just say it already? He was the man she'd been waiting for all her life. And yet, in the circle of his arms, she was more scared than she'd ever been.

He cupped her jaw in his hand and covered her mouth with his, sweeping his tongue inside to mate with hers. Without words, his kiss told her how afraid he'd been of losing her, how much he loved her.

"We need to get out of here. Do you think you can walk?" he asked gently.

She nodded, her throat clogged with a full range of emotions: Fear. Love. Confusion.

He helped her to her feet and put an arm around her waist, holding her close as they headed downhill. Five minutes later they were finally able to see the blue sky and breathe in fresh air again. She sucked it into her starving lungs as they picked up their pace on the steep downhill grade. Logan never let go, never let her stumble.

Several minutes later when they were in a much safer spot, he carefully ran his hands over her face, her neck, her shoulders, her wrists.

"Damn her for touching you," he said against her lips.

Maya threaded her hands into his slightly singed hair and kissed him. She'd never get enough of him, would never want to stop kissing him. But this wasn't the time and place for making love.

He held her tightly to him. "When I heard the chainsaw, I thought . . ."

She pressed a kiss into his shoulder. "She didn't hurt me," she insisted, knowing how helpless he must have felt, running to save her from a madwoman.

"Why was she after you? What did you ever do to her?"

"She saw us in the bar. And she was jealous. She wanted you, Logan. Badly."

When Jenny had run away, Maya hadn't wanted him to go after her. She hadn't wanted him to risk his life again, to leave her and, possibly, never come back.

Maya knew that if she gave in to what she wanted—what he clearly wanted too—if she agreed to be with him, this was the same fear she'd face every day, every night he was called away to put out a wildfire. He might end up being the target of an insane arsonist again, and she wouldn't know it until it was too late.

She put her hand on his arm. "Do you think she'll make it out?"

"She better not. This time I'll kill her."

"No," Maya said, turning her mouth into Logan's palm. "She isn't worth it."

His eyes were dark with fury. "She hurt you. She killed Robbie."

"They're just scratches. I'll heal." But Robbie wouldn't. And neither would Tony. She had to tell him. "She knew my brother. They dated."

He pulled her close. "She was obsessed with firefighters. I only wish I'd realized she was obsessed with fire too."

Maya was glad that Logan's shirt was already wet. It made her tears seem smaller.

"She says he dumped her when she got too clingy. She set the fire that killed him and said she was happy when he died. That he deserved it."

"She's insane, Maya. I'd bring him back for you if I could."

No one had ever loved her this much, enough to slay all her dragons and dry all her tears.

"When she told me she was going to kill me—" Her voice caught. "I realized I'm finally ready to start living again. It's time for me to accept that he's gone."

"Stay here, Maya. Stay in Lake Tahoe with me."

But she wasn't sure she could. Not when she loved Logan too much to lose him. Even after everything they'd been through together, she wasn't sure she could hack it as a hotshot's wife. She felt like she was wading through black smoke, trying to find her way toward the light, to a place where she would take a deep breath and feel whole again.

But she wasn't there yet. And wasn't sure that she ever would be.

So rather than answering him, rather than having to make a decision about her future—about their future—she focused on the fire. On her duties. And his.

"I need to call my boss and tell him everything that's happened."

Logan searched her eyes and she dropped her gaze. She didn't want him to see her fear. Her uncertainty.

He stroked her arms. "I know you're not ready yet, Maya, but I'm going to tell you again anyway. I love you."

She closed her eyes as his lips touched hers. He was so gentle. So wonderful. And still she was afraid.

"Will you still be in Tahoe when I'm done putting out the fire?"

She swallowed hard. "I don't know."

He didn't pressure her into making a decision or a declaration. She was paralyzed by her fear of losing him, was still convinced that it would be better to give him up now.

They moved down the trail in silence. She gasped when they got to Joseph's cabin. It was a massive fireball in the middle of a forest.

"She made me do it," she confessed in a shaky voice.

Logan squeezed her hand. "Joseph understands. He'd never blame you for doing what you needed to do to stay alive."

She held her stomach with both hands, willing herself not to hurl. "But everything you have is gone. Your memories from his cabin, and your house too."

"Joseph's going to move in with me. Or Dennis. So he doesn't need the cabin anymore." Logan pulled her against him, kissing her hard, stealing the breath from her lungs. "You're here, Maya. I don't need a house. I only need you."

Her heart broke into a million pieces at the thought of going back to San Francisco. Alone.

Suddenly, one of the cabin's windows blew out and he dragged her behind him as he ran. They didn't let up their pace until they saw the fire trucks roaring onto Joseph's driveway.

Sam MacKenzie jumped out of the lead truck. "You guys all right?"

Chief Stevens was right behind him. "Maya, thank God." His face was deeply lined with worry as he hugged her. "I could barely hear you—we had to access our recorded telephone logs to replay what you said. I wish to God we'd gotten here sooner."

"I'm fine," she said weakly. "Thank you for coming."

She felt herself weave on her feet and Logan was instantly at her side again, holding her steady. "Can you walk down the driveway?"

She blinked hard, forced the black spots away from her vision. "Yes. Of course I can," she insisted, even though it was more pride than truth.

"We'll go slow," he said as they started walking.

But he had a job to do. Which was why she was going to force herself to walk out of his arms even though she never ever wanted to let him go.

"You have to go now to see if you can salvage anything from Joseph's cabin. I'll be fine."

He searched her eyes for a long moment before he said, "Joseph's waiting for you out on the road. He'll get you a ride back to your motel."

She nodded, her heart stuck in her throat. He held her hand fast, not letting her go. "Don't worry," he said, "I'll come back to you. I promise."

And then she made herself walk down the driveway, away from the man she loved as he raced straight into the fire.

CHAPTER TWENTY-FIVE

JOSEPH WAITED for her at the end of the drive. "Welcome back from hell."

Her throat grew tight as she stood before the kind man who'd given Logan so much. "I'm so sorry, Joseph. I should have fought harder. Then maybe you'd still have your house."

He put his arms around her, his solid warmth comforting. Logan had been lucky to find a father like this.

"You did exactly the right thing. All that matters is getting out alive."

"But she got away."

Joseph's eyebrows raised in surprise. "Don't worry. I'm sure she'll end up paying big-time for what she's done. You'll see." He helped her into a waiting minivan. "Go back to your motel. Take a shower. Eat something.

And get some sleep. We'll all still be here when you wake up."

The drive back to her motel was a total blur. The man behind the wheel kept telling her she looked bad, kept saying he wanted to take her to the hospital, but she couldn't stand to have a bunch of strangers poking and prodding her. She needed to be alone, to regain her bearings and process everything that had happened.

The blonde girl was sitting at the motel's front desk watching TV when Maya walked in to get a key. "What happened to you? You look like shit."

Three days blurred together in a strange and murky cloud in her brain. "I lost my key" was all Maya could manage. She was too tired to say anything else.

The girl snapped her gum. "Name?"

"Maya Jackson."

Her name was the same, but she was a completely different person.

The girl handed her the key and Maya was surprised to see her hands shaking as she took it. Funny how you could fool yourself—and everyone else—into thinking you were holding everything together when you weren't.

Maya headed for her room, surprised that taking the stairs to the second floor felt like climbing to the top of the Empire State Building. She was so fried she could barely stand, yet at this exact moment she knew Logan was knee-deep in ashes, wielding heavy equipment and hoses to save what was left of Joseph's cabin.

Once she got inside her room, she stripped down, barely acknowledging the bruises, scrapes, and welts that covered her arms, legs, and torso. She walked into the shower and leaned her weight against the tiled wall. When she looked down, the white floor tiles were black beneath her feet. She watched ash and dirt wind down the drain until the water ran cold.

Shivering, she wrapped a towel around herself and walked into the bedroom. Heavy weights hung from her eyelids, and she used up her last burst of energy crawling under the covers. There were a hundred things she should be doing. But all of them required strength and energy she didn't have.

Additional hotshot crews and smoke jumpers from all across the West were on their way to fight the forest fire in Desolation Wilderness. By late Sunday afternoon, Logan had to make the difficult decision to bring his crew in again. With forty-mile-an-hour winds, the usual method of digging fire lines wasn't going to cut it. And while he reassessed the situation, his men could get some much-needed rest.

They'd straggled into the station, exhausted and covered in ash and dirt, each one of their faces lighting up when they saw him behind the maps.

"Logan, glad you've decided to join the party. How was your vacation?"

He'd grinned at the rookie who was as happy as a pig

in shit to be out there with the rest of the hotshots, risking his life. Logan had been that kid once. Hell, he still was, only with more responsibilities on his shoulders.

The Forest Service superintendent had already called to apologize for getting in Logan's way this weekend with the suspension. Logan told the man he knew he'd simply been doing his job. Putting him on suspension was a judgment call. Nothing personal.

He shared a chili dinner with his crew, and when they stumbled off to bed, he, Gary, and Sam discussed tactics.

Most of the guys looked beaten all to hell. Not Sam MacKenzie. Even the toughest fires didn't scare him. Nothing did.

"What's the forecast?" Sam asked.

"High winds and low humidity for the next forty-eight hours. Water is either blowing out from beneath the helicopters or evaporating before it hits the ground. Some of the guys are getting in as close as twenty feet, but it's not making a difference."

"It's been too long since these forests have burned. The trees are ripe for it," Gary added, fatigue hanging on every word.

"Both of you need to get some sleep."

Sam remained at the table. "I talked to Connor today."

Firefighters were masters of understatement, part and parcel to the life-threatening risks they took every day. But sometimes Logan wanted to jump for joy anyway.

"Thank God he's awake. How's he feeling?"

"Like shit," Sam said. "I never thanked you for saving his life."

"We did it together."

Nothing more needed to be said, so Sam pushed back his chair and headed off to his bunk, leaving Logan alone with the maps. A couple of hours later, he finally accepted that all they could do until the winds died down was keep the fire out of the trees. By dusk the next day, chainsaws and axes were going to feel like natural extensions of their hands.

When night fell, he'd sat back in his chair and closed his eyes, thinking of Maya. She was so beautiful. So stubborn. Too damn stubborn to tell him she loved him. Even though she did.

It didn't matter if she stayed in Lake Tahoe until they put this fire out. He'd find her wherever she went.

And he'd love her forever.

When sunlight finally glinted in through his eyelids, he splashed his face with water then rang the station bell. Fifteen minutes later, his men were assembled, looking sharp and ready for another killer day in Desolation. He kept his instructions short and sweet.

"Clear all low-hanging branches and chop down any burning trees. We've got to keep the fire from spreading to the treetops. Helicopters will continue making bucket drops on the hot spots as long as it's safe to keep flying in." He paused to make sure every last one of them understood his orders. "At the first sign of danger, get out.

I don't care if every house in Tahoe turns to rubble. I'm not losing any more men."

Somber eyes met his, filled with determination. He followed his men out the door to their trucks.

He thought about Maya, knew she'd learned that lesson well: *At the first sign of danger, get out.* Her casualty list was long enough already. She didn't need him to be one more name, one more firefighter she'd loved and lost.

He couldn't turn his back on a fire. And he couldn't walk away from the woman he loved. Even if it was what she thought she wanted.

The original anchor point was no longer safe, so the crew drove into a wide clearing that had been bulldozed flat. From there, Logan watched flames jumping across treetops as heat rumbled over the mountains like a fleet of jets. Entire trees were torching, exploding into flames instantaneously.

He pulled down his hood and picked up a chainsaw. It was time to get back to work.

Maya woke up stiff and sweating beneath the thick comforter as the sun set through the thin drapes on her window. Logan's face was the first image she saw. She had faith in his fire knowledge and his years of experience as a hotshot, but the madness wouldn't end until Jenny was behind bars—or dead.

Moving quickly, she brushed her hair and teeth, then

realized she had to put on her same filthy clothes again. Picking them up off the carpet, she shook them out in the shower. Her stomach growled. Grabbing her key, she walked down to the lobby.

"I need to use the phone."

The girl behind the desk shrugged. "Whatever."

Maya walked as far away from the blaring TV as the phone cord would allow. Using her company calling card number, she dialed information and got her boss's home number. He picked up on the third ring.

"Maya? I've been trying to reach you all weekend. What happened to you?"

Where should she start? So many things had happened in three days.

"We found her."

"Her?"

"The arsonist."

"The arsonist is a woman?"

"Yes."

For the millionth time, Maya wished she'd figured it out earlier.

"How'd you find her?"

Maya rubbed a hand over her eyes. "I didn't," she admitted. "She found me." She paused. "She tried to kill me from a distance and when I didn't die she came to finish the job."

How strange it all sounded when she said it aloud. Almost improbable.

Albert cursed. "You should have come home. I can't believe I let you stay, let you put yourself in danger."

But Maya wasn't at all sorry. Because if she'd left, Logan and Joseph would probably both be dead by now.

"I'm coming to Tahoe. Straightaway. Keep her in jail until I get there. And stay out of trouble."

Maya could hardly believe what she was about to tell her boss. "She's not in jail, Albert. She escaped."

"You've got to be kidding me! How the hell did that happen?"

Albert was one of the calmest men she knew, and a great boss, but obviously even he had his breaking point. Looked like she'd found it.

She summed up the past forty-eight hours in as few words as possible. "She didn't stop at setting my motel room on fire. She set off an explosion that killed a hot-shot. She bombed Logan's truck. She set two homes on fire, then taped me to a tree and nearly killed me with a chainsaw. When Logan saved my life again, she got away."

"Logan?"

"The initial suspect," she clarified. "He's one hundred percent innocent."

She waited for everything she'd said to sink in. Lord knew, it was a lot to handle over the phone.

"Are you sure you're not in any more danger?"

No, she wasn't sure, but if she told Albert the truth, he'd drive up to Tahoe and force her to get in his car and leave all the madness.

"I hope not" was as honest as she could be, adding "I'll e-mail you a copy of my report as soon as I can."

"No need. I'll be there in four hours. Where are you staying?"

She gave him the name and location of the motel, then hung up the phone. The teenage girl was staring at her with an open mouth. "You were making up that stuff about being attacked with a chainsaw, right?"

"I wish I were."

The girl looked at her with new respect. "Cool."

Heading for the downtown strip, Maya bypassed a smoke-filled diner in favor of a deli. Sitting outside on the sidewalk in her ratty clothes, she forced a turkey sandwich down, then walked into a boutique and picked out the least flashy clothes on the rack.

She threw her ruined clothes in a trash bin on the sidewalk and felt a hundred times better as she hailed a taxi to take her to the city library to look up Jenny's address, then called Chief Stevens and asked him to meet her there with a set of universal keys. He was waiting on the curb for her when she arrived.

"You've done good, kid. Real good. And you're looking much better. Did you get some sleep and something to eat?"

She nodded but didn't say anything else. She didn't want to relive it all over again. "I need to go through her things for my report to make sure the case against her is solid." She couldn't bring herself to say the woman's name aloud. Not after what she'd done. "Thanks for helping me out."

Patrick patted her shoulder. "It's my pleasure."

Thirty seconds later he had the door unlocked and open. Nothing seemed particularly odd when she first entered the apartment. A few dirty plates in the sink, a stack of *People* magazines on the coffee table, tennis shoes kicked off under a dining table.

She found it hard to reconcile the normalcy of the apartment with the madwoman who'd ruined so many lives. Patrick moved past her down the hall and she followed him into Jenny's bedroom.

The bed was neatly made, and it looked as if it hadn't been slept in for some time. Not bothering with the dresser drawers quite yet, she walked back out into the hall and tried to turn the doorknob of the second bedroom, but it was locked.

"Patrick, could you open this for me?"

Using a small tool, seconds later he swung open the door. Her eyes went wide with horror as she gazed into the room.

"My God," Patrick said in a low tone, "she was obsessed."

Every square inch of wall and ceiling was covered with photos of firefighters.

"She must have every firefighter calendar ever made," Maya said as she stood at the threshold of the room, disgusted by the creepy shrine.

"I can do this for you," Patrick offered. "You've had a hell of weekend already."

"Don't worry, I've done this a hundred times," she said aloud as a reminder to herself that she knew what she was doing. That she could handle this.

She headed for the chest in the corner, her heart racing as she opened it. She gasped and Patrick moved to her side.

They were staring at dozens of firefighter badges.

"What the hell is this?" Patrick asked. "Every guy she bagged?"

Maya started searching through the pile. And then she found the one she was looking for.

Tony's badge fell from her fingers and she stumbled backwards, out of the room, out of the apartment, unable to stop moving until she made it out to the sidewalk.

She missed him so much and wished he were still alive so she could tell him everything that had happened in the past six months.

Patrick found her there, perched on the edge of a bus stop bench, her head in her hands. He held out Tony's badge as she looked up. "He would want you to have this."

She took it from him and as she curled her fingers around the coarse fabric that bore her brother's name, she felt a bolt of love shoot through her.

And that was when she knew: Tony would have hated watching her waste her life mourning him.

He'd have loved to watch her jump off a roof, loved to see her run like a wolf through the forest.

He would have told her to risk everything, to live every day like it was her last.

He would have wanted Logan to be his friend. His brother.

And most of all, he would have wanted her to risk everything for love.

CHAPTER TWENTY-SIX

TWO DAYS and nights passed in a blur of felling trees until his arms throbbed and his hands continued to vibrate whether they were holding a chainsaw or not. Fatigue was a constant, as was the continuous threat of dehydration. As Logan's team worked the eastern hills, along the trailheads that led to what was once Joseph's cabin, he kept an eye out for a body. It was only a matter of time before they found Jenny.

And then Sam called him over and Logan turned off his chainsaw and dropped it into the dirt. He hurried to a small cave where Sam was kneeling in the dirt, searching for a pulse between the blisters under a woman's chin.

They'd found her.

"Holy shit," Sam said. "She's alive."

Despite everything she'd done, Logan was impressed with her resilience. Maybe she'd learned something from all those firefighters she'd screwed, after all.

"I've got to get her to a hospital."

Sam frowned, shook his head. "After everything she's done . . ."

But Logan had already scooped her up in his arms. Her limbs were a mass of blistering, scarred flesh and he wasn't sure how much longer she'd be able to hold on—or if he even wanted her to.

"Maybe she got what she deserved," Sam said in a low voice.

"No one deserves this," Logan said in a flat voice.

Not even the devil herself.

He headed back to the anchor point, Jenny's weight barely slowing him down. She groaned several times, her eyes fluttering but not opening before she went unconscious again. Thirty minutes later, he got in the ambulance with her, but he was thinking about Maya.

She'd stopped him from strangling Jenny just in time, and now that the intense rage had passed, he was glad for her insistence. Over the years he'd watched people die from smoke inhalation, from burns, but never at his own hands.

They arrived at the hospital and Jenny was rushed in for evaluation. Logan was itching to get back to the fire, but he couldn't leave until the doctor gave him the low-down on Jenny's condition.

A short while later, Dr. Caldwell pulled off her mask

as she stepped through the swinging double doors. "Logan, why don't you come into my office for a few minutes."

He followed the middle-aged woman into a tidy office overlooking a courtyard. "Is she going to make it?"

"Honestly, I don't know. I'd say her chances of living without life support are extremely slim." She paused. "But we found something else while we were examining her, something I think you should know."

His stomach twisted. It seemed that nothing was simple when it came to Jenny. "Lay it on me."

"She's pregnant."

He didn't bother to hide his shocked expression. "Is there any chance the baby could make it?"

"Maybe. She's already almost five months along. Do you know who the father might be?"

"Yes, I think so." Holy shit. Dennis might become a father in a few months.

"I need to discuss this with my colleagues, but my gut is to keep her on life support for another ten to fifteen weeks until the baby is big enough to take by C-section without too many complications. Could you tell the father to contact me as soon as possible?"

Logan stood to leave. "I will."

She came around her desk and put her hands on his. "I'm so sorry about Robbie. We were hoping he'd pull through."

"You did everything you could," he said, his voice the consistency of sandpaper.

His brain was overloaded with images, with emotions, as the ambulance driver took him back to the mountain.

Gary jogged over. "Good news. The winds are dying down. Humidity is up. If we continue bucket drops at this pace, we should be at least fifty percent contained by this evening."

And they'd caught the arsonist. Thank God. The end was in sight.

Gary had a good ten years on Logan. He could read between the lines, could see that there was something else on his mind. "What now? Something about Jenny? Is she going to survive?"

He shook his head. "Probably not. She's on life support. But she's pregnant."

Gary raised an eyebrow. "Dennis the father?"

Gary's question was a good one. Who knew what Jenny had been doing behind Dennis's back besides lighting deadly fires and killing people? "I sure as hell hope so."

"As long as the weather keeps cooperating, we've got this. Go tell Dennis the news." Gary dropped his car keys into Logan's palm. "And I don't want to see you back here until you've found Ms. Jackson and put a ring on her finger."

Wednesday morning, Maya walked out of the Tahoe Basin Forest Service office into the bright sunshine. When Albert had arrived in Lake Tahoe late Sunday night, he'd taken one look at her and insisted on taking her to dinner. He hadn't let her leave the table until she'd polished off a salad and a cheeseburger. Although she'd initially protested, halfway through the meal she'd realized her boss—and friend—was right. She'd been starving.

For two days, they'd hashed through the details of the Desolation Wilderness case, and by Tuesday evening, she'd finished writing up the report. Albert hadn't asked a lot of questions about Logan beyond the case. He didn't have to. Not when it was obvious where her heart lay.

"I'm staying in Lake Tahoe," she'd told him.

"Logan?" had been his response.

She'd had to laugh at herself. Clearly, love had been written all over her face. And then Albert had surprised her again. He'd felt confident that she was safe, so he was leaving town. And he'd made an appointment for her to meet with the superintendent of the Forest Service. Alone. This wasn't his case, he'd told her. And he wasn't going to take any of the credit.

William McCurdy was a very sharp man, his questions and comments concise and to the point. But she'd refused to leave his office until she was one hundred percent certain he supported Logan's innocence, even though the samples from his garage had been a match in the explosion by the housing development.

"Of course he's not guilty," McCurdy had told her. "Unfortunately, based on the meager facts initially at hand, I had no choice but to suspend him until we'd conclusively ruled him out as a suspect."

Much to her surprise, at the end of their meeting, he'd offered her a job working directly for him. The ever-shrinking line between the city and the country was putting wildland firefighters' lives in greater peril than ever before as they worked to save not only forests but houses and homeowners, often getting caught in the middle. McCurdy needed someone to keep an eye on the urban interface.

She accepted without hesitation. Lake Tahoe was now her beautiful new home.

The lake was less than a quarter mile from the Forest Service headquarters, and she made a beeline for the beach, smiling at the news the superintendent had given her that the fire was officially under control. Smoke jumpers and extra hotshot crews had been called off. Amazingly, they'd found Jenny on the mountain. Alive. McCurdy didn't know anything else, but she'd call the hospital soon enough and get the rest of the details for her report.

She kicked her shoes off as she walked toward the clear blue water. The sky had lost its look of dark gloom, the clouds quickly shaking off the gray to return to their usual bleached-white glory. She was finally ready to take in the beauty all around her.

She listened to the water lapping up on the shore, watched a couple of toddlers giggle as they rolled in the sand, and then someone was saying her name and she turned around and saw Logan standing right behind her.

Her heart pounded like crazy, just like it had the first time she'd seen him six months earlier, standing in the doorway of the bar; just like it had five days ago when he'd pulled off his helmet after running up the mountain and she'd realized he was the man she was after; just like it had when they'd finally made love and she'd known love was exactly what she felt for him.

Deep, unending love.

She drank in the sight of him. He was so beautiful, so big and strong.

And he was alive.

But even though she was desperate to be alone with him, to tell him everything that was in her heart, naked and in his arms instead of standing in the middle of a public beach, she needed closure first.

"What happened to Jenny? Is she going to die?"

Logan's eyes were dark with regret. "Sam found her. She was badly burned, but still breathing. The doctors don't think she'll live without life support." He paused. "And she's pregnant."

"She told me she was pregnant when I was taped to the tree," Maya said, swallowing hard, vividly remembering the horrific scene. "She was going to tell everyone it was your baby."

"I should have guessed. I should have known what she was plotting."

"No one could have known," Maya said firmly. "She was a jealous woman who went over the edge. I wouldn't have picked her out of a crowd."

He moved closer. "Every time I think of you with her, I go a little crazy."

"I'm not going to say I wasn't scared, because I was." She smiled at him. "But I was never worried. Not for a single second. Because the best damn hotshot in the world was coming for me."

She didn't want to talk anymore, so she launched herself at him, knocking them both down into the sand. He pressed a row of kisses along her jawline.

"I'm glad you're still here," he whispered into her ear, sending shivers up her spine.

He rolled them over so that the warm sand was at her back and he was blocking the sunlight with his beautiful face. She wasn't confused anymore. All she wanted was Logan. Forever.

"I love you," she said, the words falling from her tongue so easily. And then they were kissing again, and she was whispering the same three all-important words between their kisses, wanting to tell him a hundred times, a thousand times that she loved him, to make up for her earlier reticence, her confusion.

"So many times, I wanted to tell you I loved you." She needed to explain everything to him, knowing that she could admit her weaknesses, that he would still love her. "I was so scared. I still am."

"No," he told her as he stroked her arms, her back, her hair. "You're the bravest woman I know. The strongest."

"I didn't want to love you. I didn't want to love any

firefighter, ever again. I thought my mother was crazy sitting by the phone. Waiting. How could she think my father wouldn't come back? He was my hero. I thought he was invincible."

"He was."

"He wasn't, Logan. He died."

"And before that day came he loved you with everything he had. So did your brother."

The way he was looking at her, like she was the only woman he'd ever loved—like she was the only woman he would love for the rest of time—made her tremble with desire. And something so much deeper, so much stronger.

"I've always loved you, Maya, from the first moment I saw you, when you demanded a drink, then decided kissing me was better than getting drunk."

She stared at him, surprised by his revelation. "You couldn't have. I was a mess."

"You were beautiful. As soon as I touched you I knew you were mine."

It had been the same for her. "That day in the bar," she whispered, "you were all that stood between me and—"

"I know, sweetheart. You don't need to tell me."

"But I do," she insisted. "You were a flash of light in the darkness. The only person who could help me find my way out."

"You would have found your way without me, Maya. I'm the one who needed you. I was running. Just like you.

Every day, I was afraid of losing control, afraid of what would happen if I did."

"I like it when you lose control," she teased.

He smiled and she pressed her fingertips against his beautiful lips.

"That's just it," he said softly, his words a sensuous caress. "I can lose control with you, Maya. You make everything right. Perfect."

She couldn't stand to keep her mouth off of him for another second, so she caught a handful of his T-shirt in her fist and pulled him closer, a repeat performance of their first kiss.

His grin was swift and then his mouth was on hers and his tongue was in her mouth, tasting her, branding her as no man ever had.

"Marry me," he said later that night when they were finally alone and she was cradled in his arms, and she whispered "Yes" to the only man on earth for whom she would have dared risk everything.

Turn the page for an extract from:

HOT
AS SIN

Bella Andre

Available soon from Rouge Suspense

CHAPTER ONE

COMING TO Colorado had been a mistake.

Dianna Kelley slammed the door of her rental car shut and turned the heat on full blast, then wrapped her hands around her upper arms as she shivered on the cold leather seat.

Earlier that day when she'd flown into the small Vail airport, the breeze had been cool and steady, but the sky had been blue and clear. Tonight, however, wind howled through the trees while black, ominous clouds spat out sheets of rain all over the quickly flooding sidewalk.

She closed her eyes and fought back a heavy wave of sorrow at the emotionally charged blowout she'd just had with her younger sister in a bustling café. Dianna knew better than to expect too much from April, but she'd never stopped hoping that the two of them would finally connect.

Growing up, Dianna had longed for a baby brother or sister, so when she was eight and April had been born, she'd showered her baby sister with love. Until the horrible day when their easily overwhelmed, usually broke single mother had decided there were too many mouths to feed and gave four-year-old April up to the state.

As soon as Dianna turned eighteen, she began her fight to pull April out of the foster system, but it took four years to bring her sister home.

In the decade that they'd been apart, April had changed. The innocent, cheerful, inquisitive girl she'd once been was long gone. In her place was a hardened, foulmouthed fourteen-year-old who'd seen and experienced way too much.

Dianna's hands tightened on the steering wheel as she remembered the way April used to lash out at her, accusing her of ruining her life, of trying to control her every move like a jail warden. All through April's high school years, Dianna had tried to protect her sister. From the mean girls in her classes who thrived on picking on the new girl, from the cute boys who would break her heart just because they could, and from the teachers who didn't understand that April needed more patience and attention than kids with normal upbringings.

But it had proved impossible to protect her little sister.

As the years ticked by and she grew from a lanky teen into a knockout young woman, April retreated further and further into herself. She refused to share any details about her various foster homes with not only Dianna, but a series of therapists as well. By the time April eked out a high school diploma, they were nothing more than two strangers who passed each other at the fridge a couple of times a week.

In the two years since graduation, April had bounced from part-time job to part-time job and boyfriend to boyfriend, and Dianna worried that April was going to get pregnant and end up marrying one of the losers she was dating. Or not marrying him and becoming a broke single mother in a trailer park, just as their own mother had been.

Dianna blinked hard through the windshield wipers into the driving rain as she replayed the moment when she came home from work three months ago and found April's key on the kitchen table. Running into April's room, she'd realized her sister's favorite ratty jeans and tops were gone along with her duffel bag. At least she'd taken her toothbrush.

For seven horribly long days, she'd waited for some word as to where her sister had gone, and when—*if*—she was coming back. Finally, April left a message on Dianna's cell phone when she was taping her live television show and couldn't possibly answer it. She was in Colorado and she was fine. She didn't leave a new number or address.

Again and again during the past three months, Dianna had tried to tell herself that her little sister was simply going through a patch of self-discovery. After all, normal twenty-year-old girls tried things out and learned from their mistakes and moved on, didn't they?

But nothing about April's life was normal. Not after ten years bouncing from family to family in the state foster system. Dianna hated not being able to keep watch over her sister, hated knowing she couldn't keep her safe.

So when April finally called and asked if Dianna could come to Vail to meet with her, although it wasn't easy to shift all of her interviews on such short notice, Dianna couldn't miss her chance to connect with April.

But instead of connecting, they'd fought. And April had stormed out of the café. Leaving Dianna to helplessly wonder how she could possibly save her sister this time.

The rental car's windows were covered with condensation, so Dianna hit the defrost button, but it didn't work. Reaching into her large leather tote for a package of Kleenex, she wiped a clear circle on the windshield and slowly pulled into the street, inching forward as marble-sized hail battered her car. Every few seconds, she hit the brakes and wiped the moisture off of the windshield.

Prudence told her to turn back, but all she wanted was to be back home in San Francisco, wrapped up in a soft blanket on her couch with a novel. As it was, she was cutting it close to get to the airport in time for her flight.

The two-lane road that led from Vail to the airport was narrow and winding, and she seriously considered pulling over, turning around, and finding a nearby hotel to wait out the storm. Instead, she took a deep breath and forcefully shook off the sick sense of foreboding she'd carried with her ever since April had moved to Colorado, turning the radio on to a pop station.

I'm pulling out windows and taking down the doors
I'm looking under the floorboards
In the hopes of finding something more

Listen to me now 'cause I'm calling out
Don't hold me down 'cause I'm breaking out
Holding on I'm standing here
Outstretched
Outstretched
Outstretched for more

Her throat grew tight as she realized that this was one of the songs April had played over and over in her bedroom. How sensitive her little sister obviously was beneath her thick armor if she liked a heartbreaking song like this . . . and how hard she must be trying to hide her true feelings from everyone. Especially her big sister, who loved her more than anyone or anything.

But it had already been an emotional enough day

without some song making her cry, so she shifted her gaze to the stereo for a split second to turn it off. Lifting her eyes back to the road, she was startled by bright headlight beams from an oncoming car. Temporarily blinded, she swerved away from the light.

Too late, she realized that the only thing between her and the headlights was a wall of rock.

Dianna screamed as the oncoming car clipped the front bumper of her rental, instinctively bracing for further impact as she spun around and around in circles. The airbags exploded in a burst of white powder and thick, sticky material. Despite her seat belt, she flew into the tight bags of air, the breath knocked out of her lungs as she hit them hard.

Oh God, she was suffocating!

Ripping, grabbing, pulling, she tried to shove the airbag away from her mouth and nose, but she couldn't escape. Sharp pains ran through her, top to bottom. And yet, she didn't pass out, couldn't seem to find that numb place where everything would be all right.

Finally, after what seemed like hours, someone found her: a firefighter-paramedic, with jet-black hair and beautiful blue eyes.

"Everything's going to be all right," he said. "I'm going to take care of you."

Looking up at him, his features and coloring were close enough to Sam MacKenzie's that his words twisted up in her head, in her heart, and she was thrown back to another car crash, one that had taken everything from her.

She'd been desperately craving Chinese food, so she'd driven into town for takeout. But after throwing up all morning, she'd been so starved that she couldn't make it out of the parking lot without dipping into the mu-shu pork.

She'd mixed the plum sauce into the cabbage and meat with her fingers and pretty much inhaled it, barely having any time to appreciate the sweet-salty combination before heartburn got her, right under her ribs.

Her obstetrician said it was normal, that the morning sickness would ease as soon as next week, when she hit her second trimester, but that the heartburn would probably get worse, along with possible constipation from the iron pills and being kept awake all night by a kicking baby.

The doctor had grinned and said, "Quite a lot to look forward to, isn't there?" and Dianna hadn't wanted to admit that she was still trying to get her head around being pregnant.

And the amazing fact that she was going to be Mrs. Sam MacKenzie in a week.

The Chinese restaurant was in a trailer right off Highway 50, and knowing the road was busy year-round with tourists, Dianna carefully backed out into traffic, putting her turn signal on to make a U-turn from the center lane. When the coast looked clear, she hit the gas pedal.

From out of nowhere, a large white limo careened toward her. She could see it coming, could see the driver's horrified ex-

pression, but no matter how hard she pressed on the gas, she couldn't get out of the way in time.

She was thrown into the steering wheel, and as her skull hit the glass all she could think about was her baby . . . and the sudden realization of how desperately she wanted it.

Going in and out of consciousness as fire engines and ambulances came on the scene, she felt someone move her onto a stretcher. She tried to speak, but she couldn't get her lips to move.

Her stomach cramped down on itself just as she heard somebody say, "There's blood. Between her legs."

She felt a hand on her shoulder. "Ma'am, can you hear me? Can you tell me if you are pregnant?"

But she couldn't nod, couldn't move or talk or do anything to tell him he had to save her baby.

And then a new voice came, its deep, rich tones so near and dear to her.

"Yes, she's pregnant."

Sam. He'd found her. He'd make everything all right, just like he always did.

Somehow she managed to open her eyes, but when she looked up she saw Connor MacKenzie, Sam's younger brother, kneeling over her, speaking into his radio.

"Tell Sam he needs to get off the mountain now! Dianna was in a car accident on Highway 50."

More cramps hit her one after the other and she felt thick, warm liquid seep out between her legs.

She screamed, "Sam!"

But it was too late for him to help her. Their baby was gone.

"Can you hear me, ma'am?"

She opened her eyes and saw that the firefighter's eyebrows were furrowed with concern.

"Can you tell me if you're pregnant?"

Dianna blinked at him, belatedly realizing that she'd instinctively moved her hands to her abdomen.

Reality returned as she realized that the hero who had come to her rescue wasn't Sam. Her failed pregnancy was nothing but a distant memory she usually kept locked away, deep in the recesses of her heart.

Feeling the wet sting of tears in her eyes, she whispered, "No, I'm not pregnant," and then everything faded to black.

"I'm sorry," the doctor said softly. "Your brother didn't make it."

Dark eyes blinked in disbelief. This wasn't happening. His twin couldn't be dead. Not when they were together just that afternoon. Sharing a couple of beers in companionable silence until Jacob brought the meth lab up again, saying that they had enough money already, that they should shut the business down before they got caught and ended up in jail. Only hours ago, he'd told Jacob to go to hell, said he was the brains of the business and knew what was best for the both of them.

According to the paramedics, Jacob had been driving

down Highway 70 when his tires slipped on some black ice. He'd crashed head-on into another vehicle and the paramedics had rushed Jacob to Vail General Hospital.

For two hours, Jacob had been fighting for his life.

He wasn't fighting anymore.

The man's body rejected the news, head to toe, inside and out. Bile rose in his throat and he made it across the blue and green linoleum tiles in time to hurl into a garbage can.

More than just fraternal twins, he and Jacob had been extensions of each other. Losing his brother was like being cleaved in two straight down the middle, through his bones and guts and organs.

He needed air, needed to get out of the ICU waiting room, away from all of the other people who still had hope that their loved ones would recover from heart attacks and blood clots. He pushed open the door to the patio, just in time to see a loud group of reporters harassing anyone wearing scrubs.

"Do you have an update on Dianna Kelley?" one of the reporters asked a passing nurse in a breathless voice.

Another rushed up to a doctor, lights flashing, camera ready. "We've been told that Dianna Kelley was in a head-on collision on Highway 70. Could you confirm that for us, Doctor?"

Dianna Kelley?

Was she the other driver? Was she the person whose worthless driving had ended Jacob's life?

He'd only seen her cable TV show a handful of times

over the years, but her face was on the cover of enough newspapers and magazines for him to know what she looked like.

Blond. Pampered. Rich. Without a care in the world.

"Please," another reporter begged the doctor, "if you could just tell us how she is, if she's been badly hurt, or if she's going to be all right?"

None of the reporters had even acknowledged that there was another person involved in the crash. All they cared about was Dianna, Dianna, Dianna.

Knowing that no one gave a shit about Jacob was a big enough blow to send him completely over the edge.

"Would you like to come back and say good-bye?"

The doctor who had delivered the bad news was still waiting for him just inside the door. Her voice was kind and yet he knew his brother was just one more stranger who'd died on her shift.

Before he could respond, a tall blond girl ran past him and into the waiting room. For a minute he couldn't believe his eyes.

If Dianna Kelley had been in the crash with his brother, how was she running by him now?

It took him a few moments to realize that this girl in her dirt-streaked jeans and oversized raincoat was barely out of her teens. Although she bore a striking resemblance to the famous face he'd seen dozens of times, there was no way she could be the "important" woman the reporters were climbing over themselves to get a scoop on.

"I'm Dianna Kelley's sister," the girl said to the doctor in a breathless voice, her cheeks streaked with tears. "I saw on TV that Dianna was in a crash." She grabbed the doctor's arm. "I need to see her!"

The doctor looked between the two of them, and even in his fog of pain, he could see that she was torn between the guy with the dead brother and the girl with the hurt sister. But they both knew the famous sister would win.

"Excuse me, Jeannie, could you come help me?"

A moment later, a young nurse came around the corner and the doctor explained, "This is Dianna Kelley's sister."

"Come with me," the nurse said to the girl, whose raincoat was dripping a puddle on the carpet. "I'll need to see your ID first."

"She's not going to die, is she?" Dianna's sister asked in a shaking voice.

"I don't know, honey," the nurse said in a soothing voice. "You'll have to ask her doctor."

"I'm so sorry about all of this," the doctor said to him as she ran her badge in front of the locked ICU door. "I know how hard this is for you."

He wanted to use the doctor as a punching bag, to scream that she didn't know a damn thing about him, about the hole in his chest that was growing bigger by the second. Instead, he silently followed her down the hall into the busy ICU.

The overhead lights had been dimmed in his brother's

small room and a white sheet had been placed over his body. The doctor peeled back the cloth to reveal his brother's lifeless face, and before he could brace himself, pain unlike anything he'd ever felt before ripped through him. He felt dizzy and light-headed. As if he could drop to the floor at any second.

Moving closer and gently touching his brother's un-moving face, so similar to his own, he felt warm tears streak down his face.

"Would you like me to leave you for a few minutes?"

It was abundantly clear how much the doctor wanted to get away from him and his soul-sucking grief.

He nodded, taking his brother's stiff hand in his own. All their lives he'd looked out for Jacob, who had been the reckless one, the one who could never hold down a job, the twin who could never keep his fists in his pockets. Jacob was the reason he'd gotten into the drug trade. Manufacturing and selling methamphetamines had seemed like an easy way to support them both.

If only they hadn't fought that afternoon, then maybe Jacob would have hung out a little longer, would have realized the roads were too icy to drive and spent the night.

If only Dianna Kelley had swerved out of the way, or better yet, never got on the road at all.

It was all *her* fault.

"I'll make her pay for what she did to you, I swear it," he promised his brother.

Bending over, he pressed a kiss to Jacob's forehead.

Wiping his tears away with the back of his hand, he let go of Jacob's hand and was slowly walking out of the ICU when he saw her.

In a room a dozen feet from the exit, Dianna Kelley was lying in a bed behind a glass wall, hooked up to an IV, her blond hair fanning out behind her on the pillow. A nurse was busy dealing with a phone call just outside the room and she didn't pay him any notice as he stood there and stared.

Seeing the bitch still alive, breathing and blinking, the blood still pumping through her veins—while his brother was dead—only confirmed that she was to blame.

No jury would ever convict her of wrongdoing. She was too famous, too pretty for anyone to think she could have possibly done anything wrong. She'd killed his brother and she was going to get away with it.

Continuing to stare at her, rage and grief built up and up inside of him until there was no room left for anything else. The nurse finally noticed him and when she gave him a strange look, he turned to leave.

Just then, Dianna's sister burst in through the ICU doors, her shoulder knocking into his in her haste.

And that was when he realized that he already had the perfect weapon.

Dianna Kelley had killed his brother.

He would kill her sister.

Everything hurt like crazy, especially her head, Dianna thought as she slowly woke up. What was wrong with her? Why was she having such trouble moving her arms and legs?

She struggled to open her eyes. They felt dry, almost like they were filled with soot, and she blinked hard to try to clear them. She quickly realized she was in a hospital bed, but how could that be? The last thing she remembered, she was driving to the airport, heading back to San Francisco after arguing with her sister in the café.

She had the strange feeling that someone was standing nearby, watching her, but her vision was still too fuzzy for her to see the person's features. The only thing she could tell for sure was that it was a man, tall with broad shoulders and short-cropped hair.

Her fatigued brain instantly plopped Sam's face on the man's head. She'd spent ten years trying to forget him, but tonight she was too damn weary, too sore and achy to make much headway in dislodging her memories of a gorgeous firefighter, six foot two with midnight-black hair and sizzling blue eyes.

Was it really Sam? Had he come to see her? Or was this just another hallucination? Another vision she was manufacturing out of desperation?

Her heart rate soared, as did the faint beeping of the machines behind her.

With every breath she took, her discomfort grew. She'd never allowed herself to take more than a couple of Advil—given her mother's history of addiction—but right now, she needed more of whatever they'd put in the IV in her left arm.

Soon, a nurse moved beside her, murmuring something about another dose of Vicodin. Before Dianna could find out if Sam was really there, or merely a hallucination of her deepest desires, a cool rush of liquid settled into her veins and she fell back into painless oblivion.

Available this month from *Rouge Romance*:

Tessa Dare's 'Stud Club' Trilogy:

ONE DANCE WITH A DUKE
Spencer Dumarque, the fourth Duke of Morland, has a reputation as the dashing "Duke of Midnight." Each evening he selects one lady for a scandalous midnight waltz. But none of the ladies of the ton catch his interest for long, until Lady Amelia d'Orsay tries her luck.

TWICE TEMPTED BY A ROUGE
Brooding war hero, Rhys St. Maur, returns to his ancestral home on the Devonshire moors following the murder of his friend in the elite gentlemen's society known as the Stud Club. There, he is offered a chance at redemption in the arms of beautiful innkeeper, Meredith Maddox, who dares him to face the demons of his past.

THREE NIGHTS WITH A SCOUNDREL
The bastard son of a nobleman, Julian Bellamy plotted to have the last laugh on a society that once spurned him. But meeting Leo Chatwick, founder of the exclusive Stud Club, and Lily, his enchanting sister, made Julian reconsider his wild ways. When Leo is murdered Julian vows to see the woman he secretly loves married to a man of her own class. Lily, however, has a very different husband in mind.

THE HUSBAND TRAP by Tracy Anne Warren
Violet Brantford has always longed for Adrian Winter, the wealthy Duke of Raeburn, who is set to marry Violet's vivacious twin sister, Jeannette. But when Jeannette refuses to go through with the ceremony, Violet finds herself walking down the aisle in her sister's place in order to avoid a scandal. But keeping up the pretence with a man as divine as the Duke will take all of Violet's skills…

THE WARRIOR by Nicole Jordan
Ariane of Claredon is betrothed to King Henry's most trusted vassal, the feared Norman knight Ranulf de Vernay. But cruel circumstance has branded Ariane's father a traitor to the crown and Ranulf is returning to Claredon, not as bridegroom…but as conqueror. But though he has come to claim her lands and body as his prize, it is the mighty warrior who must surrender to Ariane's passion and her remarkable healing love.

R♥UGE
SUSPENSE

WILD HEAT by Bella Andre

Maya Jackson doesn't sleep with strangers. Until the night grief sent her to the nearest bar and into the arms of the most explosive lover she's ever had. Six months later, the dedicated arson investigator is coming face to face with him again. Gorgeous, sexy Logan Cain. Her biggest mistake and now her number-one suspect in a string of deadly wildfires.

CRASH INTO ME by Jill Sorenson

Ben Fortune is the world's most famous surfer, known as much for his good looks as for his skill. He's also a suspect in a series of brutal murders that may have begun with his late wife. FBI Special Agent Sonora "Sonny" Vasquez has been sent undercover to make friends with Fortune, but soon they have collided in an affair that is both intense and irresistible.

R♥UGE
PARANORMAL

BLOOD MAGIC by Jennifer Lyon

Darcy MacAlister is about to discover that she is a witch and the key to breaking a curse that has plagued witches and the men who hunt them. For if a Wing Slayer Hunter kills an innocent witch by mistake, the price is a piece of his soul. When gorgeous leader of the Wing Slayer Hunters Axel Locke's sister is cursed by a demon witch, he discovers that Darcy MacAlister may hold the cure...

www.rougeromance.co.uk

R♥UGE

Red-hot romance...

About *Rouge:*

Rouge is a new romance imprint for Ebury Publishing, part of the Random House group. Launched in September 2011, we will be releasing at least four new digital titles a month in a variety of categories including paranormal romance, regency, romantic suspense and contemporary romance.

Rouge Romance ebooks are available in every digital format from your usual store. Select Rouge Romance titles will also now be available in print.

To find out more about *Rouge Romance* go to
www.rougeromance.co.uk
or follow us @RougeRomance on twitter.